MAHA, EVER AFTER

Sumayya Lee

Kwela Books

Also by Sumayya Lee:

The Story of Maha

All characters in this publication are
fictitious and any resemblance to real persons,
living or dead, is purely coincidental.

For a brief glossary of terms not explained
in the text, please see end of book.

Kwela Books,
an imprint of NB Publishers,
40 Heerengracht, Cape Town, South Africa
PO Box 6525, Roggebaai, 8012, South Africa
www.kwela.com

Cover design by Michiel Botha
Cover photograph by Rodolfo Clix
Author photograph by Simone Scholtz
Typography by Nazli Jacobs
Set in Versailles
Printed and bound by Paarl Print,
Oosterland Street, Paarl, South Africa

First edition, first impression 2009

ISBN: 978-0-7957-0291-4

Acknowledgments

I express my sincere gratitude to the team at Kwela – especially my publisher, Nicola, for her astute editorial suggestions, James for his amazing editorial wand and Raj for the painstaking task of sorting out the Chaarspeak.

Grateful thanks to my family and friends – including those on Word Cloud – for encouragement and support. And Nazeera, Naseema, Farhana, Saaleha and Aziz – for attending to my never-ending questions and pointing out errors.

I am especially beholden to Dr Salduker – for taking time out of his busy schedule and patiently answering my psychiatric questions. Any errors are my own.

And to my husband, children and Neo – this would not have been possible without you!

Born in 1970 in Durban, Sumayya Lee attended Durban Indian Girls' Secondary, where an inspirational English teacher instilled in her a love of language. Her first job was as an Islamic Studies teacher to children and adults. She married at twenty and then trained as a Montessori directress.

Two children later, she divorced and spent the next few years employed at a preschool. Her passion for English led to a Cambridge Certificate in Teaching English as a Foreign Language. She is now remarried and lives, writes and counts the sunny days in London with her husband, two children and their cat.

Sumayya loves reading and eating, preferably under an umbrella on a Durban beach. She hates injustice, Islamophobia, misogyny and February in England.

Praise for *The Story of Maha*

"*The Story of Maha* is no misty-eyed myth of an African child-hood . . . it's a realistic, funny and inspiring coming-of-age story." — ROBYN ALEXANDER, *Marie Claire*

". . . we get triumph and a lively narrative with bright dialogue that suggests Lee would be equally at home writing for the stage. She is a promising new writer, with an eye on Islamo-phobia and misogyny and a novel approach to defying these." — MAUREEN ISAACSON, *Sunday Independent*

". . . a delightful sense of humour and large dollops of defiance neatly wrapped with ribbons and bows and a layer of gold dust." — AZIZ HASSIM, *Daily News*

"A fascinating glimpse into one girl's mind as she grows from a child to a woman, navigating the difficulties of adolescence and faith." — BRIDGET MCNULTY, *KZN Literary Tourism*

"A beautifully refreshing novel." — *Women24.com*

"Sumayya Lee's language is colourful, robust, unabashed and generally appealing . . ." — VICTOR O AIRE, *The African Book Publishing Record*

"Lee's first novel is neither pretentious nor an exaggeration. It is an easy yet entertaining read. I can't wait for her next one." — KASHIEFA AJAM, *The Star*

"Vivid, true to life and a definite page turner." — *Afrocentric Muslima*

This above all – to thine ownself be true.

WILLIAM SHAKESPEARE'S *HAMLET*

Humankind cannot stand very much reality.

T.S. ELIOT

For my parents, with love always,
and with very special gratitude for enduring –
with dignity and patience –
the tsunami of self-righteous Slumurbans.

Happy Birthday
Shahnaz

Wishing you many, many
more, filled with
the best of
everything!

Love + Duas
Always

Sunayya
xxx

For Richer, for Richest

⚘

"Fuuuuuuuuuuuuucccckkkkkkkkkkk!" I yelled and slapped Zeenat instinctively.

"Hey!" She recoiled in alarm. "I'm *not* torturing you deliberately, bitch! You *do* have a choice. You could always *shave* your legs . . ."

Zeenat was my dearest relative; my late mother's younger cousin who, alongside my grandparents, had spent eight years of her life bringing me up at the so-called Maal Mahal.

"In fact," Zeenat continued, smirking as she dipped the spatula back into the molten wax, "I think I'd rather have to cope with such sacrilege than deal with the physical abuse!"

I laughed. "Sacrilege! Methinks you take hair removal far too seriously!" I said, lifting my arms obediently.

"It *is* my business after all," she replied haughtily before smearing glop into my armpits. "Besides, you need to toughen up. How else are you going to push out an heir?" Zeenat let out an evil cackle, brutalised my underarms and glared at the foliage stuck to her strip of wax. "*Look* at these maadars!" she commanded.

"Gross!" I cried, turning my face away from the sight of my vile buggle baal.

I hated the pain of dealing with my own hairiness, but unfortunately Sameer, my dearly beloved husband, preferred me non-hirsute. I sighed and remained supine as she applied cream to my smarting body, glancing every now and then around the stylish two-roomed salon that took up the lower floor of the duplex she shared with her father.

"*So*, you lazy aalu," she said, finally pulling off her apron and throwing it into a basket, "are you catching forty winks there?" She walked over to the sink to wash her hands. "Have you got time for a cup of tea and fag?"

I made a face as I stretched and yawned. "Probably not, but sod it, I'll have a quick one," I said, swinging my legs unhurriedly off the side of the bed and stretching again.

"You mean that you can give *me* some of your precious time, Mrs Patel?" Zeenat said as she began to fill the kettle. "Well, I am honoured!"

I exhaled exaggeratedly and stuck out my tongue.

"So . . . how *are* you?" she asked, pulling out mugs and milk. "Recovered from Eid at the Palace?"

I grinned. "*What* can say?" I replied while buttoning my shirt. "*Have* to recover! Back to *normal* routines and all. Was up at seven, too . . . but shame, can't complain . . . *must* make shukar! Sorrr nice husband I got, sor nice mummy, daddy, everyone."

Zeenat snorted as she sat down next to me and lit a fag. "Ah, Maha the duryi dorternlaw!" she teased, shaking her head.

"Fuck off! I have no choice! Sameer is *such* a duryo poyro. How will look if his wife too one wild thing?" I mocked à la Gorinani the Goat – my mother's annoying aunt who lived in Maal Mahal's buggle and was thus an ever-present trial in my life.

She shook her head resignedly. "And there I thought I was going to manage a nice cherr! Sor grown up you came way, Maha! Ayyo, I can't cope!" Zeenat drawled aunty style.

I giggled. "Yeah, I'm all mature and sensible . . . now, if only this bloody province would get with the programme all would be well with the world! It feels like the killings never stop!"

The kettle boiled and Zeenat got up to make the tea. "I think if Buthelezi stopped inciting his supporters it would help, but then again, there are all these Third Force rumours . . ." She sighed. "Ey, you news junkie . . ." she whined, "forget the gloomy politics for once and choon some Palace gossips."

I shook my head with resignation. "You know how dangerous it can be to share Palace intelligence with you! If you happen to mention it to some big-mouthed client it'll go through Slumurbia like veld fire."

"Honey, you are *so* scared of Palace news being accredited to you . . . You must have nightmares where *you* are some kind of news reporter: 'This is Maha Patel, CNN News, The Palace!'" she guffawed as she made her way back across the room, the mugs of tea sloshing dangerously in her hands.

"Hey, put down the tea if you're going to act savage . . ." I said, puffing gratefully on my fag.

The Patel's new satellite dish had created an almost insatiable appetite for real news though Zeenat seemed to think the duryi dorternlaw moonlighted as a reporter for the Palace. Asking for a verbal agreement to the stock confidentiality clause had become standard practice before the pronouncement of Palace news. I'd burnt my fingers on that front pretty early on and was not partial to masochism.

"So *choon*, you mean chuth!" Zeenat said, handing me my tea.

I stuck out my tongue at her epithet. "Well, firstly, dearest Zeenat, *I* am not a chuth! However, as you well know, two wonderful specimens do reside at the Palace."

She leaned forward and patted my arm maternally. "There, there . . . you can cope, beti . . . come tell Aunty Zeenat *all* about the chuthias."

"Very funny!" I sipped slowly and frowned. "Nothing new with them, thank goodness! More a case of same shit, different day . . ."

The two in question were my not-so-fabulous siblings-in-law: Naseem, the younger brother, who had once upon a time amazed me with his sensuous good looks, and Fayza, the only sister. Naseem had recently bought his way into university, and I'd watched with barely concealed horror as the arrogant arse played by his own anarchic rules. As much as Sameer was revered and banked on – perfect first-born heir, sensible *and* married – Naseem was pandered to and bankrolled as an irresponsible baby. Dwelling on him, *or* darling Fay for that matter, was futile – there was sod all I could do about the two gorgeous thorns in my marital bed of roses.

Zeenat appeared lost in thought and I cleared my throat. "I guess I should start moving my arse . . . you look tired, woman!"

She nodded. "I've been busy . . . Which is not a bad thing, I suppose, mus make shukar and all. And you can manage another five minutes! Ey, I tell you! That Katy Patel got you by the gaanbaals . . . see how you rushing-rushing and all . . ." she sniggered.

I stuck out my middle finger. "*Fine*, then. I'll stay another five minutes."

"Yah, yah, go if you must." She waved me away tiredly. "When am I going to see you, muthlabee? When the bhaji grows in your buggles again?"

I giggled at the image of my armpits sporting herb patches as I grabbed my bag and keys.

Zeenat chortled, beaming triumphantly. "I knew I'd make you laugh once at *least*!"

I shook my head as I moved to give her a quick hug. "You *know* it's not like I don't *want* to see you . . ."

"Yes, I know, Meesees Cherrable! Hey, have you spoken to Naani this week?" she asked, changing the subject.

I nodded, my maternal grandmother called me with alarming regularity. I adjusted my clothes and re-attached my orhni – bandannas had failed to achieve a Palace seal of approval and I'd relegated them to my bottom drawer.

"Naani's okay, considering the Goat and her never-ending bleat about the Mahal's overcrowded backyard," I said, trying not to dwell on the image that had popped into my mind of me cramming myself along with my bandannas into the rather capacious bottom drawer in our fabulous closet. "Oh, and she got cross 'cos I refused to take her to Makro!"

Zeenat giggled. "Yah, I know . . . She called to moan and insist that

I take her. She heard that they had more essentials in, apparently!"

I laughed. *"She's* got enough to see her through the next millennium already! What more does she need?"

Zeenat nodded. "Yah, and about the overcrowding . . . I reminded her that it was sawaab nu kaam, and that managed to calm her down."

"Good work, Zeenat, 'a blessed act' indeed. I'd like to hear what the Goat has to say to *that*! I mean, how can helping fellow humans be a *bad* thing?" I sighed, blew a kiss in her direction and headed for the door.

"The Goat's gaan!" she declared. "Forgot to choon," she continued, grinning as she followed me out to my car, "her precious child Samiha, your *favourite* relative, was here to have her moosh and tshebe waxed . . ."

"Poor you! Tough week then?" I giggled.

Plump Samiha and her older, plumper sister Nabiha had haunted me since childhood, which was the reason I had christened them the Heifer and the Calf, aka, the Cows.

Zeenat shook her head gloomily. "No choice . . . families and all . . ." She leaned against the door frame as I unlocked the car. "She went on and on about duryo Sameer . . ."

I paused and squinted at her. "Oh, *yah*? What brought *that* on?"

She shrugged. "Apparently, every time she and Nabiha go to the shop Sameer actually leaves all his kaam and comes down from the office to see if they are okay . . . Ayyo, how *you* got sor nice husband with sor much izzats . . .?" she teased.

"African luck?" I said, and grinned. Sameer Patel was certainly Mr Thoughtful, I thought as I took my seat and made my salaam.

He always sent flowers on birthdays and anniversaries – not just to me, but also to his mother, sister *and* aunts!

"Salaams, Maha," Zeenat said, waving. "Hamba kahle," she called after my departing form.

⚜

Pausing at an intersection as I negotiated the light traffic on the roads between Zeenat's salon and one of Durban's premier locations, I grinned at the graffiti: *Help your local branch of ANC/IFP on 27 April – beat yourself up!* The actual razing of rural Natal, where suspected ANC supporters lived, was unamusing, but our National Sense of Humour was certainly alive and well, I thought as I drove towards the Palace, tucked conveniently just off Musgrave Road.

I sighed as I crossed another hairy intersection and turned into The Grove, the cul-de-sac off which the Palace was situated. Two years down the line and the grand entrance – with its six feet of wrought iron flanked by amaphoyisa – still created a *frisson* of excitement inside me. Maal Mahal paled by comparison. This was like entering a foreign world and, glitz aside, the Palace also boasted the most incredible views of the sprawling city.

George, the phoyisa, stepped out of his hut, rolling his newspaper into a tight scroll. "Sawubona, Maha. Howzit?" he said, waving it in greeting.

I wound down the window, grinned and raised my thumb. "What about you, George? How's everything?"

"Eish, Maha! You see this newspaper?" He unrolled it with an air of disgust.

I plucked it out of his hands and glanced at the front page. Great! Now the good King Goodwill wanted independence for Zululand!

I shrugged. "The madness never ends."

George shook his head. "Ey, I am sick of these malkops, man. Every day you see the peoples running from the farms. You must see the jondols now! Eish, I tell you, no space to move even!"

I sighed. "Are your family all in Durban?" I asked.

Sarafina, Naani Maal's maid, had her surviving relatives currently ensconced at the Mahal – the act of kindness that had put Gorinani's nose out of joint – and Happiness, the Palace kitchen maid, had found her daughter, Mary, wailing at the gates a few days earlier, having managed to escape the burning of their village down the coast. Faction fighting between Buthelezi's Boys and the minority ANC in Natal – an IFP stronghold – was tearing the countryside apart.

Mummy had been highly affronted by Mary's unannounced appearance, though of course she had no cause for fufuyaan. *Her* busy life – involving social engagements, migraines and overseas travel – *would* go on, come what may! However, seeking drama was one of Mummy's main pastimes, and such an occurrence provided the perfect motivation for an impromptu performance: "Just now all the maids' families will pitch up!" she'd wailed.

George nodded. "Eish, lucky they all here! Nothing by the farms now . . . is all burnt . . . finish and klaar! Ey, how's one ugwayi, Maha?"

I held out the packet. "Yah, they *are* lucky, thank God! What *can* we do? We must keep praying for peace!"

"Yah, is true that, Maha. Siyabonga!" George said, tucking a cigarette behind each ear. "You know that Sameer's friend Ba, with the nice car? I see him by the jondols also . . ."

"Oh?" I asked curiously. Ba – the Memon word for brother – spotted in a jondol, nogal? Then again, of all Sameer's bras, Vaalie Shahzad – Ba's given name – was probably the only person I'd expect to find in the vicinity of a slum. According to legend, he'd transferred to the University of Natal's Durban campus after having his heart broken by some half-Bruinou, half-honky chick who had been pregnant with his child at the time.

"Nkosi sikelel' iAfrica!" George shouted abruptly and scurried back to his post.

I glanced into my mirror automatically as the car behind mine revved impatiently over the thumping bass. Sighing, I inched forward as the gates swung open, Prince Naseem roaring behind me, the sound of "She don't let nobody" rocking the Palace gardens.

Naseem screeched to a halt and headed for the main entrance without even a backward glance as I swung into the garage and switched off the engine. Sitting in the car I dwelt for a moment on the song he had been playing – Chaka Demus and Pliers. Why, I wondered, would anyone want to be called Pliers?

I sighed. There was no point in postponing the inevitable, so I gathered up my bag and headed for the back door. Stepping into the temperature-controlled formal kitchen area – kitted out in stainless steel and wood; state-of-the-art German appliances gleaming in every corner – I thought again what a patently high-maintenance, low-use waste of space it was. The main kitchen – where actual work was done – was connected to it via a glass-walled archway. No less fancy, though with marble counters instead of wood, it also boasted a full range of appliances designed for use by professional caterers.

I gazed around; all was quiet and apparently calm. Pulling up the nearest chair I sat down, exhaling slowly as I slapped the newspaper on the table and began to read – averting my gaze carefully from the good King's demands that would no doubt result in increased disorder. Someone pottered about in the scullery, and the distant sound of Mummy's voice implied she was busy on the phone – the instrument via which she monitored and controlled her kingdom.

⁂

Mrs Kathija Patel – Katy to those near and dear – faced the world primly. Her strict no-sun policy meant that the face she presented was flawless and paled to perfection, belying her age and increasing her status twofold. Mummy hailed from a well-known family across the Vaal, and was revered by all as an inter-provincial woman of power, sophistication and class. She served willingly on numerous committees – and did so immaculately turned out, not a hair out of place (thanks to Terry Scott, who maintained her meticulously tinted golden-brown bob).

"*Have* to be fashionable and all," she regularly saw fit to remind me, highlighting the great responsibility that had become mine when I married into the Patel Empire. Katy's idea of being fashionable was built around a chain of boutiques called Trends, which had spread its mantra – *It's all in the name* – along the Natal coastline. Palace policy upheld this motto in every respect and augmented it with an interest in the latest gadgetry – which meant that all of the

Patels could currently be seen at any given moment talking on the *de rigueur* cellular phone. Internally, I rebelled against living by such maxims – a one-woman resistance movement – and remained determinedly aloof from the gadgetry. But externally Katy was only acquainted with Maha the dutiful dorternlaw, who smiled and nodded during her endless monologues on appropriateness and Palace culture. Like my hapless bandannas, my opinion on matters that raised my ire had also long been packed away.

The intercom shrieked and I recoiled. Two years and counting. Would I *ever* get used to the ghastly thing? I wondered.

"Salaams," I chirped sweetly.

"Wa 'alaikum salaam, Maha. Foi just *wouldn't* put down the phone, you know," Mummy began.

"Hmm," I responded.

"Yah, so now they *all* coming from Reservoir Hills for supper tonight, so I think we must take out the fish *and* the prawns. You made the salad? It will be enough, you think?"

"Yah, there's enough salad," I announced calmly – by now I had become amazingly adept at cooking industrial-sized quantities for every meal.

Foi and The Vankers – Daddy's sister and family – resided high in the hills, not too far from the landmark reservoir, but this lack of proximity did not deter them from coming to dinner whenever they felt like it. It was, after all, bhai nu ghar – brother's house and all.

"Okay, then, I'll just read my namaaz and get ready . . ." Mummy said. "What you doing now?"

"Umm, just reading the paper," I responded. "I'll start in the kitchen . . . salaams."

Replacing the receiver and casting the broadsheet aside, I yanked open the enormous American fridge – which I reckoned would just about hold even the bulbous Foi – and pulled out the fish curry *and* the king prawn curry, along with two salads and a quiche as starters. More than enough food, I mused as I shuffled off to the scullery in search of Happiness – a woman of forty whom much to my disgust was still referred to as the kitchen girl!

I found Happiness busy ironing dishcloths and folding them into neat triangles, exactly as Mummy liked.

"Howzit, Happiness."

"Siyaphila, Maha Missus."

I grinned. "Table for twelve, please."

"Hawu! Who is coming?" she asked, looking up in alarm.

"Your favourite . . . Foi!" I teased. "And Dada is around as well, I think." Dada was Sameer's paternal grandfather and only surviving grandparent.

She smiled. "Let me finish with my dishcloths first."

I nodded. "Sure, we'll probably eat at six thirty, so no need to rush."

This was a good time to escape for a fag break, so I slipped out via the scullery door and scuttled off to our gorgeous studio flat that stood across the back lawn – well within reach of Mummy's custom-designed apron strings. Once inside I stripped down to my underwear, strode into the bathroom eagerly and dropped a few bath towels onto the closed bog. I relaxed on my makeshift armchair before lighting up contentedly.

I sucked in deeply before shuffling around in my basket for my Walkman. Much to everyone's amusement I remained stubbornly attached to cassettes despite the advent of the CD. I jabbed the play button and giggled – if only Foi could see me now!

As the music washed over me my mind flitted to Sameer's cousins. Haroon, Foi's son, was an obnoxious fart who did not even deign to speak with me – for his holiness, ignoring women was a prerequisite for sadhu status. Zaahida, his delightfully demure and dignified sister, who donned her sincerity like her cloak – from the outside – was equally annoying. She would no doubt chatter nonstop, boring me senseless while her husband remained mute.

Zaahida had started out by lulling me into a false sense of security. Naively newlywed and traumatised by my new sister-in-law Fay's antics – trawling through my wardrobe without asking and helping herself to an armful of my favourite clothes – I'd vented gratefully on Zaahida's faux-friendly shoulder, only to have her repeat and embellish all I'd said to her darling mother. Before one could say Fat Fuck Foi, she'd foisted herself upon us midway through the main course of a dignified dinner. "Better sort her out early," she'd instructed Mummy and Daddy, "otherwise hu ne hu kehe?"

This pronouncement – of who knew *what* I'd spread around Durban – heralded my first experience of Joe Patel's incredible ability to morph from Daddy to wildehond. Rising from his seat with a savage roar he had hoisted the table from his end. Thankfully, it was a moerse lump of solid oak, topped by half an inch of maxi-strength glass, and the wildehond had only managed to raise it a few inches, causing dishes to clatter and echo in the petrified silence, while I sat stunned and sickened.

"Fucking bhenchodh can't even eat in peace," he'd roared as the table crashed back to the floor. "One fucking meal in peace too I can't have? If I fucking hear one more *maadarchodh* story about *anyone* in this house, anytime . . . they must just fucking go! I don't want to see their faces again!"

Everyone had glared at me while Sameer pointedly avoided my gaze.

Some partner he had turned out to be, I had thought as I laboured through the rest of my dinner.

I stubbed out the cigarette and methodically removed all traces of my habit. It was time to face Fat Fuck Foi and the Vankers.

I brushed my teeth vigorously and glared at my reflection for a few seconds. At least my clothes were decent enough. Foi was not averse to tugging at a shirt she deemed too short or tight. I reapplied my make-up with a small sigh and smoothed down my artificially straightened hair. You're good to go, Mrs Patel, I reckoned with a frown. Smile, woman! I ordered.

I stepped out of my zone and onto the paving stones. Chubby, the neighbour's cat, purred and rubbed herself against my ankles. I paused to stroke her and smiled – tonight Sameer would be home and not off with the boys.

The first and only time I'd complained about Sameer's social schedule, Mummy had materialised in my kitchen at six in the morning, blathering about how she'd been up all night worrying about the state of our marriage.

"What?" I'd asked, rubbing my sleep-addled eyes, completely perturbed by her assault.

"What *what*?" she had shrieked, squeaking unbecomingly. "Sameer said you was complaining about his squash and cards and club and what and what!"

Sameer had complained to his *mother*? I had busied myself with mugs and politely offered her a drink.

"How can I drink anything," she'd whinged, "with such worries on my head? If you stop your husband from playing sport and having boys' time, then you must see! He'll go do *other* oondha dhandhas. Yah! Then you won't like that! *Then* how you'll feel?"

Upside-down nonsense – I had flinched at her words, sloshing boiling water onto my hand as I had tried to make tea. Mummy had insinuated that if I stopped Sameer from going out to play he'd sleep around.

"Don't suppose *you* have such pains in your life, hey, Chubs?" I asked the cat as she fell onto her back and proceeded to lick a paw.

I sighed and stepped into the kitchen. My hands concerned themselves with the food while my mind dawdled over the possibilities that lay ahead. Sameer managed quite well with his multiple roles: perfect son, businessman, mate *and* husband of mine whom I loved to bits. I smiled; lying in bed with him definitely numbed me to the prickling thorns.

"Asalaam 'alaikum, Maha. I can smell dhania. What you cooking?" Foi walked into the kitchen and took a deep breath before beginning to lift the pot lids for a quick glance and sniff. "*Prawns!*" she cried seconds later. "You know Haroon don't eat prawns at *all!* *We* eat *some*times only."

No one cares, I thought, smiling sweetly.

Foi frowned as Happiness walked past. "I see *that girl* is working nicely," the Slumurban skandemeester pontificated. "How's her daughter? I heard their whole house got burnt and she got raped even."

I dropped the pot lid I had been holding with a clumsy clatter. "Mary wasn't raped!" I muttered. How could she speak about someone's daughter like that? Is rape fuck all if you happen to be black? I subdued my scowl and Foi thankfully shifted focus to her own daughter as Zaahida sauntered in with a self-satisfied smile on her face.

I centred on the task at hand. Prior to the presence of a daughter-in-law, Mummy had employed a khaala to cook and serve. Now, of course, they had me. In spite of the trendy Palace image, expectations regarding the daughter-in-law were based on archaic cultural models. Early on in our marriage I had naively explained the Islamic perspective to Sameer.

"What the hell? So if you cook we must *pay* you? Where the hell do you come up with such wild ideas?" he'd asked, laughing.

"It's not a joke, doofus, it's the way of the Slumou."

"Oh, well, your UNISA fees are being paid for you . . . I reckon that's a fair exchange."

"Hmm," I had responded, concealing my dismay and fleeing to the bathroom.

I'd puffed furiously on my fag while fighting back tears and persuading myself that, along with the credit cards in my name, it was an okay deal; and we spoke of it no more.

Now, I walked across to the capacious dining area, where as expected everyone was already seated. Shit! The prawns were *in* Haroon's face. I swapped the dish swiftly with the fish, but as usual he ignored me. He was probably pissed off at having to sit at the same table as haraam Coke, prawns and females.

Resignedly, I took the only available seat – between Zaahida and Foi – and flashed Sameer a quick grin.

"Oh, yah, lucky it isn't Sameer's club night or anything," Zaahida piped up, never one to miss a trick.

Foi scooped a healthy portion of rice onto her plate. "You still go to your naani's house on club night?" she asked, staring at me for a few seconds before returning to her plate.

I nibbled on my slice of quiche and shook my head.

"Too much work, isn't?" Zaahida piped up. "You must use that time to do your readings and assignments," she pronounced.

Foi nodded sagely. "Yah, must *listen* to Zaahida, she got *all* her timetables and all in her study. You know they built a new study?"

I nodded and smiled. How could I not have known of their ever-so-painful and expensive renovations? Zaahida had started with the master bedroom prior to her wedding and then attacked her marital home room by room.

"Hey, Sam! I checked your bra Ba today," Naseem piped up.

Dr Forjee Vanker, Foi's oily spouse, peered over his pudgy nose. "You're *still* friends with that Memon?" he asked Sameer, with a small sniff.

The Memon were fellow Chaarous who, like the Surtis (the Patels, Vankers et al), had come to South Africa from Gujarat. The two were divided along linguistic lines, and Memon and Surti alike were responsible for perpetuating the archaic village mentality which declared "the other" inferior.

Sameer nodded politely.

Haroon paused mid-chomp. "He's a sharp ou, that Ba . . . last time I saw him he said he was on his way to the shacks! He must be doing some lekker business!"

Naseem laughed. "He must be cracking it there!"

23

Dr Forjee harrumphed. "What can any *decent* person want by the shacks?" he asked.

"How *is* that Shahzad?" Zaahida asked, turning to me. "Is he *still* not married?" She prided herself on knowing everyone in our lives.

"Still not married," I responded vapidly.

"*Can't* understand!" she declared. "He's sooo handsome and plus super-rich!"

Naseem perked up as the words "handsome" and "rich" floated down to him, and smiled extra sweetly in our general direction.

Foi paused masticating. "Who that? That Memror? Oh, yah, I met his aunty at ta'leem last week. She say they all *so* fed up with him. His dhaadi was *dying* and begging him to settle down with one nice cousin . . . and *still* he never listen."

I kept the smile pasted on my face, rolled my inner eye and served myself some prawns.

"What about *Riaz*? You see *his* wife, isn't?"

I sighed. Trust Zaahida to go down this path. Riaz Patel, Sameer's chief choobie and cousin, had unfortunately chosen Rozina Kareem, the daughter of a Hedroo gangster, as his wife. The Urdu-speaking Chaarous were looked down on by Surti and Memon alike – never mind that her father was the Don of Lenasia.

Rozi's petite frame boasted curves in all the right places, bright blue contact lenses covered her brown eyes and blonde streaks highlighted her waist-length hair. She dressed as she pleased, smoked in her mother-in-law's presence and left the house whenever she got the urge – without telling her mother-in-law where-where she was going, too! Socialising with outwardly outrageous Rozi was thus a big black mark in my book.

"Sometimes, yah . . ." I mumbled. "Hey, is that shirt from Queenspark?" I deftly changed the subject.

Zaahida snorted. "The *whole* world goes to Queenspark! Mummy told Sameer to drop off some samples last week from Trends. He never tell you? You know, they have *such* nice things in their sample room."

I smiled and nodded, allowing what I hoped would pass as utmost interest to colour my features.

Time to clear up and serve dessert. I gathered a few empty dishes and made my way back to the scullery. Tonight, thanks to a sudden increase in numbers, dessert would be uncomplicated, albeit home-made ice cream that had been poured into flower-shaped moulds.

"So, what time those people coming, Katy?" Foi asked as she and Mummy barged in and glanced around.

I perked up. So this dinner was merely a precursor.

"They said around eight," Katy replied. "So I think we should serve dessert one time with tea when they come," she said, turning to me.

"Oh, I didn't realise," I said. "I'll put the ice cream back then. What about the tea things? Do you want me to take out some biscuits?"

"Nor, no need to worry about all that," Foi harrumphed. "*We* brought enough and everyone likes Zaahida's chocolate crunchies! Where that gaandi girl put all the Tupperwares?"

Mummy glanced around the immaculate kitchen. "Oh, she must have left them in the main kitchen . . ."

Main, my arse! "So who's coming for tea?" I asked, while empty-ing leftovers into appropriately sized containers.

"Oh, some men from that Muslim Party. You know they trying to get money for all this election nonsense."

"Well, the tea and dessert trolley is ready for twelve. How many extra things do you need me to put?" I asked politely.

"Oh, just add one or two," Mummy stated. "You can go now if you want. Naseem is going out and I think Fay also."

One would never think that Fay was in matric – her nose was seemingly made for powdering and was miles away from the grindstone.

"Yah, Maha," Foi encouraged, "Happiness is still here and you look *so* tired also."

It was pretty obvious that my absence was being demanded, and I couldn't care less – I'd been up and on the go since seven, over twelve hours on the trot, plus I had a night of pleasure ahead if the wannabe politicians didn't stay too long.

"Well, if you're *sure* you can manage, Mummy," I said, smiling benignly as I walked over to Foi. "Salaams, Foi, see you soon." I bent to offer her a polite peck.

"Yah, yah," she offered her cheek grudgingly, "inshallah, inshallah."

"See you in the morning, Mummy, salaams," I called out as I unwound my apron and threw it into the laundry.

Stepping out into the clear night I caught sight of the Olympic-sized swimming pool, the water glimmering in the glow from the garden lights, beckoning me like an oasis. I found myself taking the longer route back to our studio flat, pausing to run my hands through the warm water, watching the ripples as they spread out across the pool. I gazed out at the night – another endless summer night, warm and shimmering with promise.

I was humming as I pushed my front door open and walked straight into a fug of smoke. Sameer and Naseem, having long left the table, were puffing away while Fay peered intently into the mirror, lashing on her mascara.

"Hey, Maha . . ." Sameer broke away from his brother and walked over, his pretty-boy face breaking into a lovely smile.

I stepped gratefully into his embrace. "I missed you," I said.

He stroked my hair. "You had a nice day?" he asked and took a drag on his fag.

I disentangled myself, led him to the nearby couch and pulled the cigarette out of his hand. Sameer glanced instinctively at his siblings, both of whom were oblivious to us, hellbent on their own missions. I gave him a glare for giving a shit and pulled contentedly on his fag.

Naseem was now on his new cellphone. "We *need* a fucking fourth man, you maadar!" he yelled. "*You* sort it out." He cut the call with a flourish and paused to admire his state-of-the-art toy.

"Anyways, bru," Naseem looked at Sameer, ignoring me as usual, "seeing as you're not vaaing anywhere tonight, I'll use *your* wheels. Got an important thunnee match on!" He rubbed his hands gleefully.

Sameer shook his head even as he reached into his pocket for his keys. "I'm warning you, Nas, you'd better be careful. And please clean my car . . . I don't want to find *any* of your shit!"

"Oh, stop nagging, fuck face!" Naseem snapped.

Even I wouldn't have minded using such words when the supremely anal Sameer Patel made me strip the sheets post-sex posthaste *and* replace them instantly, nogal!

Naseem grabbed the keys and after checking his appearance, flashed his brother a wave and was thankfully gone.

"I'm using Nas's car," Fay drawled slowly.

Was she on something? I wondered. I was completely mystified as to how she planned to pass matric, but I had learned to keep my thoughts to myself. Any mention of his family and the shutters fell over Sameer's eyes. If I dared continue, I was silenced with, "It's not your problem, don't interfere, okay?"

Sameer stood up, preparing to go back to the house, while Fay fumbled around for Naseem's key. "Ey, I think that arsehole took his keys with him!" she finally said. "Hey, Maha, lend me your wheels." She held out her hand wilfully, purposefully avoiding my gaze.

I sighed and shot a glare at Sameer's back. Everyone knew my views on unlicensed driving – an occurrence I'd found disturbingly *de rigueur* when I'd first moved into the Palace. At the time it had been Naseem hurtling around sans licence, clocking up speeding fines and summonses in Sameer's name. The fact that he'd tried to evade a roadblock, been involved in a car-chase with real amaphoyisa and had made it home only to crash into the garage door hadn't made a fig of a difference.

Perhaps I was unconventional, but the incident had me suggest rather forcefully that the hoodlum be held accountable for such flagrant violations of law. The brat had responded by flouncing off to his room in tears, locking the door and refusing contact and food for two whole days. My rational explanation on responsibility resulted in Dada Patel grabbing every opportunity to spit in my face about "people who thought they were too clever". In response I had learnt to hold my tongue, which bore teeth marks as a result.

Sameer turned to Fay. "You know where the keys are," he said. "Please drive carefully."

"Yah, yah," she replied, waving away his concern. "See you. Bye."

"Salaams," I called out resignedly as she yanked the keys off the hook and stomped off towards the garage.

"Well, *I* have to get back to the politicians," Sameer said as he watched his sister disappear.

"I know," I sighed and walked over to kiss him. "I'll be waiting up for you."

"Great," he grinned. "Something to look forward to."

While Sameer strode back to the Palace I lit a fag, grabbed the phone and dialled a number automatically.

"Salaams, Rozi, howzit?" I said, flumping into the nearest chair. "It's Maha."

"Hey, Maha. Was wondering when you were going to call!" She chortled. "Mothernlaw chooned your fat-arse foi was around!"

Rozi was the only family member with whom I could whinge about the family without fear of reprisal since – sisters in arms – she was even more anal than I was about Patel news being accredited to her. But she was happy to pass on all she gleaned from Aunty Gori, her mother-in-law, who called Mummy at least twice a day to keep abreast of Palace news. Perhaps Aunty Gori felt it was her duty to keep in touch, given that – as the *poor widow* – she received a monthly Palace handout.

"So? How did it vaai?" Rozi asked. "What are you up to now? Finished very early, I see!"

"Just came home . . . The siblings have gone out as usual, but Foi & co are *still* around. Apparently they would rather *I* was not there to welcome the tea guests."

"Oh, yeah? So let me guess . . . some dudes from the Muslim Party, right?"

I giggled. *"God!* Is there anything your mothernlaw doesn't know?"

I drew on my fag thoughtfully as she launched into a description of her latest shopping spree. The Don of Lenasia made up for his poor parenting with regular cash-filled envelopes. These deliveries, always made by some shady-looking character, always got Aunty Gori in a right tizz, but Rozi was less concerned – she reckoned she'd be vilified regardless of her conduct and jauntily cultivated a min gepla attitude.

"Anyhow, I'd better go before Riaz throws a tantrum!"

"Your husband adores you and can't bear to have you out of sight!" I replied, slapping away an image of the fawning Riaz Patel.

She snorted. "Yah, right! Anyhow, take care . . . choon tomorrow." She made kissing sounds and cut the call.

Tomorrow was another sodding Saturday, meaning that Sameer would be out of the house by seven and I would have to be ready for Baking Day at the Palace by eight. Joy was a weekend when the family were invited elsewhere, I thought as I walked into the bathroom and began to fill the tub.

Half an hour later my eyes shot open, the water still deliciously warm. I relaxed for a few more minutes, knowing Sameer wouldn't return any moment soon. I dried myself and anointed my body before selecting a sexy sliver of silk and throwing myself onto the king-sized bed awash with squishy cushions. I deliberated between a book and a film. Sameer was not partial to Chaar flicks, I mused as I flicked through the ones on offer, but he also wasn't around . . . *1942 – A Love Story*! Rozi had enthused about it, so I stuck it into the VCR and made myself comfortable.

Three hours, a few laughs and some tears later, the movie came to its grand finale. Bollywood had taken a turn for the better, I decided as the credits rolled. Still *no* sign of Sameer, though. Fuck it, I thought grumpily and hauled the phone towards me.

"Why are you calling me on my cell?" he muttered tersely, not giving me a chance to speak. "You know how expensive it is!" He paused. "I'm still busy with these politicians. Sleep if you're tired!"

I replaced the handset, berating myself for disturbing him and closed my eyes with a sigh.

⚜

I prepared for a night out with husband and friends while gaping at footage of the devastation in horror. I tugged on my jeans angrily. Would Terreblanche and his band of civil war doomsayers be proven right? I paused to take in Buthelezi's response to the Shell House Massacre: "We will fight to the finish!" he pontificated.

"Oh, grow up, Gatsha!" I snapped at the screen and switched it off angrily. Forget Mississippi: sunny South Africa was burning, in rubber garlands of shame, nogal. I squirted some perfume and headed downstairs to the car.

The News Café – Sameer teased that it had been built especially for me – was a knot of bustle and bright lights. Rozi clunked down her cup, shrieked and stood up to hug and kiss us as we entered the courtyard. Her husband, Riaz, predictably turned his focus to his beloved Sameer's order before we could take our seats.

Rozi lit a fag and made small talk. I followed suit quietly – she was sure to make her way to her preferred topic – reminiscing about the good old days when they were all part of a crazy, carefree gang at varsity.

"Hey, Sam, remember how you paid Riaz twenty bucks . . ." she began as if on cue, "for every tampon he managed to tie to a first year's backpack?" She chortled at the memory.

"Unused, I hope!" Shahzad said dryly.

I sipped on my exotic coffee – laughing and exclaiming at appropriate interludes – annoyed that she always managed to make me feel like an outsider.

"Oh shit!" I clunked down my tall mug, handed Sameer my fag and rolled my eyes as Raeesa and Anwar – in coordinated ensembles – entered the café.

Raeesa and Anwar were first cousins and married, nogal. They were both grandchildren of Nana Maal's youngest brother, Chota-nana, who had spent most of his life in the bundus until the recent violence had forced him to relocate. We had a long history of not getting on, though all that seemed to belong to a bygone era since I had landed one Sameer Patel.

"Who's that?" Rozi asked, squinting at the newcomers. "Oh, it's your irritating cousins . . . *fab*! I bet they'll come over and act all pally-pally," she grumbled as she lit another fag and sighed theatrically.

Let the games begin, I thought and pasted on a smile as they drew closer.

Riaz Patel glared at me as he clunked Sameer's refill onto the table. "Great, Maha! Did you *tell* your relatives we were going to be here?"

"Thanks, Riaz, my man!" Sameer smiled at his cousin. "How much do I owe you?"

Riaz took his seat a fraction less grumpily. "Oh, don't be stupid, man!"

"Fine then," Sameer flipped open his wallet casually and threw a note onto the table.

"Oh, Maha!" Raeesa squealed, excitedly foisting herself upon us. "I didn't expect to see *you* here . . . Oh, how *lovely*!"

She embraced me heartily, bestowing extravagant smacks on each cheek. Behind her Anwar was already dragging two extra chairs to our table.

I sighed as she disengaged herself. "You know Rozina and Riaz . . ." I said, gesturing at the table. "And this is Shahzad," I pointed to Sameer's famous Memon buddy, "also lovingly known as Ba."

Shahzad held out his hand and smiled lazily. "Nice to meet you, Anwar, Raeesa."

Raeesa was instantly dazzled and gawped at his toned body, shown off perfectly by his fitted T-shirt. Rozi and I sometimes argued over whether he was more Brad Pitt or Johnny Depp, but either way he was an altogether disconcerting package for any female.

Riaz ignored the forlorn hundred rand note and everyone else, and sipped churlishly at his coffee.

"Hey, you know . . ." Shahzad started, chipping at the ice, "there's some brilliant graffiti around at the moment!"

I giggled. "The writing's on the wall?"

He chortled appreciatively. "Exactly! In fact, I was at my folks up in Pretoria last week and saw this brilliant piece. *AWB, voetsek!* some-one had written. *We cannot survive on pap and Boere-force!*"

We all laughed, apart from Riaz who remained surly, with Rozi struggling to catch his eye.

Anwar grinned inanely, pleased to be seated next to Sameer. "Ey, what's this hundred bucks lying here?" he squeaked. "So big tip you leaving?" And with that he launched enthusiastically into a profound discussion about the cheapest places for coffee.

I sipped slowly, listening to the conversations going on around me. Shahzad was happy to steer the polite chitchat, and Raeesa remained enthralled by him. I turned my gaze heavenward and shifted focus to the bigger, prettier picture above – starlight, star bright. Brushing away my irritation I wished for peace in my province.

For Better, for Worst

The house phone shrieked, echoing in the empty-as-a-morgue kitchen as I wiped away the final crumbs of the day.

"Patel residence! Hello!" I sang politely, as instructed by Mummy.

"Maha! It's *me*, Farah!"

Farah and Sabah were old schoolmates. Sabah was studying abroad and Farah was in Joburg, training to be a doctor.

"*Farah!* Are you okay? What's wrong?" I asked as a heavy knot of fear settled in the pit of my belly.

"I'm at the hospital," she spluttered, her voice breaking as she succumbed to the tears she had been holding at bay. "My folks got hijacked this evening driving back from my aunt in Lenz . . . They shot my father . . ."

I took a steadying breath. "Oh my God! Is he okay?"

"I'm not sure," she choked. "He's in . . . in theatre at the moment and they won't let me in to see what's going on." She paused to blow her nose. "Listen, I've got to go . . . I can't leave Ma alone. She's not coping . . . Please pray for him, Maha. Salaams."

The phone went dead. I set off to find Sameer.

As I made my way through the house Mummy swished down the staircase, clutching onto the banister.

"Who phoned at *this* hour?" she asked.

"It was my friend Farah," I replied flatly. "You know her father, Dr Osman? He has his practice in Umlazi . . . Well, he was hijacked in Joburg. He's in the hospital. They shot him."

"Arreh Allahpaak!" she cried, clasping her jaw in shock and rushing down the stairs. "Oh, yorl heard?" she announced, flinging open the door to the study. "That Umlazi Dr Osman got shot dead! Can you believe it? Arreh, what this country is coming to? It's getting *worst*, I tell you!"

The words "shot" and "dead" sank in slowly.

My eyes sought Sameer's. "Farah's father," I explained, "and he's in theatre at the moment. He's *not* dead!"

Daddy looked suitably aghast.

Sameer frowned. "I'm still busy with Daddy," he said slowly. "I'll come over in a bit, okay?"

Fine! It was clear where his priorities lay. I swallowed my anger, headed for my haven and curled up on my bed, overcome by thoughts of violent crime and poor, poor Farah.

⚜

Dr Osman's funeral was held in Joburg the following afternoon; a devastated Farah had called me at five that morning to let me know that he had passed away. The Patels didn't think my attendance was necessary, so my mouth moved in silent prayer for my friend as I waded through the daily drudge.

Farah and her mother flew back to Durban the day after the funeral. In the midst of her turmoil, Farah had decided to rent out her flat in Joburg and transfer to the local medical college. I accepted this change with a heavy heart – happy on the one hand to have my good friend near but unable to feel any joy given the circumstances.

The days after Farah's return passed in a blur as I helped her through the mourning rituals. Even the deployment of peacekeeping troops, as our province officially entered a State of Emergency (brought about by the interminable faction fighting), seemed to be something that was happening in another, faraway world.

I clung to my tenuous band of hope as I tried to balance Palace responsibilities with holding Farah's hand as she tried to find a way through her monumental grief. Sameer was surprisingly considerate about my time away from the Palace, and even bought me a cellphone with which we could stay in touch.

"I've put some numbers in for you . . ." he said, clicking on the phone.

I peered at the screen, unsure of my ability to master the contraption. "Are you sure it's okay with you?" I asked him. "I mean, I don't have to spend time there when *you're* not going out . . ." I felt vaguely uneasy that he was treating my sudden absence from the Palace with such nonchalance.

He shook his head and depressed another button. "Nah . . . no problem . . . look," he pointed, "this is for typing messages." He handed over the device du jour and shrugged. "I can always get extra work done, and Ba is around if I'm bored."

I handled the cellular phone gingerly. Perhaps I was fortunate to have a man who didn't begrudge me supporting a friend in her time of need. Mummy, on the other hand, had made no bones about *her* concerns the first Saturday post-funeral. "So *when* will you do all the baking?" she'd asked with a compassionate smile plastered across her face.

✺

We were technically into autumn, but Durban refused to succumb to such labels and remained stubbornly summer-like and cheerful. Of course, any feelings of hope faded under the shadow of never-ending crap. The Rwandan Genocide was sickeningly under way, and on the home front the bloodshed continued unabated.

With our first democratic elections around the corner, Mummy and Daddy announced their decision to host a lunch on Voting Friday – after they had voted. My African luck: I would be marking *the* most important day in our country's history with a bloody daawat.

In between churning out tubs of ice cream and frying more fucking onions than I cared to count I called Ouma Galiema. Ouma Galiema was my orphan father's aunt – the woman who'd taken him in when he'd pitched up on her doorstep with Maryam Maal, my mother, in tow. Unlike the Maals, who'd ostracised my poor mother for running off with a Cape Malay mongrel, Ouma had pressed her tiny garden cottage on the newlyweds, and I had thus spent the first eight years of my life in her backyard.

"Salaams, kleintjie. I was just now thinking of youse, truesgod!"

"Hey, Ouma . . . Are you ready to vote?"

Ouma giggled. "Of course, of course . . . . I can't believe I have actually lived to see this day, algamdoelillah!"

"So who are you voting for, Ouma?" I teased.

"Ag, sies, Maha! What kind of question is that? Tell me, I must give my vote for the man who stopped me from voting all these years?"

I laughed. "I'm teasing you, Ouma. I think my parents would roll in their graves if you *didn't* vote ANC!"

Ouma laughed and coughed, and then carried on coughing for a while.

"Hey, are you okay, Ouma?" I asked when she finally managed to catch her breath.

"Ja, ja, stop fussing . . . . It's my age mos . . . I'm not getting younger . . ."

"Yah, Ouma, I know that. Are you having regular checkups? Are you eating properly?"

"Moenie worry nie, Maha darling. Anyways, if I can live long enough to vote I think I will die happy. I have seen too much suffering in this country. Now I want to see peace and hope."

I swallowed the unbidden lump in my throat. "I'll call you after you've voted, okay?"

"Ja, Maha, I think I'll make some koesisters for the celebrations also . . ."

"Ag, don't, Ouma. You know I crave your koesisters!"

"Youse got cravings? Are youse expecting?"

I snorted. "That's all you people ever think about! Babies!"

"Ja, well, it would be lekker to see your kleintjie before I go . . ." she teased.

"Well, then you better plan on sticking around, Ouma, 'cos Sameer is not interested in babies at the moment."

⁂

The first day of voting was Wednesday, 27 April. I sighed as I did my face, wrapped a small scarf around my head and kicked aside the heels that matched my ensemble, rebelliously slipping on flats instead.

As I walked across the lawn I wondered at the surrealness of the moment. It was hard to believe that I would forever look back at this point in history and recall only the interior of the glorious Palace kitchen!

By the time I arrived in the aforementioned kitchen, Khaala and her sister Mayroon – kitchen helpers employed during daawats – had already started with the meat washing.

"Salaams, Khaala, how are you?" I asked.

"Salaams, beti, so mashallah too you looking and all. Ey, Mayroon, see Maha," she instructed her sister.

Mayroon looked up and smiled shyly before resuming her work.

I reached across and switched on the small television that stood on the counter. Everyone paused simultaneously and gasped at the image of people queuing under blue skies – miles and miles of patient, peaceful people.

Happiness finally shook herself and bustled off. "We mame, can't believe . . . Eish, Nkosi!"

Buoyed by the sudden peace that had descended on our beautiful if troubled country I whirred contentedly into action, sorting out the endless jobs on my lists.

Friday dawned clear and bright. I dressed carefully and climbed into the cool interior of my car, shivering with excitement. I was going to *vote*! A free and fair election for a free and rainbow nation. I smiled as I zoomed along the quiet roads that led to the Mahal.

"Salaams, Naani, Juma mubarak!" I said as Naani climbed into the car beside me.

I waited for her to sit before leaning over and planting a kiss on her carefully moisturised cheek. She smelt exactly the same as she'd done fourteen years earlier when I'd first moved to Maal Mahal: a comforting combination of Pond's cold cream and baby powder.

"Wa 'alaikum salaam, Maha," she finally said, exhaling loudly and tugging on her seat belt half-heartedly. "Nice you take. Nana too gor sor early voting."

"Yah, he said he had a meeting this morning. Come, Naani, I'm waiting . . . please do up your seat belt!"

"Ey, Maha, this thing too tight . . ."

I leaned over and pulled on the strap until it stretched across her ample torso. Then, with Naani wriggling about resentfully, I swung out of the driveway and headed for the nearest polling station.

"All kaams finish for daawat, Maha?" she asked once we were on the road.

I nodded.

"Where Sameer? He gor shop today?"

I nodded again and smiled. "Don't worry, he'll be there after Juma . . ."

Naani smiled. "Arreh, bechaaro."

Poor thing? "He's not a bechaaro, Naani!" I said, turning into the entrance to the polling station.

After I had found a place to park, I guided Naani towards the glass doors of the hall. Inside we walked towards the first table we saw, presented our deep-green ID books and allowed our hands to be stamped with invisible ink. The hall, normally used for weddings and baby clinics, was set up unfamiliarly, and I had to steer Naani awkwardly towards the smiling face that hovered above piles of ballot papers.

Having seen Naani into her booth, I stepped excitedly into mine. After a few minutes of blinking at the blank wall, I took a colossal breath and shakily marked my page. I stared at the unfamiliar sheet for a few seconds, absorbed by my two ostensibly tiny marks – two mammoth leaps for a nation – then I shivered and popped it into the box.

"Hey, Naani!" I waved. "I'm done! Can't believe we just did that!"

Naani shuffled forward, impervious to my excitement. "Chaal, Maha . . . must gor home now . . ." she said, grabbing my elbow and steering me towards the exit.

Gorinani huffed her way towards the entrance just as we stepped outside, Goranana a pace behind her. "Ey, asalaam 'alaikum! Maha! What *you* do here? *Beeg* daawat by your house! We also got daawat!" Her cheeks wobbled as she nodded heartily.

"Ey, yorl finish vote and all?" she clucked and peered curiously through the glass doors. "Sor much ghar-bhar for voting! Yesterday too Maria, Sarafina leave all kaam and run for voting. Then, night time, big naach they have by their room. Ey, I tell you!" Her jowls jiggled indignantly.

Good on the maids! I thought. The enfranchisement of a nation was certainly cause for naach! "Salaams, Goranana," I said, ignoring the old woman and reaching out to shake her husband's hand.

He patted my head distractedly. "How you, Maha, dhikri? We coming your house for lunch today . . ."

I smiled. "Jee, I know," I said, urging Naani forward. "I'll see you later . . . salaams!"

Gorinani stepped aside reluctantly. "Hah jah by your house," she called after my departing form. "How you let bechaari mothernlaw do all kaams? Just now she get *fresh airs*!"

"What are fresh airs, Naani?" I asked, trying to quash my irritation as we climbed back into the car – I was not about to allow the Goat to taint this special day.

Naani grunted, yanking on her seat belt. "Ha, ha, you dornor? Can get high blood –"

"– pressure!" I said, interrupting her and giggling as I caught Naani's *moue* of disapproval.

"Don't worry, Naani, Katy Patel does *not* have high blood pressure . . ." I reassured her.

❧

The biryanis were full steam ahead and I was busy adjusting the temperature on the oven when Rozi burst into the kitchen with her mother-in-law hot on her four-inch heels, the poor woman already deep in a Palace-induced trance. I hugged Rozi and kissed her soundly, whistling at her sexy salwaar khameez as Aunty Gori enveloped me enthusiastically. "Salaams. Oh! Sooo mashallah you looking. New set you wearing?" she asked, fingering the jewellery in question. "Sooo many diamonds, Maha, can't even count . . ."

Rozi rolled her eyes and chewed on her ever-present gum – part of her insouciant persona – as her mother-in-law peered intently at the necklace.

"I'm going to find your mummy now . . . where she?" Aunty Gori flapped excitedly.

"Umm, she's outside with some people."

"Oh! People came *already*? *See* Rozina? I *told* you must rush . . . sor *long* you take to get ready!" she complained before dashing off.

"Thank goodness for that," Rozi said, shaking her head. "The woman is driving me nuts."

"So? Did you vote?" I asked as I pulled a stack of trays towards me.

"Oh, puhleeze let's *not* discuss voting! *Everywhere* I fucking go, that's *all* people are talking about . . ." she replied.

"How can you be like that?" I demanded, puffing myself up with indignation. "It's history, bonehead! How can we not talk about it! We did it! Finally!"

"Yah, yah, whatever . . ." She flicked her hair.

"So, what plans for this weekend?" I asked as I began to artfully arrange a platter of bite-sized savouries.

"Well, everyone seems to be celebrating the *voting*." She grimaced. "Riaz is hosting the boys' braai tomorrow, and my father is in town, which means I have to socialise with the thugs."

I didn't blame her for looking downcast. Her father, in true gangster style, had married, divorced and stalked at least a dozen women – meaning that family gatherings involved a truly motley crew.

"Well, it's bound to be interesting at least . . ." I tried to console her as I garnished the trays with sprigs of mint and parsley.

"Yah, fuck it, at least there'll be plenty of drugs . . ."

My eyes widened a fraction, but luckily Rozi hadn't noticed. I was constantly forced to keep a check on my disquiet as she relished any opportunity to wax lyrical about my naivety.

I glanced at the clock. Mummy dearest would start panicking in a few minutes. "Do you want to go outside?" I asked Rozi.

"Nah, I'm going to your place for a pre-lunch fag!" she said, picking a pie from a passing tray and setting off towards my flat.

"Fine," I said enviously, preparing to play hostess. "See you later . . ."

I spotted flashes of Sameer every so often, working the crowd and then disappearing – probably off smoking or shooting pool in the games room. Mummy was obviously in her element, flitting from group to group, ensuring she was up to date with the latest tattle, and Dada kept me running around as anticipated, forever dissatisfied with the manner in which I saw to his needs. I shook my head as I handed over his dratted serviette.

"Anything else, Dada?" I asked, ready to kill for a mug of tea and fag.

He gave me a cursory glance. "I'll send for you when I need you, now gor see if your mummy needs anything . . . And find that Riaz Patel, what kind wife he got? She don't even come make salaam with me!"

I scanned the crowd for Riaz and found him engaged in earnest conversation with a few of Daddy's friends, but where was the shameless Rozi? How could she be so daft as to forget the old sod?

I *needed* a fag break, so I slipped out through the scullery door heading for the apartment – and almost walked into Ba.

"Oh! Shahzad!" I cried out in shock as a weird sense of déjà vu washed over me.

"Maha! Fancy bumping into *you* here!" he teased.

Shahzad, apart from his Don Juan reputation and congenial persona, was a fellow news junkie, which gave us something relatively impersonal to discuss at friendly meetings. However, he was not averse to the odd bursts of soul-searching and now was definitely *not* the time . . .

"Out of my way, bru!" I ordered. "I'm on a mission!"

"Oh, really?" He sniggered. "Would that involve state secrets and cigarettes?"

I laughed. "You know that if I tell you, I'll have to kill you!" I growled with a grin.

Ba stared at me thoughtfully for a few seconds. "You sure you don't want to talk for a bit first?"

I paused, turned around and glared. "I didn't say I *wouldn't* talk to you . . . I just invited you to choon over a fag, so I can kill two birds with one stone, get it?"

"Eish, calm down, woman. Sounds like you definitely need your nicotine fix! But hey, it's so beautiful out here, why don't we smoke around the back?"

"Are you nuts? That is a serious risk for an undercover agent like myself! My cover will be blown!" I said and grinned.

Ba mumbled, scraping his shoes on the paving.

I shook my head. "Why aren't you socialising, silly?"

He rolled his eyes. "I'm actually fleeing society. That Haroon is a hectic ou. He cornered me and went on and on about his fucked-up notion of evil women!" he spluttered irately.

I furrowed my brow. "That actually sounds quite *interesting*! Listen, I would love to chat, really, but I'm *desperate* and have limited time . . . so I'll catch you later. Oh, and if you see Riaz, please tell him Dada Patel is looking for him *and* his errant vrou!"

He responded with a smart salute.

I pushed through the front door of my apartment and took in the carnage. It looked like a small army had already made a pit stop in my kitchen for a fag break. Well, that was fine for them, but the only place it was safe for *me* to smoke was behind the locked door of my bathroom.

I sighed as I slipped off my heels and padded slowly up the carpeted stairs. The bedroom door was slightly ajar and as I gave it a light prod I immediately spotted an overflowing ashtray on the precious cream carpet! Shit! The last thing I needed was Sameer going ape-shit: his calm veneer shattered at the sight of even a speck. I took a step closer and looked casually towards the alcove at the far end of the room. I'd give anything to simply throw myself onto my bed and just lie there, I thought. Then I frowned, blinked and froze.

It was Rozi's back, but her arms were wrapped around someone that was evidently *not* Riaz! Shahzad? No, I'd *just* seen him outside. I didn't want to look, but I couldn't tear my eyes away. *Sameer?* My brain iced over as he opened his eyes, which rapidly widened with shock.

The afternoon light danced playfully through the gently billowing curtains, oblivious to my paralysis. Then, suddenly, adrenaline stormed through my veins and my body slipped effortlessly into survival mode. I fled, frozen brain or no, pausing only to grab my sandals.

You remembered your *sandals*? I thought, shaking my head at myself as I sat on the lowest step and slipped them on. I listened for the sound of Sameer running down behind me to explain, but there was only the sound of distant chatter wafting over from the party. And, anyway, how exactly was he going to explain being caught playing tonsil hockey with Rozi? Rozi! That whore of Babylon!

You are *calm*, I instructed myself firmly as I teetered down the garden path, attempting to unclench my jaw and rearrange my face so as to appear as normal as possible. Whether it was an insane calm, I didn't care. At that moment I'd take any brand of calm.

Mummy was fussing around the kitchen, all flustered. "*Where* you went?" she cried. "Everyone's waiting for tea now. Where you put all the baking?"

"Everything's ready, Mummy," I said placidly. "It's all in the dining room. We just need to take it outside."

"Come, *come* then. Get the girls to help you. It's getting late."

My breaking heart se *moer*. I grimaced as a sharp pain seared through my chest, but there was no time for that. Time for tea, Maha! *Focus!* I closed my eyes, attempting to shut out the image of Sameer and Rozi, and steadied myself. Grabbing a tray of intricate biscuits I focused on the swirling icing as I made my way outside to the heaving trestle table.

Naani and Gorinani pounced as soon as they spotted me. "Ey, Maha," Gorinani said, pinching my cheek. "You dorn look right."

Smile, Maha, smile!

Naani smiled warmly. "You coming our house after?"

I shrugged. "Depends on what Sameer is doing," I responded robotically, realising with a dull ache that I had *no* fucking clue what

Sameer was going to be doing! "Try the chocolate cake, Gorinani, it's a new recipe from Mummy's sister," I continued, clutching onto the table for support as a wave of nausea hit me. "If you like it I'll give Samiha the recipe . . ."

"Cut small piece . . . Got sugars too, can't eat too much cake-bis-coot," she replied.

I stabbed at the cake and sliced violently. Perhaps I *would* go to the Mahal and catch my breath. *No!* That would allow time for my brain to thaw and the thoughts to flow, and that was a bad idea. Handing out the plates, I muttered incomprehensibly and fled to the kitchen as the puke rose threateningly in the back of my throat.

Mummy walked in, trailed by her entourage of Foi and Aunty Gori, just as I lowered my forehead onto the cool metal of the cold tap.

"What's happening here?" Foi asked immediately. "Ey, you look sick! I must call Forjee to see you?"

"No, no, don't bother him . . ." I croaked. "I'm fine. Just feeling a bit weak . . ." I'd have rather given Dada a sponge bath than have the delightful Dr Forjee Wanker examine me!

"These girls today," Aunty Gori said before Foi could get another word in, "they don't look after themselves, they don't eat properly too, they run-run everywhere every day, going gym and where-where . . ."

Foi nodded in agreement. "Have to look after yourself, Maha. Now see? Big-big daawat and you can't do nothing. Must just sit here like one paari."

I turned on the tap and sipped some water from it. Paari? She called *me* – slave *par excellence* – a fucking malingerer?

"So now," Mummy asked worriedly, "what you doing?"

"Nothing, I'm just resting for a few minutes. I'll be fine. Don't worry . . . I'll finish up."

"Professor Laher invited me and Daddy for supper," she went on, smiling at Aunty Gori. "They taking us out, I don't know where . . . and isn't Sameer and the boys got that mosque braai tonight?"

"Yah, yah," Aunty Gori yapped eagerly, "Riaz too got daawat for that braai. All the boys from the mosque. Plus tomorrow night 'nuther braai by our house!"

"*Who's* preparing the gos for tonight?" Foi suddenly asked worriedly. She believed that the Patels simply couldn't tolerate anyone else's cuisine.

"Oh, no! Bhengori from Reservoir Hills is giving the masala. She gives like us!" Mummy responded derisively, and swept out of the kitchen, aghast that Foi could dare presume that she wouldn't have checked on this pertinent detail.

⁂

The kitchen counter heaved with a seemingly endless sea of dishes but I worked my way through them methodically, sorting them into manageable stacks and packing away any leftovers. By the time the tea trays made their way back to the kitchen, the food had been seen to and the dishes cleared away by Happiness and her small army of washer-dryers.

When I finally clicked the last Tupperware lid shut, I walked across to the scullery where the maids formed a chattering blur through the steam. Happiness's daughter had also been roped in, her arms elbow deep in soapy suds. She looked up with a shy smile.

"Hey, Mary! I didn't know you were here! How *are* you?" I asked, squeezing her arm gently.

"Good, Maha, just busy . . ." she replied, smiling shyly.

"Yah," I made a face, "I can see that. I see your mother's got you working . . ."

"Not *her* mother," Happiness whispered as she wandered by, balancing an enormous tray of glasses. "*Your* mummy. She tell me: 'Go get your ntombi. I give her ten rands.'"

My eyes widened. "Oh? Okay, then . . . Anyway, I just wanted to say thanks for helping out. I'm done now. You can finish the dishes and then wipe, sweep and mop, okay?"

"Eish! So fast-fast you finish too, Maha! Where you running?" Happiness asked.

"Nowhere. I'm staying over at my naani's 'cos everyone's going out . . ."

The bile rose instantly as I stepped out through the scullery door and looked up at the familiar and now forever tainted view before me. Just. Don't. Think, I told myself as I gritted my teeth and made my way across to the apartment.

No one had bothered tidying up downstairs. It had been left to me to empty the ashtrays, straighten the cushions and wipe down the small counter. All this I did and only when it was impossible to postpone the inevitable any longer did I kick off my sandals and pad up the carpeted stairs.

The door was still ajar, the curtains still billowing, but the overflowing ashtray had been cleared away. The fading sunlight cast a jaundiced veil across the room. Sameer had no doubt given vent to his OCD and removed every trace of "crap".

Sameer! I heaved and fled to the bathroom, flinging my head into the loo just as my innards convulsed and brought up the biryani.

Falling back onto the cool tiles I tried to catch my breath. Stop it, Maha, I lectured myself. Just wash your face, pack your bags and go!

I flew into my closet, pulled down an overnight case from the top shelf and started throwing random items into it. Three minutes later I hefted the case, swung my handbag onto my shoulder and stomped down the stairs, hoping to get to the car without crossing anyone's path. Mission accomplished, I collapsed thankfully into my seat, pulled out my phone and typed a message to Farah: *Slmz. Staying over at Mahal. Please come. Need you. Bring drugs. Need oblivion. Serious stuff. X*

See you around 8. X, she responded as I put the car into gear, reversed slowly out into the driveway and nosed towards the main gates.

Someone was chatting to George. Fuck! I slowed to a halt and wound down my window. It was Shamini from next door.

"Hey, Maha. Big jol, I see . . ." she said.

"Hey, Shamini, howzit. I didn't know you were around. I saw your ma at the lunch, but she didn't say anything . . ."

"Yeah, her head's full of stuff, she keeps calling me Chubby, who as you know is the cat." She laughed, shaking her head. "It's my sister's eighteenth this weekend," she continued. "We're having a bit of a jol ourselves . . ."

"Oh, yah, I think Fay and Nas are invited, not old fogeys like me," I said and managed a false snigger.

"Well if you're old, then I'm old . . ." she said and grinned. Although we shared the same birth year, our lives were worlds apart.

Shamini lived on her own in Joburg, where she practised law at a high-powered firm.

"So, why are you prancing around The Grove?" I asked.

"I'm meeting some mates at Musgrave and my sister's taken my car," she said, running her hands through her closely cropped hair. "I was just trotting along when I saw George, and stopped to chat."

"Why don't you hop in?" I asked. "I'll give you a lift . . ."

"Hey, cool, Maha, that's great," she said. "See you later, George, bhasobha kahle."

He grinned, waved and let us out.

"So, where are you off to?" Shamini asked as soon as she had strapped herself in and kicked her bag under the seat.

"I'm going to my grandparents' place for the weekend. It's been a crazy week and I need to relax. As you can imagine, the elections were by the way. Priority was preparing for the luncheon!"

"The bloody Chaarous are still the same . . ." she said and laughed.

I pretended to peer at the road and cast a quick glance at my silent cellphone – still no word from the bastard!

"Hey, I've got some hot gossip . . ." Shamini said, breaking the silence. "I bet no one at the Palace knows. You know John . . .?"

"Tshabalala?" I asked, swinging onto the main road.

"Yeah . . . He's in matric this year. Anyhow, he's in lurrveee."

John Tshabalala was their maid's son. He'd grown up with the Pillay sisters and fortunately for him attended the same schools.

"Good for him. Who's the lucky lass?" I asked.

"You'll never guess . . . Mary, Happiness's daughter!"

I laughed. "But she's only been here a few weeks. How is that possible?"

Shamini shrugged. "Who knows?" she said. "But she's quite a look-er, so I'm not surprised." She paused. "You're actually looking quite pale. You sure you're not ill or anything?"

"Nope, don't think so anyway," I said, gritting my teeth as we pulled up outside the centre. "It's just been a busy week . . ."

"Nice catching you," she said, leaning over and kissing my cheek before opening the door. "Thanks for the lift . . ."

Maal Mahal's welcoming lights blinked comfortingly through the dusk, a sturdy presence on a familiar road. I drove up and parked haphazardly, grabbed my bag and ran around to the back door.

Naani was bustling in the kitchen, her prayer orhni still draped around her upper body. "Asalaam 'alaikum, Maha, sor late you come . . ." she clucked and fussed, looking at my bag. "Only one night you stay? Why you dorn stay whole weekend? Sameer can come way also . . ."

As if. Naani dear still hadn't cottoned onto the fact that her be-loved Sameer would never sleep away from the Palace.

"You read Maghrib?" she asked.

"I've got my period," I replied brusquely. "I'm going to have a bath and then a nap. Farah is coming over later, and . . . umm . . . don't worry about supper."

"Har *hu* supper? Sor much biryani we eat and come. Nana too want torst and chur after he come from masjid."

My insides churned. "I'll come down and see him later, after my nap . . ." I said.

"Haaru, beti, gor rest, sor tired too you look . . ."

Minutes later I shed my clothes and slipped into the warm welcoming depths. Grabbing a towel, I rammed it into my mouth, biting down savagely on the material as I began to howl, letting out the emotion I had denied myself since I had caught them together. My mind replayed the snog and I gagged in agony – I had *no* words, just plaintive mewls that wracked my entire body and stirred a tsunami in my bathtub.

Twenty minutes later I climbed out of the tub, cocooned myself in my old robe and settled under the heavy godhru and soft blanket – the perfect combination of weight and warmth. I shifted my head around, found a comfy spot and closed my eyes in preparation for the *ultimate* escape.

⁂

The incessant ring of my distant mobile tugged at the edge of my consciousness, dragging me reluctantly out of slumber. I fumbled around for the wretched thing and spat out a chunk of hair.

"Hello?" Shit! I hadn't even looked at the number. It could be *Sameer*! Suddenly, I was fully alert.

"Maha! I'm here . . ."

It was Farah! Thank goodness! "Hey, Farah, sorry, I was asleep . . . I'm coming down."

"'K . . ." she said and cut the call.

I struggled out of the tangled blanket and godhru, straightened out my gown and hair and made my way downstairs.

"Hey, Farah," I wriggled my fingers at her in greeting. "I just need to go and see my nana quickly. You can go up to my room if you like . . ."

"Cool, thanks. I'll see you there."

"Do you want tea or something?" I offered automatically.

"Tea's good," she called as I made my way to the kitchen.

Nana looked up from his toast. "Asalaam 'alaikum, beti. How are you?" he asked kindly.

"Wa 'alaikum salaam, Nana." I paused to kiss his cheek. "I'm fine, alhamdulillah."

Nana smiled. "Allah keep you happy, beti . . ."

I busied myself, turning away and scowling at the kettle. "Aameen, Nana . . ."

Happy? I wouldn't know happy if it ran over and slapped my arse!

A few minutes later the kettle clicked to a stop and I poured the steaming water. "I'm going to be in my room," I told Nana. "I'll see you tomorrow, inshallah."

"Yah, beti, go and rest, you must be very tired after today."

"Salaams, Nana," I said, hefting the tray and then almost dropping it with fright as a car horn blared outside.

Nana stood up. "Sameer aawo!" he called out excitedly, scuttling towards the entrance. Like every self-respecting Slumurban, the grandparents subscribed to the philosophy that keeping jamai happy meant a happy union, and thus they zealously ensured his every comfort while showering him with the utmost respect.

"Jaldi kar," Naani urged. "So much hooting, he rush, Maha!"

I stepped outside, seething with frustration. Nana was already engaged in earnest conversation with the wonderful lad, and I watched as the chuth wove his magic, nattering away in the lingo. I waited until Nana had his fill of golden poyro and stepped aside reluctantly, muttering about mosque braais.

"Get in," Sameer finally said.

Anger surged, but I swallowed it quickly and made my way to the passenger side.

⚜

Sameer waited until Nana was safely back indoors before turning to face me. He reached for my hands, but I snatched them back angrily.

"Don't be like that, Maha, please?" he coaxed. "Look, I'm here . . . Why do you think I came?" He leaned back and pulled out a tired BP bouquet. "I got these for you," he said, thrusting them onto my lap. "Listen, what you saw *never* happened before. I promise. And the only reason it happened is 'cos Rozi, the idiot, popped some pills, so she was out of control and just attacked me!"

"You seemed pretty happy for someone being attacked!" I muttered, pulling at a petal and avoiding his gaze. Rozi popping pills and morphing into a succubus was not improbable, but I remained aloof.

"Fine, Maha, suit yourself. If you want to act all funny with me for something that wasn't even *my* fault . . ." He sighed theatrically.

So now I was the bad one for acting funny! I was fucking far from amused.

"Listen! If you're not going to speak to me, don't waste my time. I'll just carry on to this braai!"

"Fine then . . ." My words escaped with some difficulty through gritted teeth.

Sameer glared. "I'm warning you, don't you dare mention what you saw to *anyone*, understand? It was a one-off fuck-up . . . End of story!"

57

I nodded tersely. "I'll see you on Sunday," I managed and fled back inside, leaving the wilted blooms behind.

⚜

Farah was reclined on my bed and sat up as I put down the tray and locked the door. I gave her a pained look.

"Sorry it took so long. Sameer turned up." I sighed and flumped down beside her.

"Yah, I heard the famous hooter!" She stretched across for her mug and grinned.

"Thanks for coming . . ." I smiled wanly.

"Don't be daft. Now what's so serious? I've got drugs, so bring it on, baby!"

I perked up at the thought of narcotics. "Oh, what did you bring?"

"Well, it depends on what you need . . . I brought my pa's bag with me." She shrugged. "I wasn't sure what the emergency was."

"Well," I sipped, swallowed and took a breath, "you know I've been busy all week?"

"Yeah, 'cos of today's luncheon at the Palace." She sipped her tea. "Sorry I couldn't make it . . . So? Did something happen there?"

I took her through the fag break and my altercation with Ba and then . . .

Farah stared at me in shock. "Rozi, the bitch!"

I breathed deeply, but the dam had already burst and a few seconds later my body was wracked by my sobs.

Farah was suitably aghast and pulled me into her arms, rocking me soothingly. "What *did* you do?" she muttered into my ear.

I snorted through a sob and looked up at her. "Me? Hah! Well,

58

let's see . . . I froze . . . I went numb . . . I fled . . . " I sniffed, yanking the nearest cloth and blowing my nose. "And then I went like the perfect dorternlaw that I am and served tea! Can you believe? I served high fucking tea at the Palace!" I screeched hysterically.

Farah stood up and surveyed the garden below. "I think it would help if you had a good cry and let it all out . . ."

"Yah, right, and have Naani pound on the door to find out 'Hu che? Gorinani can hear fufuyaans from our house!' "

Farah leaned against the windowsill. "So what the hell did he want just now?"

"Oh, he stopped by to explain. Apparently Rozi was high. She attacked him!" I filled her in succinctly.

"Yeah, well at least he is sorry!"

I sighed. "Yes, I know . . . I know . . . But I just can't believe it!" I groaned. "Sameer and Rozi!" I burst out angrily. "I mean . . . Rozi! Rozina? Riaz's wife! And Sameer 'Poes' Patel?"

Farah shook her head and shrugged. "To be honest, I'm glad this week's finally over," she said. "It was a tough one for my ma, 'cos my father, well, he'd been really excited about the elections, you know . . ." she trailed off broodingly.

I picked at the carpet with my hand, nodded and focused on Uncle Faizal.

She smiled wanly. "Look at the two of us sorry sods. I reckon we need a good night's sleep."

I nodded, standing up to switch off the lights.

Farah plumped her pillow and handed me my pill. "There you go, take this like a good girl now . . . We can't have you sobbing along to Toni Braxton all night!" she said and smiled.

"Hilarious! Why do I have to live the damn cliché?"

"Hey, I'm not the one who was born on a dark and stormy night . . ." she said, collapsing tiredly against the pillows.

I sat beside her and picked up a pillow. "How dare you . . ." I began, thwacking her with my pillow, "call my life a cliché! Well, fuck you!"

She held up her hands defensively. "Good, that's it, get it out of your system. I can see you've been aching to punch something . . ."

I hit her half-heartedly. "I love him, you know . . . and I have no idea what I'm going to do!" I muttered.

"Well," she raised her head and rested it on her hand, "you don't have to think about it right now. I reckon you should go to sleep and maybe tomorrow we can call Zeenat and have a chat?"

"Yes, oh wise and sensible friend."

She inhaled noisily. "Yah, okay, whatever you say . . ." she slurred. "I'm going to pass out any second now . . . We can choon tomorrow . . . Tomorrow is another day . . . The dawn of the new South Africa . . ."

Thank goodness for that! "Sweet dreams . . . Salaams," I whispered.

I shut my eyes with a deep sigh. The day was over – at last!

"Hey, Farah?" I nudged her gently. "If my life is one big fat cliché," I mumbled, "where's my happily ever after?"

But Farah was already snoring gently.

To Have and to Hope

Winter sojourned in Durban – typically brief and mild – and by the time it was over Mandela had long been sworn in. I'd watched the historic event while chopping coriander for sambals. My country had officially rejoined the world, but I was almost entirely unmoved, too busy trying to keep a lid on the unappetising kachumbar of jealousy and rage that was roiling inside me to be anything more than mildly amused by the motley array of royalty, Ivy-League presidents, tin-pot dictators and revolutionaries on the guest list.

In the end I had chosen to believe Sameer – I had *had* to – and had somehow found the energy to forget about the indiscretion and lumber on, a part of me preaching that marriages were not to be flung aside at the very first pothole. Putting it all behind me, I focused compulsively on work and could always rely on the kitchen for a constant supply. I crowded my days by upping the ante with my

UNISA degree – meeting my deadlines with new-found fervour – and offering to run errands for Naani. I was now first out of bed – up at six to get my caffeine and news fix and squeeze in some reading before reporting for duty.

As the historic year wound down, I acknowledged that I had become a bona fide Round Roti; I had indisputably morphed into the type of female I had derided as a teenager. Gone were the days when I had relaxed after a busy day, anticipating the return of my man. Our passion post-ordeal saw a primeval collision of rage, lust and guilt, which though physically satiating was tainted by after-action dissatisfaction.

Unfortunately, Rozi was still very much a part of our lives. Old friendships run deep and there was no way I could avoid her if I wanted to socialise with my husband. I was content to believe that she had no recollection of her whoring, though I held back from re-newing our friendship and only ever asked of her if I was desperate. Her self-centredness continued unabated, and the only irritations in her life were Riaz's recent nag about babies and her mother-in-law's desire to visit India now that full diplomatic relations had been restored.

⁕

Mummy stood with hands on hips and a firm set to her jaw. "Fayza and Naseem ate something funny," she said. "They both sooo sick. You must help me look after them."

Sick? My left tit! More like hung over. Fay remained unbothered about passing matric – her dire grades would not thwart Katy and

Joe's plan for her to *read* English at UND next year – and Nas, well, Nas was just Nas.

"Oh, yah, and it's Sameer's club Saturday, so he won't be here today," she continued. "Daddy is resting. And, lucky, Dada not coming today."

Satisfied that I was completely in the picture, she sighed theatrically and set off to look for Happiness. I'd played lady-in-waiting to the bedridden brats before, and I efficiently rounded up two trays and a pair of everything else. Tea and toast for the royal spawn first, then I could see to my own needs.

"Club Saturday," I bitched as I stood in front of the toaster, yanking its lever savagely. The Club boasted Sameer's great-grandfather as one of its founding fathers, a historical fact that blessed each of the male Patels with life-long membership (as with any gentleman's club, women were strictly barred). "Sod it," I griped as the toast popped – the weekend had barely begun and already it seemed like it was over.

I would, however, have a brief interlude in the afternoon, I reminded myself as I took the trays up to the prince and princess. Farah and I had waxing appointments with Zeenat – which, though painful, would also be a chance to chill, choon and have a laugh.

Having delivered breakfast to the ingrates I returned to the kitchen to spend the morning preparing enough cakes and biscuits to last the week.

⁂

I was late for Zeenat's. As soon as Mummy had got wind of my appointment, she'd instructed me to pack a selection of baked goods and drop it off at the Vankers. This meant a long and unnecessary detour to Reservoir Hills, but there was no way round it.

Farah was already waxed and relaxed when I burst into the salon breathlessly. "Salaams, sorry I'm so late . . . never-ending errands!" I said, pausing briefly to hug and kiss them both.

"Do you want a drink?" Farah asked as I stripped and prepared to endure the imminent torture.

"Tea," I demanded, climbing onto the bed and closing my eyes. "I want a nice mug of tea that I can drink in peace . . ."

"So, Mrs Patel, what news from the Palace?" Zeenat asked as Farah rummaged around for a tea bag and put the kettle on to boil. "It's been ages since we had a chance to sit and choon. You need to bring me up to date!"

"Same old, same old," I replied. "Just work, keeping me sane. Why don't you ask Farah for her news . . ."

"Okay," Farah said, "shall I choon the story of Ba?"

I nodded as Zeenat stubbed out her fag and prepared herself for waxing, eager as always for other people's tales.

I had arranged for Farah and Shahzad to get together for coffee a few weeks earlier, and they had apparently hit it off like a Memon house on fire. Farah had succeeded in getting to the bottom of many things, including his slumming in the jondols, and I had been abashed to learn that the time he spent there was given over to charitable work as opposed to shady deals! However, his past had remained a closed book. That was, until now.

"Well, apparently, he was in lurrveee," Farah began as Zeenat started to smear the molten wax onto my legs. "He was completely besotted with this chick Melissa, a half-Bruinou, half-Boere chick from some village near Laudium. They dated for years, and then she fell pregnant, so he immediately offered to marry her, despite the fact that his family had major fufuyaans and threatened to disown him if he went ahead."

Zeenat whistled. "That would mean losing a truckload of dosh! Wow!" she said as she pulled viciously and I gritted my teeth.

"Well," Farah continued, "the way Shahzad tells it, he was prepared to walk off into the sunset with her with only the clothes on his back."

Zeenat peered for strays and ingrowns. "I'm impressed," she muttered as she jabbed with her tweezers. "Didn't think the lad had such balls."

"Yeah . . ." I groaned as she plucked a hair.

"So what went wrong?" Zeenat asked, starting to smooth her soothing cream onto my legs. "'Cos he's sitting pretty with all his flats in the city . . ."

"*All* his flats?" I asked. "I didn't know he owned more than one."

"Well, from what I hear, he has about half a dozen, prime locations, etcetera," she replied.

Finally, Zeenat was finished and I jumped off the bed, grabbed my mug from Farah and flopped down beside her. "So, what happened?" I asked.

She sighed. "Yah, what happened was that the love of his life saw her meal ticket slipping away, so she cut her own deal with his family and dumped poor old Ba!"

"What a bitch!" Zeenat said, washing her hands. "And was she *really* pregnant?"

Farah snorted. "Oh, yah, she made sure she had the kid. That way she knew she'd get support for life!"

"Un-fucking-believable!" I said and took a greedy gulp of tea. "So why did he end up in Durbs?"

"After it was all over his family decided that he needed a change of scene and packed him off to Durbs."

"Hmmm . . ." Zeenat said, drying her hands. "He was lucky he came as a student . . . Easy to meet people and make friends."

I reached out for a fag, sighed and lit it, taking a deep drag. "Ooh," I squealed as "Endless Summer Nights" floated over the airwaves and into Zeenat's salon, "I haven't heard this in *ages*!"

Farah giggled. "Does it remind you of carefree adolescence?" she asked. "Oh, and speaking of adolescents, I meant to ask you how Mary's doing?"

Zeenat looked up from her mug. "Who's Mary?"

"Our kitchen maid's daughter," I said. "She's finally attending the local girls' secondary." I paused. "Mummy didn't want to let her go, but I managed to persuade Sameer to nag her. Well, he fucking owed me a favour . . . But surprise, surprise, she still has to work part-time at the Palace to 'pay' for her education."

"And *your* assignments, how are they coming along?" Farah asked, changing the subject. "Are you on track?"

"Yah, it's going well, actually. Been working religiously, so I've actually managed to get loads done *and* revise!"

"You're killing yourself, woman," Zeenat clucked. "You've got to take it easy or you'll crash and burn! Gor relax and see flim!"

They chortled and I laughed along – determined to deal with the stress as there was simply no time off from dorternlaw duty to do anything other than study.

Sameer arrived home one evening waving tickets for a Christmas break in Cape Town. Since so many months had passed since his transgression, it was perhaps a little late as a conciliatory gesture, but I still couldn't help feeling a faint lifting of my spirits. It would be my first time back in the Cape since I'd left over a decade earlier and my thoughts immediately turned to my political-activist parents, martyred by the apartheid regime. I felt my heart break all over again as I imagined how they would have welcomed us at the airport, how they would have driven us around the peninsula, how we would have eaten together, laughing and catching up. Thank God for Ouma Galiema, I thought, at least I would have time to see her.

Unfortunately, I had all of five minutes alone with the old woman as, immediately after greeting her, my bourgeoisie husband claimed to have developed a migraine and announced that he'd be waiting for me in the car.

Ouma pulled me aside furiously. "Just who does your husband mos think he is, Maha?" she demanded crossly. "We is not goed enough for him? First time mos youse come back to Cape Town, he can't see *all* your daddy's families is here?"

I didn't blame her – she had cooked a feast fit for royalty and invited the entire Jacobs clan – but Athlone was clearly not good enough for Sameer's snobby sensibilities.

"I'm sorry, Ouma," I said sadly. "I did beg him, you know?"

"What is this begging nonsense, kleintjie? For what must beg your husband for anything? Youse want to beg, Allah is there for that, hoor?" She took in my stricken face and pulled me into her warm embrace. "Leave the koelie, never mind now, darling . . ." she said, trying to console me, but her words had cut me to the quick.

I blinked away the tears, slapped on a smile and went through the motions of saying hello and goodbye to my non-Chaarou family.

"So, where's your handsome husband, Maha?" Tante Gabiba, one of my father's cousins, asked innocently.

"Umm, he's not feeling too well . . ." I shrugged apologetically. "He's waiting in the car."

"Ag, shame," she offered sympathetically and smiled. "Well, youse must come to us for tea at least!"

I winced at her kindness.

"Hey, Nadima," she said, yanking her niece towards us.

"Howzit, Maha. Nice to finally meet you . . ." She smiled. "Come meet the others quickly," she said, leading me away from her aunt and towards a group of relatives clustered around a table. "Will we see you again while you're here?"

I smiled, hiding my discomfort at the question. "I'm not sure. Mrs Abrahams also invited us for tea, but Sameer may have other plans," I answered lamely, silently hoping Sameer wasn't smouldering in the car.

Nadima cackled madly. "Mrs Abrahams? Eish, Maha, jy is mos malkop! Tante Gabiba will klap you if you call her that!"

<hr/>

There was hope in the world, I acknowledged as I studied Robben Island from the top of Table Mountain, but whether it extended to my plans to see Ouma Galiema again before we returned to Durban I couldn't say. Much to Ouma's annoyance I had pretty much given up on the itinerary she had put together with the rest of the Jacobs clan for my time in Cape Town. I had assuaged her with promises of a final visit, which I still had to engineer somehow, but as Sameer glazed over every time I brought the subject up I had decided to take Ouma's advice for the time being and abstain from begging the koelie.

Sameer caught up with me and smiled as I drank in my Mother City, sprawled open armed before me. "Isn't it our anniversary next month?" he asked.

I offered the city of my birth a long-suffering smile. "Three years!" It felt more like thirty!

"Seems like I've been with you *all* my life . . ." he mused.

"Poor you!" I offered unsympathetically.

"Don't be stupid!" He gave a feeble smile and moved to put his arm around me. "It's the best thing. You know that."

"Do you want to go back down?" I asked, squinting up at him.

"Yah, let's go." He broke away from me and stuck out his hand, which I took compliantly.

⁂

I called Ouma and arranged to pop over while Sameer did a spot of shopping – infinitely more exciting than in Durbs as Cape Town had a slew of independent local designer stores and a wider range of shops stocking delectable foreign fare.

Ouma was busy dunking her freshly fried koesisters into the thick syrup when I arrived. The smell assaulted me as soon as I stepped in, sparking off an unexpectedly vivid flashback of returning from school and running into her kitchen. I caught my breath and gulped.

"Hey, Ouma, salaams," I said. "It smells lekker in here! You didn't have to go to all this trouble . . ."

She wiped her hands hastily and embraced me warmly. "Ahh, Maha, my darling. Kom, kom sit . . . Tea?'

I nodded, flopped down on a chair and looked around the kitchen. There were shoeboxes on one end of the table and larger boxes stacked neatly in a corner. "Hey, Ouma, what are you up to?" I asked. "Cleaning?"

"Ja, Maha, I was sommer sorting through stuffs . . . So many things everywhere and jus now He calls me," she gestured heavenward, "then who's to do all these jobs?" She placed a brown-and-orange striped mug full of tea in front of me. "I kept this," she said. "It's for you, it was your daddy's favourite mug . . ."

"Oh!" I held the mug in both hands and summoned up a vision of my daddy, sitting and sipping out of this very mug. I smiled. "Thanks, Ouma, this is now officially the best mug of tea in the world . . ."

Ouma Galiema finished up with her cooking and sat down across from me at the kitchen table, pushing a shoebox towards me as she did so. "See here, Maha, I got this small box for you. The rest of the stuffs," she shrugged, "I don't know if you want to go through and check . . ."

I nodded. "Thanks," I said, looking carefully at the box she had produced. "I'll have a look but I'm sure most of it can go to people in need, Ouma. What's the point of hanging on to it all?"

"I also got a big box of all Achmat and Maryam's books," Ouma Galiema continued. "I'll post it to Durban for youse. Ag, they mos liked to read, your mummy and daddy!"

"Don't worry about posting anything. I'll take the books with me,"

I said, picking up a koesister and taking a bite. I paused, letting the soft, sweet dough melt in my mouth before I swallowed. "So, what's in this box?" I finally asked, jerking my head towards it.

She chortled. "Bits and pieces, en mos the dishcloths we wrapped you in when you was born . . ." She shook her head at the memory. "I've got a small box of koesisters for you to take too . . . When youse going?"

"Our flight's tomorrow morning . . ."

"I thought youse came by car?"

I shook my head. "No, Sameer just hired one from somewhere in town."

Ouma nodded. "That Sameer, he is looking after you, Maha, klein-tjie?" she asked, her gaze boring into me.

I blinked and looked away. "Yah, Ouma. He can be a bit odd, but he's good to me!"

She nodded. "Goed, goed, I like to know that jy is mos happy."

***

The following morning we took a taxi from the hotel to the airport. As the driver drove us through the slowly awakening city Sameer lay back in his seat with his eyes closed, but I was alert, my window wide open, my eyes blurry with tears as I drank in every flashing sight. As the taxi passed the first of the rush-hour traffic, I found myself wondering whether I would ever meet up with my darling Ouma again. My heart squeezed painfully against my ribcage at the thought, and I bit my lip, but I knew there was nothing I could do.

I stood patiently at the check-in counter while Sameer paid the excess baggage costs without complaint.

"I'll get the driver to take them to your nana's . . ." he said, grabbing the boarding passes and moving away. "You've got space for all this junk in your old room."

The words hurt, but I nodded in agreement, grateful to be able to fly back to Durban with all the reading matter my parents had amassed during their short lives.

To Love and to Perish

The year kicked off with an eruption of love as Sameer "The Accountant" used our third anniversary to balance his books. A box of Swiss chocolates supplemented the usual bouquet in the morning, while the evening involved candlelight and a sparkling eternity ring.

That evening already felt like a lifetime ago when I stepped out into the back garden a few weeks later and glanced up at the sun, which had already gained sufficient strength to fill the air with a stodgy haze, signalling the impending squall of steam. Looking back down at my hands I saw the light glinting off my new ring. I sighed as I made my way to the Palace kitchen.

Naseem rolled in at eleven, demanding a full English breakfast. Still no sign of Fay, I mused as I pulled out the macon, tossed the sausages in a pan, cast the eggs into the sizzling ghee and waited for the toast to pop. Finally, I placed the heaving plate before the unsavoury prince, who, predictably, ignored me and tucked in.

The phone rang and I answered automatically.

"Hello, is it possible to speak with Dumisile Dlamini?"

"I'm sorry, I think you have the wrong number . . ." I ventured politely.

"Well, I'm calling from Overport Girls' . . . I have a student called Mary Dlamini. This is her contact number. Does her mother work there?"

"Oh, Mary! Yes, that's right, her mother works here. Is there a problem?"

"Well, I'm Ms Potter, one of her teachers . . . She's not well. Can someone come and pick her up?"

"Oh, shame, of course someone will pick her up," I responded.

"Thank you, just come along to reception and ask for her. She's lying down in the sickroom now."

I replaced the receiver. Mummy would be annoyed by my sudden absence, but sod her.

"What was that about?" Naseem blurted as I picked up the detritus of his breakfast.

"Nothing. I have to go!" I muttered.

"Oh? Where?"

I gave him a shrewd stare. Since when had Prince Naseem taken an interest in staff issues? I shrugged casually, whipped off my apron and set off to find Happiness, who was beating the kitchen rugs on a distant patch of lawn.

"Hey, Happiness, Mary's school called," I called to her as I made my way across the garden. "She's sick."

"Nkosi! What happen?" she asked, pausing her rug-bashing worriedly.

I shrugged. "Must be the flu or one of these viruses. Don't worry, I'm going to fetch her now, she can rest at my place while you're working."

"Eish. Siyabonga, Maha," Happiness said, turning her attention back to the rugs.

⁂

Stepping through the big doors I gazed in awe at the old honky state school – awards boards and framed photographs lined the hallway that led to the reception.

The secretary smiled. "Are you here for Mary? Are you the madam?"

I shrugged. "Umm, kind of," I muttered, and followed her into the sickroom.

Mary lay huddled under the thin blanket, her face flushed and her breath raspy. She struggled to sit up. "Maha!"

"Hey, Mary, you look awful! Come, let's get you sorted out." I held out my hand to help her up.

Mary leaned heavily against me as we shuffled out towards the main entrance. I paused to sign the leave-slip, thanked the secretary and helped her into the car. I reclined against the door and caught my breath before heading back to the Palace.

I waited impatiently for George to let us in, eased down the long drive and spied Mummy making her way across the lawn.

"Maha!" she waved, shouting across and almost stumbling over Chubby.

The poor cat flew deftly up the bordering tree, and promptly com-menced cleaning his face. I parked outside the garage and turned to Mary. "Why don't you go and lie down on my sofa? I'll be with you just now."

She nodded and shuffled off.

"Salaams, Mummy," I called as I gathered my things and made my way out unhurriedly.

She reached the car huffily. "Where you went?" she asked. "What happened to the girl? Naseem said the school phoned! What she stole?"

I slammed the door harder than necessary and clicked on the alarm. "Mary is not a thief. She's sick, so she needed to come home!"

"Oh! Where she now? I hope her mother don't go running-running to the room whole day!" She sniffed.

"Oh, don't worry, I told her to lie down on *my* sofa," I said through gritted teeth. "I'll keep an eye on her, so Happiness doesn't have to worry."

She clucked impatiently. "And *now*? You just going to sit and look after that girl?"

"Well, it won't take too long to sort Mary out, give her some tab-lets and then I'll do some work," I answered politely.

"What she got? Flu? Ey, everyone is getting flu. Naseem too said his head is paining whole morning." And with that she harrumphed and turned to hobble back to her lair.

⚜

Mary swallowed the extra-strength Panados gratefully and sank back onto the sofa. "Everything hurts," she groaned. "I feel so weak!"

I nodded sympathetically. "Yah, but let's see how you feel after the pills and some rest. Your mother knows you're here and I'm sure she'll stop by to see you . . ."

Mary nodded slowly.

"You should sleep," I instructed. "Are you comfortable enough on the sofa?"

She stretched out and wriggled down as I drew the blanket over her. "Yah," she yawned. "It's nice and warm here . . ."

"Good. Well, I'll be upstairs so shout if you need anything. I'll leave this glass of water here." I smiled.

She managed a weak grin and shut her eyes.

⚜

My desk heaved with books and files. "I'll be with you soon," I muttered in their general direction and stepped out of the climate-controlled interior onto the balcony that looked out over the city. Easing myself into the single wicker chair, I lit a cigarette, inhaled and blew out a plume of smoke and relief. It was a perfect moment and the only improvement I could envisage would be the calming motion of a rocking chair. "Yes, Dhaadi Maha," I said out loud, mocking myself as I brushed away the image of me sitting in the exact same spot as a grandmother. Taking another drag of my fag I fished out my cellphone. *Salaams. What time do you want to meet for supper? Legends at 7?* I typed.

Dropping my phone into my lap I focused on the gorgeous expanse of aquamarine horizon before me and let my thoughts wander. Ramadan was around the corner. Great! The season to be holy – *Palace* style. Nana and Naani had brought me up with the philosophy

77

of Ramadan being a time out from the grind of everyday life – altering one's focus and concentrating on the spiritual. Nana reckoned that abstaining from food, drink and acts of a sexual nature – not because you thought it was a good idea, but because your Creator asked you to – made focusing on the spiritual a *physical* reality. The Palace doors, however, opened magnanimously during Ramadan, allowing high society to rub shoulders with the hoi polloi from sunset until the final post-Taraweeh stragglers wandered in.

My phone beeped and I clicked on the message: Sameer.

Salaams. Everything okay? See u at Legends at 7:30! X

The phone rang moments later. Shit, it was Rozi.

"Salaams, Rozi! Howzit?"

"Bored out of my fucking mind, as usual. Whatcha doing?"

"Nothing much," I muttered.

"Lucky bitch! I had to help fill a hundred dozen samoosas! By the end I was ready to stick a fucking samoosa into the mothernlaw's eye!"

"Shame," I replied, sniggering, "sor good dorternlaw you are!" At least I didn't have the pain of geometry in the kitchen – samoosas at the Palace were delivered monthly: boxed, labelled and ready for the freezer.

She snorted. "I'm on a fag break and then it's back to the bloody pasting and packing."

"Yah, I'm also taking one of those, and then I need to work on my next assignment: 'To speak of woe that is in all marriage . . .'"

She grunted. "Who wrote that? Shakespeare?"

"No," I laughed, "Chaucer. *The Wife of Bath.*"

"Hmm, whatever . . . I heard you guys are going out for supper tonight!"

That was quick! I stretched lazily. "Yah, Sameer felt like it."

"Lucky you!" she groaned. "Old lady's invited some bloody relatives who are down from goodness knows where!"

"Oh, so what did you cook?" I asked.

"Me? You think I'm going to cook after samoosa torture? *She* prepared some stuff yesterday; *her* visitors, *her* problem!"

I sighed. "Well as long as she doesn't moan to Riaz about you, I guess it will be okay," I offered.

"Fuck 'em. Let her moan if she wants and let him sulk if he wants! Anyhow, fag's finished. I'll see you soon, okay?"

I cut the call and flopped back with relief. Was I *ever* going to see the light at the end of this tunnel? I wondered. Or would my life just roll along with me escaping every now and then to my balcony? I stubbed out my fag and headed back inside to work.

⚜

I paused to chew my pencil as, downstairs, the door opened. I rubbed my eyes, glancing at the clock: one thirty. Happiness had probably brought Mary some lunch, I thought as I stood up lazily and began a slow shuffle across my room, my mind struggling to disentangle itself from the Chaucer I had been reading.

I heard the crash just as I got to my door and immediately picked up speed.

"*Shit!* Bloody bitch! See what you've done!" Naseem yelled.

I raced down in time to see him standing furiously above poor Mary with his fist raised.

"Hey! Naseem! What the *hell* do you think you're doing? Are you crazy?" I shouted.

He spun around and gestured to his soaking trousers. "Just look at this! She threw water all over my new chinos!"

"Calm down!" I glared at him as I caught my breath. Had he really been about to *hit* her for *that*? "It's only water!"

"Now I have to go and change," he griped and stormed off.

"Hey, are you okay?" I asked Mary as soon as Naseem was out of earshot. "He didn't hurt you, did he?"

Mary shook her head and averted her gaze. "I'm sorry," she whispered. "I didn't mean to wet him . . . Promise that you won't say anything to my mother?"

"What? Your mother? About what?" I was confused.

She nodded. "Yah, my mother. Please don't tell her about the water and Naseem, or anything else . . ."

"What else is there to tell?" I frowned as a finger of fear unfurled. "That he looked like he was about to hit you?"

She didn't speak for a while, gazing off into the distance. "He came and sat here . . ." she finally said, gesturing weakly at the couch. "And then he said, 'Oh, *poor* Mary, she's sooo sick . . .' and put his hand under the blanket and onto my leg . . ."

What the fuck? I stared at her wide-eyed. "Did he . . . did he . . ." I stammered, struggling for the right words.

She sniffed. "I moved my leg away, but he went to touch me again, so I tried to knock the glass over, thinking you'd hear the crash and come down . . . Only I knocked it the wrong way, so it all fell *on* him . . ."

What the hell had he been trying to do? I shuddered as the possibilities ran through my mind.

"Please, Maha," she sniffed, "please don't tell my mother anything.

She has enough to worry about, and if she knows about this she'll start to worry about the meesees finding out, and *then* she'll worry about losing her job." She twisted her fingers. "You know how hard it is to get a good job *and* she has to buy groceries for her aunty in the jondols. You know, the one who used to look after me by the farm."

"Okay, maybe it *is* better if she doesn't know," I said, "but please stay out of Naseem's way. And if you find yourself alone with him just run or shout or something . . ."

She managed a small smile. "Thanks, Maha."

I stared thoughtfully. "I will say something to Sameer, though . . ."

Mary's eyes widened. "Are you sure?" She bit her lip.

I nodded. "I think *someone* needs to help the arsehole before he does something really stupid!"

"But Sameer won't say anything to his mother?"

I shook my head. "No, he won't want that . . . Too much drama, and Sameer doesn't like drama!"

She smiled shyly. "Okay. Thank you, Maha."

<hr>

I drove carefully through the sultry night and parked close to the lifts. A short walk later, I stepped into the gentle bustle of Legends.

A trendy waitress materialised. "Table for one?" she asked.

"Uh, no, two actually."

"We've got that table for three in the corner if you like . . ." she said, pointing to the far end of the room.

I nodded. "Thanks, I'll take it."

I sat back in the upholstered seat and surveyed the crowd in the restaurant. It was still predominantly honky, but there was a definite smattering of rainbow. Ten years ago, I wouldn't have dreamt of eating out as one nation, I mulled, fiddling with the drinks menu.

"Planning on getting drunk?" Sameer asked, appearing suddenly and unbuttoning his suit as he prepared to settle down. He leaned across and kissed my mouth.

He sat back and smiled. "You're looking nice . . ."

I un-wrinkled my brow and managed a small smile. "Did you have a good day at work?" I asked.

He shrugged. "Usual. Nothing special. So? What's new? How was your day?"

I glanced away and studied the legends gracing the walls. "I managed to get some work done." I made a face. "But then it turned somewhat shitty."

Sameer feigned a look of concern as he fished around his pockets for his fags and phone, which shrilled to life just as he aligned it alongside his cutlery.

He picked it up, throwing me an apologetic look. "Salaams, yah, I *can* hear you . . . what's up?" It's Ba, he mouthed at me. "Am at Legends with the vrou! Is it *that* urgent? Oh, okay then . . ." He placed the phone back in its spot and lit a cigarette.

"Sorry, there's some sort of problem with Ba and Nas," he said. "He says it's urgent," he shrugged, "so I told him he could stop by. You don't mind, do you?"

I shook my head resignedly and waited for a waitress to appear so I could order a drink.

Shahzad arrived ten minutes later, shedding his jacket immediately and flopping into the empty chair with a huge sigh. "Salaams, guys, sorry to spoil your romantic dinner for two."

I patted his hand soothingly. "It's okay, besides I wouldn't mind a distraction. I've had a strange day."

Shahzad ran his hands through his hair. "I love this joint!" he said, looking around for a waitress. "You should check it out after the movies when it's overrun by Chaarous!" He laughed. "Did you know that their first coffee shop at the Playhouse got *genuine* culture shock when Chaarous discovered *Friends* and café culture? That's when they fled to these larger, more accommodating premises!" he declared.

"Hey, Shaz," a sexy waitress said as she sidled up to him, "didn't think I'd see you tonight. What can I get you?"

He beamed at her. "Yeah, urgent work . . ."

"The usual?" she offered.

"Great, thanks . . . Hey," he said, turning to us, "can I get you guys drinks?"

"I'm okay, thanks," I said, indicating my Appletiser.

"I'll have what he's having!" Sameer said and laughed.

Shahzad threw me a worried look. "Are you sure, Sam?"

"Why? What's your *usual*, Shahzad?" I asked curiously.

"Bacardi and Coke," he replied, lifting his hand warily. "I know, I know, I'm a *bad* boy! But trust me, I *need* it to ease the pain. Either I dop or die!" he pronounced theatrically.

"Oh, really?" I turned to my husband, who was fiddling sheepishly with his cutlery. "And *you*? If you don't phuza will you also ifa? Do your folks *know* you drink daaru?" I asked him sweetly.

Duryo Sameer drank daaru? I rolled my inner eye. At that moment

I wouldn't have been surprised if a UFO had landed outside the restaurant and Marilyn, Elvis *and* JFK had stepped out of it and yelled "surprise!".

Sameer shook his head, ignoring me totally and focusing instead on the groups of people entering and leaving the bustling eatery.

"Okay, let's get down to business . . ." Shahzad began, fixing Sameer with a firm stare. "Your bru has completely lost it. He called me yesterday saying he had a consignment of cellphones and was looking for a buyer. Of course, I asked him if they were kosher. 'Yah, yah,' he choons, 'don't worry, it's all above board. I just want to move them fast 'cos I need the cash to buy more . . .'" Shahzad paused as the waitress brought the drinks he had ordered.

"I'll be expecting a nice tip, Mr Moosa!" she said, jabbing his cheek with her long, varnished nail.

I watched as Shahzad paused to take a greedy gulp of his Bacardi and Coke before continuing with his story. I was amazed at how quickly I'd quelled the horrific thought of pidelo Sameer. It was probably thanks to my current state of agitation, brought about by Naseem's clumsy attempt at molesting Mary. In fact, I realised as I eyed Sameer's untouched drink, *I* was capable of downing it myself!

"Anyhow," Shahzad continued, "he's your bru and all, so I thought I'd help the laaitie out. I chooned okay, he brought over the phones and I gave him the cash. Anyhow, today I try and use one, and guess what?"

Sameer looked at him questioningly. "They were blocked?" he asked.

"You're damn right they were blocked. Blocked as a Surti's arse! The maadar sold me fucked phones, which I can do nothing with!"

I sniggered and Sameer glared. "Oh come on, Sameer, it was funny – Surti's are famous for having carrots –" I started.

"Yah, yah, whatever," Sameer cut me off.

I ignored him and smiled sweetly at Ba. "Memons are not exempt," I whispered, "although theirs are gold-plated."

Shahzad laughed.

"Maybe he didn't know they were stolen?" Sameer offered lamely.

Shahzad gave him a withering look. "Yah, right, and I'm Madiba!"

"Don't worry, I'll speak to him. We'll have to make a plan to sort out this mess . . ."

"Cool, bru, ten grand is ten grand, you know!"

Sameer downed his drink as though his life depended on it and I studied him, waiting for some metamorphosis.

"Anyways, I'm off," Shahzad said, grabbing his jacket.

"Hot date?" Sameer asked moodily.

Shahzad wrinkled his nose. "I wish! Nah, I'm going to crash."

"Will you manage driving?" I asked.

He laughed. "Trust you to worry, Maha. I'll be fine. I'm walking back. My new place is not too far from here, you know."

I shrugged. I didn't know. Ba's flat was the domain of the boys. I'd never been invited to his old place on the beachfront, and I didn't expect to be invited to his new place, no matter how close it was to our regular haunts.

"I'll call you later," Shahzad said to Sameer as he moved away from the table. "Salaams. Check you, Maha!" And with that he was off, pausing to greet someone else on his way out.

Sameer sat back while the waitress put our coffee orders in front of us. "So, are you going to tell me your story or what?" he muttered grumpily, fingering his Irish coffee.

"Mary's school called today," I began, and took a sip of my innocent latte before relating the events of the last few hours.

Sameer looked outraged as I got to the end of my monologue. "What are you so pissed off for?" he whispered fiercely and took a hearty slug of his coffee. "From what you say, my brother didn't do anything!"

"Well, there's no question that he was definitely trying to do something . . . And I *saw* him standing there with his fist raised, about to strike! Isn't it bad enough he tried to abuse her?" I replied belligerently.

He grunted.

"Anyhow, she seems okay, but your brother needs help!"

Sameer sighed and lit a fag. "Shit, man, I suppose I'm going to have to sort him out, what with this phone shit and all . . . And preferably without Dada getting wind of anything!"

So, the phone shit was the more heinous crime, I thought, but I bit my tongue.

"Shall we go home?" Sameer asked.

I nodded and he gestured for the bill.

"Are you okay to drive?" Would one Bacardi and Coke plus an Irish coffee make a person drunk? "Where are you parked?"

"Oh, no, I parked at home," he replied. "Riaz popped by after work to borrow a suit, and I got him to drop me off . . . So, honey," he leaned forward and I spun away from his rancid breath, "you're driving."

86

All was quiet upon our return and I started tidying up the evidence of Sameer's post-work stopover while he grabbed the mail and headed for the stairs.

"So, do you drink often?" I called after him casually.

He paused and turned around. "Don't you think you would have noticed if I did?" he asked and laughed.

I shrugged. What did I know about daaru? My knowledge of drunken behaviour began and ended with watching the occasional gardener sway and sing drunkenly along a Slumurban road.

"I don't plan when I'm going to do it, if that's what you want to know," he offered.

"Don't you feel bad?" I couldn't help but ask.

He yawned loudly. "Yah, I suppose I feel bad, but we're only human . . ." he said as he continued up the stairs.

I emptied the ashtray – the last of the mess – into the bin and followed Sameer tiredly up the stairs. What a fucking day! I still had to endure the last weekend of January, followed by the entire month of abstinence – the year had barely begun and I was fed up already.

"I think it would be better if you spoke to Naseem here," I suggested as I walked into our room. "That way he can't lock himself in his bedroom."

Sameer slammed the door shut and flung his jacket onto the bed. "Can you just shut your bloody mouth about Naseem? I said I'll speak to him," he shouted as he stripped off his clothes. "Now leave me alone!"

I needed no further invitation, and grabbing my packet of fags I fled out onto the balcony, sniffing back my tears.

In spite of having crapped all over me, Sameer took my advice and invited Naseem to our place, using the pretext of discussing business. I hovered on the landing above, straining to catch their drift while they mumbled and muttered downstairs.

"What?" Sameer finally said, raising his voice for the first time, clearly frustrated. "You fucking needed the money for rock?"

The schmuck was smoking crack!

"Are you fucking mad?" Sameer yelled. "Now you better fucking listen to me or my vrou will choon Mummy everything!"

I clenched my fists furiously. So, my big mouth was the ultimate threat? I pushed open my bedroom door angrily, heading for the balcony as Naseem responded to Sameer's words with a thunderous bellow and a string of expletives.

I exhaled as I closed the balcony door behind me and reached for my fags. I blinked in the unexpected brightness and peered surreptitiously over the railing. Shit! Doctor fucking Forjee! He must be on yet another of his seemingly endless house calls to Mummy. I dropped the packet, fled back indoors and careened down the stairs to warn the warring brothers. Too late, I realised as the bell chimed and door handle turned almost simultaneously.

The good doctor surveyed the scene in front of him before turning in my direction. "You can go, Maha," the slimeball said, waving dismissively, "we don't need you for family business."

"Yah, Maha," Naseem snarled as I turned and strode back upstairs, "we don't need *your* big mouth here!"

"Yah, lucky I came when I did," Dr Forjee pontificated as soon as he thought I was out of range. "I could hear yorl swearing and shouting from the driveway! I came to give your mummy her migraine injection. Lucky she doesn't know what and what is happening. She's in no position to deal with this nonsense!"

I assumed my former position at the top of the stairs, but the good doctor had adjusted his volume considerably and I could only shift about restlessly as they murmured to each other.

"And you know what he said, Forjee?" the crackhead suddenly whined, raising his voice. "He said his wife was going to tell Mummy everything!"

"You need a few thamachos for that!" Forjee ranted at Sameer.

My husband needed a few slaps?

"Your wife is an outsider! She's not family! How can you involve *her* with her half-brains also?"

I seethed silently as I waited for Sameer's response, but there was no word from him. Did you really expect him to fly to your defence? I asked myself.

"Naseem, you must come right . . . one time too!" Forjee continued. "I want to see you five times in the mosque, you hear? No more cellphone nonsense. And as for that girl, nothing happened so forget about it. If I hear one more thing, I will tell your mummy to fire that luchee and her mother. Nowadays *everything* is rape-rape and they walk around half naanga! What these women expect?"

So, Mary was a slag! She was the one leading him on. I fumed at the top of the stairs, rage oozing from every pore as their voices returned to a level that I couldn't hear.

❦

"Can you believe your fucking uncle?" I exploded apoplectically as soon as Sameer made his way through our bedroom door. "How can he speak such drivel!" I roared, banging the thick textbooks on my desk. I could feel the Round Roti I had become start to crack.

"Shut up!" Sameer snapped. "Don't speak like that about my uncle!"

"Oh, for once in your life, *think* about what he's saying! Blatant sexism, bru . . . You can't deny it! There was no fucking need to refer to Mary as a slag!"

"Yes, but women *are* supposed to dress modestly . . ." he countered belligerently.

"That may be true," I ranted, "but men are supposed to treat women with respect. Blaming *women* for men's depravity is just an easy option."

"Yah, yah, *you* know everything!" he said, turning away. "But don't you dare say a fucking word to anyone about Naseem, you hear? He can't help himself right now . . . I'm sure you heard me shout about the drugs and all!"

It took all of my self-restraint to stop me from punching his smug-bastard face – blame the drugs, not the dope that took them – but I managed a peremptory nod and slammed my Chaucer file onto the desk.

"And what about Mary?" he continued arrogantly. "Will you tell her to shut her mouth?"

"She won't say anything," I countered. "She doesn't even want her mother to know anything happened. But what about Naseem? Are you going to take him to a shrink or what?"

"Yah, Forjee is organising Dr Sheikh . . . He'll see Nas at home. That way no one will spot him at the rooms," he replied.

I grunted.

"You know that whole thing with the stolen phones? It was only to get quick bucks for his rock. So we have to sort it out before he gets in trouble with thieves and gangs," he offered earnestly.

I understood his concern – crack addicts were legendarily socio-pathic – and conceded that the fake Sheikh was better than nothing.

Forever and Ever

⁂

I'd met my deadlines, sweated through my exams, passed and grad-
uated – an achievement that had been markedly ignored at the Palace
and remained the biggest nonevent of the previous year. My new
challenge was an HDE, a qualification that would allow me to teach
the subjects I'd studied and which would require me to be assessed
in a classroom. The Palace had responded – without consulting me –
by asking Dr Forjee to arrange my teaching practice at Islamia
College, the Slumurban school headed by his brother. Simulating
gratitude was the only course of action, but I was pleased at the
prospect of a respite from the endless tedium of the Palace.

Fay was under some kind of enforced work schedule now that
varsity mid-year exams loomed. Naseem had developed a sullen
sulk ever since the confrontation with Sameer the previous year –
and sometimes disappeared for days on end, allegedly with his mates.

Mummy, of course, maintained that he was "just stressed" and called upon Dr Sheikh to increase his visits and the dosage of whatever he was on. It was unclear whether prescription drugs were the *only* thing he was taking for his problem, but I knew my worthless place and held my tongue.

⁂

The Palace hosted its biannual ta'leem barely a week after I completed my teaching practice. Twice a year, the entire neighbourhood and extended family made the effort to attend. Even Fay had been bribed into taking the day off from varsity and putting a smile on her overly made-up face.

Mummy was well aware of the more conservative Ta'leem Tannies' disapproval of socialising pre- or post-gathering – they preached that the sole purpose of the gathering was to speak of religious matters. Yet she ensured that High Tea was served according to Palace custom. The rabble partook excitedly while the Tannies and their entourage left in a huff, pausing only to survey the spread dismissively.

The post-ta'leem dawdlers – including Rozi's mother-in-law, Aunty Gori – continued to drink tea and gossip in the Palace drawing room. Rozi had promptly followed me to my apartment where I was busy getting ready for an evening out with Sameer. I had barely seen him for almost a month – what with his late-night meetings and never-ending trips to Joburg. This was his first work-free night for absolute ages and I was determined that we were going to have a good time.

Rozi dragged deeply on her fag, stared at my ensemble and shook her head while blowing out a perfect smoke ring. "*Love* the pants! Verrreee sexy, but the top's *too* much," she said.

I whipped off the top and strode to my closet in the low-waisted, hip-hugging, soft-leather trousers that flared gently above my sparkling sandals.

"How's this book?" Rozi asked, picking up *Nine Parts of Desire* and peering at the cover as I slipped on a white shirt.

"It's fucking brilliant, fascinating stuff," I called back to her over my shoulder. "Shahzad brought it from England . . ."

"I was thinking of Shaz today, 'cos of the news . . ." she said, interrupting me as she cast the book aside dismissively.

"You've been watching the news?" I asked and snorted.

"Not really! The mothernlaw had it on and I just happened to be there . . ."

"So what was on the news? I've been too damn busy preparing for today's chur-bur!" I'd worked my skinny ass off for the High Tea and was thankfully done with dorternlaw duty for the day.

"There was another bomb in London, apparently. Thank goodness Shaz's back here!"

I flopped on the far end of the bed and placed the book carefully on my bedside table. "Yah, I saw that. It happened last weekend. And it was in Manchester, not London!" I sniggered derisively. "So you reckon Shahzad is safer here in KZN, where we've been unable to hold local elections 'cos of the ongoing violence? I mean, for goodness sake, the King has had to actually beg the people to stop killing each other!"

"So, what time do you want me to drop you off?" Rozi asked, changing the subject.

"Half an hour?" I said, gritting my teeth and transferring the glare that had settled in my eyes to my watch.

She nodded and I stood up, casting cellphone, make-up, tickets, wallet and tissues into my bag. Enduring Rozi was the price I had to pay for not wanting to drive to Musgrave Centre. It was pointless, I reasoned, as Sameer would drive straight from work, and it wouldn't be much of a date if we drove back in separate cars!

⋘⋙

As I stepped onto the escalator that would take me up to the cinema in the Musgrave Centre my mind drifted to the agenda for the following day. Dada Patel was due at the Palace. I shuddered as I remembered that he had recently taken to lugging around an odious, sputum-filled spittoon, something that I would have to empty on the hour every hour. Luckily, I would be able to escape to help Mary with her English in the afternoon – she was now in matric and was blooming in her new school. I thanked the Lord silently.

Minutes later, I made my way into the cinema and settled myself in my carefully selected seat, placing my drink in the space provided. The theatre was already filling up, so I took a sip and fished out my phone. *Where are you?* I typed. *Am in seat. Have refreshments. X*

My phone beeped as I crunched on my popcorn. Finally!

Leaving in a few minutes. Sorry. C u soon. XXX

But by the time Helen Hunt burst onto the screen Sameer still hadn't turned up and I shifted focus to the wild storms in *Twister* – forgetting all about his absence right until the scene with the flying cows.

Flying cousins! My mind conjured images of the Heifer and Calf in full flight and I giggled as I clicked on my phone. A missed call. Shit! Sameer had called? Well, if he'd called – I refocused on the big screen – then it was probably to say he'd been held up, so no point in stressing. I sighed stoically. So much for my romantic night out.

I checked my messages as soon as I stepped back into the bright light. "You have one new message," the annoying voice intoned.

"Salaams, Maha, it's Sameer. Listen, we've just had a hold-up at the shop. Thank God, we're all okay, so don't worry . . . I'm at the police station, statements and whatnot . . . So sorry, sweetheart, I'm not going to make it. I'll call you later . . ."

Fucking hell! Literally held up! Robbery! Taking a steadying breath I dialled his number.

"Maha!" He sounded stressed. "Listen, I'm not done. I'll call you in an hour." And with that he cut the connection.

I glared at the phone and redialled.

"The subscriber you have dialled is not available . . ."

I exhaled slowly and made my way as calmly as I could towards the escalator. Well, at least no one had been hurt, I consoled myself as I headed towards the exit. Was I really going to take a taxi home? I stepped out into the night and looked around. Perhaps a coffee first – some small compensation for a screwed-up evening.

"Hey! Maha? It is you! All alone, nogal!" a familiar voice called out as I sat down heavily at a small table outside one of the on-street cafés.

I looked up with surprise. "Shahzad! Salaams! Yah, I'm all alone . . ." I shrugged. "Haven't you heard? There was a hold-up at the shop. Probably just as Sameer was locking up."

"No way! Is he okay?" he asked, taking the empty seat at my table. "What happened?"

I shrugged. "I'm not sure. Sameer left a message on my phone, but

I was at the movies . . . I tried calling him but he was still too busy with the police to speak."

"Oh, crap, man, you poor thing, but at least you know that no one was hurt, right?"

I nodded. "I know, that *is* something, I guess . . ."

"So what did you see?" he asked and smiled. "At the movies, I mean."

"*Twister*. Wild storms and flying cows!" I smirked.

He sat back, lighting a Marlboro and observing me quietly. "You're looking really nice, by the way," he said and smiled gently.

"Thanks . . . All dressed up and no husband to appreciate it," I griped with an overtly doleful expression.

He laughed. "Well, I'll keep you company if you like . . . Shall I get you a drink? I think you should have some chocolate, good for the shock, you know."

"Ah, Shahzad," I stretched out my legs tiredly, "these days when *you* offer me a drink, I'm not sure *what* exactly you're offering, but your company will be most welcome . . ."

He shook his head. "You're nuts! What coffee would you like? Cappuccino?"

I nodded. "Yah, that's fine, thanks . . . So, tell me, how was the UK?"

Shahzad motioned to the waitress. "An espresso, a cappuccino and one Death by Chocolate, please?" he said when she approached.

She nodded and I looked at him curiously. "Death by Chocolate?"

"Awesome chocolate overload," he pronounced authoritatively. "And you need it."

I nodded.

"As for the UK," he flicked the ash from his fag expertly into the ashtray on the table, "everyone's miserable, and I for one don't blame them. They've had an arse of a year so far; the Dunblane shooting, all that IRA crap and now mad cow disease!"

Our coffees arrived and I busied myself with the sugar.

"So, how's your HDE going?" Shahzad asked. "Belated congrats on the graduation, by the way."

I frowned. "I'm plodding along with the HDE. It's okay. I just finished my practice teaching at Islamia, and they've offered me some cover work for the last term."

"Hey, well done! Good for you, Maha Patel!"

"Very funny." I poked out my tongue and took a sip of cappuccino.

"By the way, how are you getting home?" Shahzad suddenly asked.

"I guess I'll get a cab. There are always cabs outside . . ."

"Don't be daft, woman, I'll take you." He sipped his espresso. "Go on, have some cake," he urged.

I broke off a tiny sliver and forked it into my mouth. "That's divine . . ." I muttered with a glazed expression, quickly scooping up another, larger forkful.

Shahzad grinned. "Good. Eat. Enjoy."

⁂

Cake and coffee finished Shahzad stubbed out his stompie as I stood up quickly, grabbing my things. "So, where's your car?" I asked.

"At home." He stood aside to let me pass. "A short walk, hope you don't mind?"

I shrugged. "If I can *work* in these heels, I'm sure I can *walk* in them! Lead the way, kind sire!"

I click-clacked along the quiet pavement, past the subtly illuminated window displays, following Shahzad as he led the way to his flat.

"So, what happened with you and Farah?" I asked after a few hundred yards. "I really thought you guys were hitting it off?"

Shahzad smiled. "Yah, we do hit it off. She's a lekker bra."

"So, what are you saying? There's no spark?" I quizzed.

He laughed. "Spark? You mean passion? Desire?"

My phone beeped as he looked at me inquisitively, waiting for an answer. I blushed and scrabbled in my bag, grateful for the interruption.

Hey, Maha, it's JT. Do you know where Mary is?

John, the neighbour. I dialled the number of his newly acquired cell and he answered immediately.

"Hey, Maha, sorry to trouble you so late."

I cleared my throat. "Howzit, John, no problem. Have you checked my place? She sometimes studies in my kitchen."

"Oh, okay, I'll go and check . . . Is it okay if I go?"

"Yah, of course! Sameer should be there soon . . ."

"Hey, thanks, Maha. You're a star!"

I switched off my phone and looked across at Shahzad where he had come to a halt outside an imposing gate. "It's here," he said, waving towards the tall, circular building set behind the gate.

A security guard ambled over. "Hey, Wiseman, my boss! Howzit vaaing?" Shahzad greeted the beaming guard.

"Ba, my bra! What you doing?" He looked at me. "Eish! You found someone! A nice one too!"

I laughed and shook my head. "No, no, we're just friends," I blustered.

Wiseman was instantly woebegone. "Eish! *When* this boy going to find the vrou?" he grumbled, shaking his head.

"Pray for me, Wiseman, my man!" Shahzad countered, even as he looked up and pointed into the sky. "One day Nkosi will bless me with the right one."

Wiseman nodded.

"Aameen," I said and Shahzad flashed me a grateful smile.

"I'm getting my car, boss. I have to drive the lady home, so open for me, okay?" Shahzad told Wiseman.

The guard flashed a thumbs up, opened the gate and wandered away to resume his duties as we made our way through the grandiose entrance.

"Wow, this place is huge!" I said as I gazed up at the tall structure. "The view from the top must be awesome!"

"Oh, yah, it is," Shahzad said as we walked towards the parking lot and a black, floor-hugging car that was standing on its own in the corner.

"Is that a new car?" I asked curiously.

"When was the last time you examined my wheels?" Shahzad asked with humour in his voice. "I've had this for two years now. I'm not a Patel, I don't change my car twice a year!"

Shahzad unlocked the car and held the door open politely for me. "Oh, sorry!" he said as he realised the passenger seat was covered in a pile of papers, stooping to gather them up. "Shit! I need to pick up the mail from my old flat." He stuffed the pages under his arm and ushered me into the car. "Do you mind if we do that first?"

I glanced at my silent phone. "Let me try Sameer," I said. "If he's home I'd prefer to go back right away, if you don't mind?"

Shahzad shrugged. "Yah, of course," he said, shutting the door behind me and moving round to the driver's side.

I dialled and waited. Damn! His phone was still switched off. I stuffed it crossly into my bag and leaned back as Shahzad started the engine and drove towards the gates.

Shahzad frowned worriedly at the look on my face. "You're not stressing are you? The main thing is that you know everyone is safe, okay?"

I nodded. "Yah, yah, the details will come eventually. I'm just not the most patient person, you know?"

He shook his head. "Actually, I think you're a very patient person."

Too deep, Mr Moosa. "So, what awesome CD lurks within your fancy player?" I asked, ignoring his comment.

Shahzad pushed a few buttons and the player whirred and clicked into life. "This is a cool mix of old and new . . . Good soul!"

"Shahzad Moosa, a man with soul!" I said happily, grinning as Diana Ross came through his state-of-the-art sound system. "I know what's beautiful looking at you; in a world of lies, you are the truth," she sang.

I opened the window, allowing the wind and music to whip around my head as we approached the ocean. I sniffed appreciatively. "I love the smell of the sea," I said, smiling as my hair whirled against my face.

"What? You mean you love the smell of dead fish?" Shahzad teased.

"Unappreciative Vaalie! So which one's *your* building?" I tore my gaze away from the rolling waves and peered at the buildings to our right.

"Not far." He pointed. "That face-brick one."

"So . . ." I gazed up at it, "do *you* have a penthouse?"

He grinned. "Nope, I'm not that greedy. My old flat's on the ninth floor . . . and I own one lower down which I rent out. One of the penthouses, by the way, belongs to Rozi's ballie!"

"Ooh! Nice! Rozi never mentioned it."

Shahzad turned the car into an underground parking lot and stuck a card into a slot on one of the machines. The boom rose.

"I won't be long, I promise," he said as he unbuckled himself and grabbed a bunch of keys. "You can smoke in the car if you like . . . Shall I leave the CD on?"

I shook my head. "No, no, switch it off. I wouldn't want to press the wrong button in your fancy car."

He sniggered. "It's not a Batmobile, you know? It won't bite."

I unstrapped myself and flumped into the seat, fished around for my phone and stared at it irately – still nothing from Sameer.

Two minutes later the heavy door to the stairwell clanked in the distance. It couldn't be Shahzad, I mused, still glaring at the phone; it was way too quick. I heard voices – a man and a woman. Definitely not Shahzad, then. I played around with the buttons on my phone as the voices began to get louder. Unable to hold back my curiosity any longer, I peered cautiously out of the passenger window.

I was mortified. In front of me, in the middle of the parking lot, a couple were locked in hardcore embrace – *his* hand cupping her breast, *her* grip on his rather sexy bottom. I promptly refocused on my phone, hunkered down and blushed, clueless as to why I was embarrassed when they were the public spectacle, but embarrassed nonetheless.

"I . . . have . . . to . . . go," the woman moaned. Her heels clicked, she laughed and her car alarm bleeped. "See you tomorrow, Sammy darling . . ." she trilled over the sound of slamming car doors.

Even as her words pierced my eardrums and shot across my brain the phone was already falling from my hand into my lap. It felt like my body had been cleaved right down the middle, and I clutched at my chest while the blood roared in my ears. Ohmygod! I thought. Ohmygod! Ohmygod! Ohmygod!

My phone beeped. I fumbled agitatedly in my lap, stabbing wildly at the buttons.

Slmz. On my way home. C u soon. X

"Fucking bastard!" I roared, scrabbling for the door handle, the incriminating evidence clutched in my hand. "Fucking bastard! Fucking bastard!"

I burst out of the car in stupefaction, staggering against it as my legs trembled and I began to breathe in rapid gasps. The phone clunked to the floor and I kicked it brutally. It emitted a strange wail as it came to rest forlornly on the concrete floor, but that was the last of my strength. I sank down against the cool metal of the car, tears coursing down my face. When had I started crying? I couldn't remember.

***

The door clanged in the distance. "Maha! Are you okay?" Shahzad called out, hurrying towards me.

"I seem to have dropped my phone," I choked.

"Leave the phone!" He squatted in front of me. "What's wrong? What's happening?"

"I think," I strangled a sob, "I'm having a heart attack."

Shahzad rubbed my back soothingly. "Take a deep breath," he said. "It sounds like a panic attack. Has this ever happened before?"

He spoke quietly as he wrapped his arms around me and eased my body back into the car. "Here," he held out some water, "sip this slowly. I'm going to get your phone. Okay?"

I managed a nod and stared blankly at the bottle.

He leaned in and unscrewed the top. "Do you want me to *make* you drink this?"

I shook my head. "I'll manage," I whispered and exhaled slowly, quickly taking another deep breath.

I sipped slowly as I watched Shahzad pick up the pieces of my phone. He returned, frowning at the battery as he tried to slot it back into position.

"I think it's actually okay," he said. My phone beeped as he brought it back to life. "Unbelievable!"

"Is that a message?" I asked.

He shook his head. "No, it's just starting up. Do you need to call someone? You can use mine if you like," he offered, pulling it out of a special holster on his belt.

"No, can we just not move for a while? Just stay here? And then you can take me home," I said.

Home? What home? What marriage? What fucking husband? Suddenly I couldn't breathe. The tightness in my chest was overwhelming. Sameer! The lying bastard! I'd believed him! Believed *them*!

I opened my window as we eventually purred out into the night, blinking at the sudden brightness of the golden mile – a blurry kaleidoscope of night lights flashing through my tears. I sipped on the water in a bid to quell my nausea. Stop crying, Maha, you stupid wuss, I told myself as I kept my eyes firmly averted from Shahzad's obvious concern.

"Would you like to talk about it?" Shahzad asked, interrupting my thoughts.

I shook my head.

"Are you sure?" he asked, raising a single eyebrow.

"What do you want me to say?" I babbled. "This is Maha Patel, CNN News, the Palace. Tonight, breaking news: Sameer Patel and Rozi Kareem are lovers!"

"Lovers?" He frowned. "You sure? I know that they *were* together in varsity, but Sameer said there was no point in chooning about the past . . ."

"Trust me, they're together."

"So, how did you find out?" He slapped his forehead. "Shit! You saw them at the flat!"

I nodded and took another sip.

Shahzad drove at a leisurely pace, evidently weighing his words carefully. "What are you going to do?" he eventually asked, his tone sombre as he turned into The Grove.

I barked dementedly as I fished about for my remote. What was I going to do? Fucked if I knew. "Anyhow," I sighed, "thanks for the lift."

"You're welcome," Shahzad replied, pulling the car over on the side of the road outside the Palace gates. "Glad I could help . . . Listen," he searched his pocket, "here's my card. All my numbers are on it, including my personal cell, so if you ever need to choon or anything, please call me . . ."

I thrust it into my bag and winced as the Palace gates swung open without warning. A speeding ambulance careened out the driveway onto the road, sirens blaring, with Daddy's car hot on its tail.

⁂

"Maybe It's something to do with Sameer's grandfather," Shahzad said as we both stared after the ambulance, but he didn't sound convinced.

I shuddered, clutching onto my handbag as Shahzad eased his car slowly through the gates and made his way up the driveway.

"Here we are . . ." he said, finally drawing to a halt outside my apartment.

I thanked him automatically, unlocked the door and stepped out. "Salaams."

"Ey, Maha!" Mummy hollered from her kitchen window. "How you came? Where you went? You even know what's happening? Come here right now!"

I hastened towards the open door and stepped in warily.

"Daddy's gone with the ambulance. I'm just going to get changed and then Naseem will take us also," she said, flapping agitatedly.

"What happened?" I managed to ask.

"Ey, everyone says the wife is always last to know!" she pronounced in wonderment.

My heartbeat picked up speed.

"You know about the robbery?" she asked.

I nodded.

"Yah, shukar no one got hurt . . . They just took some money from the tills, but then . . ." She glanced at the clock. "Ey, I'd better get ready, just now they'll take him to surgery . . ."

"Take *who* to surgery?" I asked with more than a trace of impatience.

She glanced up sharply. "You don't speak to me like that!" she snapped. "*My* fault *you* don't know your own husband got stabbed in his own house? No. Not my fault."

I clutched onto the table as my legs buckled. "What? How?" I exclaimed.

"Ey, don't ask me, I never see . . ." She spun away from me. "Ask Naseem, if you want, or that lucho, John, from next door. Saalo ran away like one chorr!"

"John is not a thief," I said out loud, much to my horror.

Mummy paused, turned around slowly and glared. "What *you* know, Maha? You think just because he goes varsity like some big baas he got proper brains? You don't know. If the baal is waanku, the brains is also waanku. Can't come right!"

I blanched and gulped for air. Like me!

"Hurry up and get ready for the hospital now," Mummy called over her shoulder as she swept out of the kitchen. "We leaving just now!"

"I'll come in my car," I uttered shakily as I dug in my bag for my battered phone.

"John?" I whispered as I scurried back to the studio flat. "Are you and Mary okay?"

"Maha! Eish, don't ask. Mary went to the bathroom, and I was waiting in the kitchen," he exhaled noisily as I stepped inside and latched the door behind me. "Next thing I knew, that savage Naseem was there shouting at me like some thief! As if he doesn't know who I am!"

"So what did you say?" I asked.

"I just said that I was waiting for Mary, but he got violent, opened one of your drawers and pulled out a knife. I was trying to make him see sense when your husband walked in."

"Oh, my goodness!" I slumped against the wall.

"Sameer also tried to reason with Naseem, but, eish, man, I think he's on drugs or something, he just wouldn't stop . . ."

I grunted, incapable of speech. "Yah, so then," he continued breathlessly, "Sameer tried to take the knife from him and the next thing I knew it was stuck in his side!"

"I see . . ." I muttered tonelessly.

"I grabbed the nearest phone, and dialled the ambulance, but by the time I got through Naseem had run off . . ."

I emitted a strange blend of yelp and snort. "Is Mary okay?" I asked.

"Yah, she's fine. She stayed in the bathroom until it was all over."

"Thank goodness for that," I said, already starting to mentally prepare myself for the scene that would greet me at the hospital. "Well, I have to go . . . Take it easy now . . ."

"Oh, Maha!" Mummy gasped as I finally entered the waiting room. "They just took him into theatre now. Mister Khan is operating."

I nodded. Khan was the famous General Surgeon who had put much of Slumurbia under the knife.

Daddy patted my arm awkwardly. "Now, you mustn't worry. He got saved. Lucky Naseem was there . . . So he phoned the ambulance immediately!"

My gaze flickered towards the alleged hero where he sat slumped in a chair with his eyes closed.

"Everyone is asking why you never come home *with* Sameer?" Mummy frowned. "If *you* was there then all this wouldn't have happened!"

"So, what exactly happened?" I stared at her shrewdly.

She wrung her hands and pulled me aside. "That John from next door and Naseem was fighting in your apartment," she took a breath, "and then Sameer came and tried to stop them, and *then* he got stabbed!" She squeezed my shoulder.

"So who had the knife?" I asked.

She drew back in horror. "That Kaaryo had the knife! *Who* else going to have a knife?" she demanded.

I patted her hand half-heartedly. "Actually," I murmured, "I spoke to John and he said that Naseem had the knife."

Mummy inhaled sharply.

"What fucking difference does it make?" Naseem bellowed. "No one's pressing any charges or anything. Mummy is going to tell everyone he got stabbed during the hold-up, so shut up or fuck off!"

I recoiled with revulsion while Mummy grabbed my hand and

pressed her mouth against my ear. "If Daddy hears any stories about Naseem you will be in big trouble," she whispered. "So don't go and open your big mouth, you understand?" She stepped away and scowled accusingly. "Now see, you upset Naseem more! You can't see he's already so upset and all!"

My mouth hung open as I marvelled at her audacity. Katy Patel had it all worked out and was ready to spin the web of lies she had concocted to protect her Precious Prince.

A door opened and the tall, dark and handsome Mr Khan stepped through and pulled down his mask. He surveyed the room sombrely and focused on Daddy. "Well, the worst is over, alhamdulillah," he began. "He's lost a lot of blood, but nothing was badly damaged, thank goodness. Inshallah, he should heal nicely."

Daddy offered his hand. "Thanks, Goolam, appreciate it."

"No problem," the doctor said, shaking the proffered hand. "Listen, Joe, we're moving him to the ICU just now, okay?"

Daddy nodded and followed him out into the corridor while Mummy and Fay collapsed with exaggerated relief.

⁂

I got my first chance alone with Sameer the following day. Foi and Mummy adjourned their vigil and returned to the Palace to show face and have tea with the people who had congregated to support the Patels during their time of greatest need.

My jaw ached as I relinquished the tight, polite smile that had been plastered across the lower half of my face for the previous twelve hours. I sighed with relief as I walked over to his bedside. "Hey, Sameer! Wake up!" I said.

He shifted about restlessly, mumbling incoherently.

I tapped his sallow cheek. "*Sameer!* It's Maha! Can you hear me?"

He blinked slowly and licked his dry lips. "Water . . ." he rasped.

"Here," I bent a straw to his lips and he sucked gratefully.

"How are you feeling?" I asked when he had had his fill.

"Groggy . . ." he mumbled.

"Can you hear me okay?"

He nodded slowly.

"Good! Then listen up, Sameer. I'm not going to wait until you're better, 'cos who knows when the hell that's going to be?"

"What's wrong?" he spluttered.

"I'm sorry about the hold-up, and I'm sorry you got stabbed . . ." I began. "But I don't care if you're sorry about what you did the other night."

"What? What are you talking about? I didn't do anything." He looked down at himself. "This was done to me . . ."

"I wouldn't call mauling Rozi's tits *nothing*!" I spat.

His pallid features turned ashen. "What has she told you?" he muttered hoarsely.

"Rozi? That lying two-faced chuth? What is she going to tell me, Sameer? Fuck all! That's what. I fucking saw you," I growled.

Sameer closed his eyes. "Where?" he asked tiredly.

Where? He was concerned about where?

"Don't you dare go back to sleep, you lying, cheating bastard," I shouted. "Look at me!"

He opened his eyes. "Look, maybe you're confused . . ." he mumbled, groping around for my hand. "We'll talk about it when I get out of this place, okay. Please, let me sleep now . . ."

I whipped my hands away and drew back viciously. "Confused!" I roared. "Are you out of your mind? I *saw* you in the parking lot with her, you fucker!"

He turned away, stubbornly shutting his eyes.

"Oh, no, Mr Patel!" I jabbed his arm. "You don't get to sleep in peace after fucking around for all these years!" I shouted. "We are over! Kaput! Finito! Khalaas! Finish and klaar!"

He exhaled slowly, his eyes resolutely shut.

I couldn't cope. I'd confronted him with the truth and all he could ask was *where*? I grabbed my bag and strode out of the oppressive room. Then, thinking better of it, I paused, turned around and marched back inside.

"And I'll leave it up to *you* to explain the situation to your folks," I said as calmly as I could. "We don't *have* to drag your name through the mud, so 'irreconcilable differences', okay?"

He opened his eyes long enough to glare at me for a few seconds.

I glared back and stormed out, not pausing until I'd reached the furthest corner of the parking lot where I promptly burst into tears. What have you done? I chastised myself. What have you done?

❦

I drove to the Mahal – pausing at the Palace to pack a few bags.

"Jamai sleep nice?" Naani asked, taking in my dishevelled state. "You come for shower? You want breakfast? What time you go back? Today Juma too. Lort people will come way to see after . . ."

I suppressed my sigh. "I'm going to shower and then I'll have breakfast. I have to sort out some of Sameer's things before I go back to the hospital."

"Oh, I make soup, you must take and gor. Gorinani make fresh naan too."

"Thanks, Naani," I said, excusing myself and making my way up to my bedroom.

Upstairs, I kicked the door shut behind me, stepped out of my shoes and threw the case onto my bed. "Hello, bedroom!" I announced. "I'm back!"

⚜

The nurse had handed me a bag containing everything that had been on Sameer's person the night he had been brought in, and after my shower I sat down, lit a fag and pulled out the clear plastic bag, emptying his phone, wallet and keys into my lap. I held the phone in my hands for a few seconds, took a deep breath and clicked on messages received. The last one was from Rozi:

Sammy darling! R u done playing cops & robbers??? I'm at JK's. Not wearing underwear! X

I scrolled sluggishly through sent messages. The last SMS he had sent was the one he'd typed to me. I selected the previous one with trepidation.

On my way, sexy. Can't wait to eat you! XXX

I gagged, but there was no way I was going to delete it. Even though I couldn't see myself unleashing Sameer's sordid messages upon Slumurbia, I would *definitely* be hanging on to every incriminating piece of evidence I could lay my hands on.

Putting the phone aside, I opened his bulging wallet and relieved it of its cash, transferring every last cent into my purse. It was not often I had cash in hand, I reflected, studying the credit cards in my

113

purse thoughtfully. Perhaps a shopping spree to stock up for the hard times ahead was in order, I thought. After all, all's fair in love and war!

I stowed away the incriminating evidence and glanced around my old bedroom. Ouma's boxes – the smaller shoebox standing on top of the larger, book-filled one – stood forlornly in a corner and my eyes filled instantly. I grabbed the shoebox and stuffed it completely out of sight – at the bottom of my wardrobe behind a pile of jumpers. Right now, I didn't have the energy to deal with any more emotion.

Naani was still in the kitchen; a neatly packed basket stood waiting on the table. She glanced at me with a small frown. "Why you dorn wear nice punjabi? Juma too today, Maha! Sor nice clothe they buy. Next time mus gor change by *your* house . . ."

I kissed her cheek. "I'm going back now. I'll see you later."

❧

Rozi and Aunty Gori entered the ward just as I turned the corner. I slowed down, tightening my grip on the basket and shopping bags. Well, they *were* bound to come, I told myself. What did you expect, Maha? I took a deep acquiescent breath and pushed open the door.

Aunty Gori immediately set upon me tearfully. Rozi hovered, waiting for her turn to console me. I allowed Aunty Gori to mumble platitudes in my ear and thanked her politely as she wiped away her tears.

Then it was Rozi's turn. She stepped forward, stretched out her arms and wrapped them around my stiff body. "I'm so, so sorry," she said as she squeezed me. "May he get better quickly."

I cupped my mouth to her ear. "Don't worry, he'll soon be up and running to you, you whoring bitch!" I whispered.

She jerked back with a frown, but I had already moved away.

"Let me just put these away," I said to no one in particular, arranging the magazines and snacks on Sameer's bedside table.

"Can I get you some tea or something, Aunty Katy?" Rozi piped up sweetly.

The chuth.

"Oh, I don't want to trouble you," Mummy replied.

Aunty Gori leapt up excitedly. "No, no, *what* trouble? Good idea, Rozina. Go get some tea," she babbled.

Rozi swung her bag. "Come and help me carry them, Maha!"

I grabbed my bag and followed sullenly. With all eyes on me I had no alternative.

I caught up with the slag as she waited for the elevator. "So, what the fuck was all that about?" she asked, a scowl on her face.

I glowered. "Don't mess with me, you bitch!" I snarled. "I know all about you and Sameer! A single solitary stoned mistake, my arse!"

She had the good grace to blush. For once, Rozi was at a loss for words.

Till Death do us Part

I was finally allowed a night off from nursing obligations – Mummy had laid down the law and I had neither the strength nor the inclination to fight her. As far as I was concerned this was my final stint as duryi dorternlaw. I was looking forward to some decent sleep when Farah and Zeenat burst into my bedroom and promptly locked the door behind them.

"So what happens now, Ms Maal?" Farah cut to the chase with a worried look.

I sighed. "Well, I suppose I will *have* to have a chat with the grandparents, but not tonight, darlings, I'm shattered!"

Farah gave me a look of empathy. "So, what about Sameer? Have you had words with him?"

I smiled wanly and filled them in on my conversation with Sammy.

"So, do you reckon she married Riaz so that she could stay close to him?" Farah asked, lighting a fag and passing over the packet. "Why didn't Sameer marry *her* in the first place?"

I lit one and shrugged nonchalantly. "God knows why she married Riaz, but Dada Patel would never have tolerated a Hedroo dorternlaw for his precious poes heir, so Sameer and her were a nonstarter."

Farah nodded in agreement. "You may feel like an idiot, but they've managed to pull the wool over everyone's eyes!" she declared.

Zeenat patted my arm. "They are both obviously sick, manipulative, egocentric gaanbaals!" She grimaced. "Turns out that you were the only normal one in that place. Well, for the most part anyway."

"What do you mean *for the most part*?" I puffed moodily.

Farah took a deep breath. "Don't take this the wrong way, but you have to admit you did get swept up by the Palace." She shrugged. "You know, lost sight of yourself . . . I understand how important keeping up appearances is to the Patels, and it's always easier to fit in and try to be the perfect Round Roti, but, darling, I was beginning to fear that you weren't just acting like a Round Roti, I was beginning to think you believed that you *were* one!"

I snorted. "I was just focused on getting things *done* . . ."

Zeenat stubbed out her fag and stretched lazily. "So jika-jika also? No *thinking*, just lying back and doing it for Africa?"

I pinched her. "Oh, shut up, Zeenat! Not perfect, but not bad. No complaints!"

"Well, at *least* you had orgasms!" Zeenat patted my head placatingly. "*Never* mind, beti," she said, imitating Gorinani, "*mus* make shukar at least he make you come and all. In *our* times . . ." She chortled.

Farah and I burst out laughing. "I can't remember the last time I laughed like this!" I exclaimed in awe.

"There you go, then. Something else to be grateful for," Zeenat responded.

Farah shook her head. "Well, orgasms well past their sell-by date are not going to keep her warm at night . . . she needs *hard currency* now."

Zeenat snickered.

I punched her lightly. "Actually, I've been thinking about currency . . ." I turned to Farah. "I'm going to draw up a list of all I want and then write him a letter, so that there is proof of my sensible request," I said seriously.

"Well, make sure you make a few copies and certify them," Zeenat said bossily. "Get them stamped at the bank or the police station. That way no one can ever say that they aren't true copies of the originals."

Farah nodded. "Yah, you never know, he might tear it up and accuse you of all sorts."

"Oh, come *on*, he's not exactly in a good position, is he? I have his phone, which is filled with SMSs to the chuth!"

"Which you're not going to share with anyone," Farah countered. "He knows it's an empty threat."

I hooted scornfully. "Trust me, whatever I say Katy will put such a spin on my revelations that everyone will believe *I* was having it off with Rozi's boiled-vegetable bhailo husband."

"Yah, but at least your grandparents might find it easier to swallow!" Farah replied.

Zeenat snorted. "Oh, I am extremely grieved to break this to you, but Naani will most likely choon 'Kaynee, bhen, mathera am kare . . . Mus make sabar'!"

Farah frowned uncomprehendingly.

"Never mind, sister, mens do like this . . . Mus make patience!" I translated.

Zeenat stood up and straightened out her clothes. "Well, just be prepared for resistance. No one is going to say, go, Maha beti, without creating a stink."

"I'm hoping that by the time they let him go home, everything will have been done and dusted," I said. "I'm going to tell Sameer that he needs to sort it all out with his parents *before* then. There's *no* way I am going to move back to the Palace and play happy fucking families *and* Florence Nightingale!" I shuddered at the thought.

"Do you know how long he's going to be in hospital?" Zeenat asked. "Because I'm telling you right now it'll take ages for such a stench to clear."

"I'm going to speak to the doctor and find out," I said. "But I'll give him my list of requests as soon as I can."

⁂

The next morning I made my way to the hospital with my letter for Sameer – copied and certified – tucked into my overstuffed bag. I pushed open the heavy door and eyed the bastard where he lay propped up in his hospital bed, flanked by Foi and Mummy.

"I see your Boesman jaath came out *one time* too, Maha!" Foi spat.

The cat was officially out of the bag and I steeled myself.

"What *nonsense* is this?" Mummy snapped. "What bladdy divorce rubbish? *So* much-so much we do for yorl! What you short of?"

I started at Mummy's expletive, walked over to the window, and hooked my bag over a chair.

"Ey, Katy, leave this stupid. Must talk to her nana-naani! For what you wasting time and getting upset also. Dada *won't* allow talaaq!" Foi declared decisively, grabbing Mummy's hand and steering her out of the room.

"We'll see you just now," Mummy muttered ominously.

"So," I sat down and looked at Sammy, "feeling better?"

He looked up from his drink and nodded. "You're looking nice . . ."

"Thanks," I replied curtly. "So what exactly did you say to them?"

"Just that we were over and getting a divorce." He sighed. "They promptly burst into tears, started scolding me and asking why."

I made a face. "And? What was your reason?" I persisted.

"I said that we . . . we didn't get on . . . not suited . . . that kind of thing . . ." he trailed off tiredly.

"Incompatible?" I asked.

He nodded wanly.

"Oh, well, I hope you added that it was a joint decision?"

He shook his head. "They just assumed that it was all *your* idea. They wouldn't let me explain . . ."

"*Fabulous!* Well, you'd better set that straight when they come back. And I *don't* care if your dada is with them or not!"

I pulled out the envelope and handed it over to him. "Here, these are my humble requests. And I have certified copies, so don't even think about messing with me!"

He opened the envelope and scanned the contents.

"You're right. You're being very reasonable," he said, flashing me a glum look. "But I just can't believe this is you. You're so cold."

I swallowed and averted my suddenly tear-filled eyes. I was not going to reveal how hellish it was maintaining the sub-zero temperature I was radiating.

"So, you really are serious then," he muttered dourly. "You want to call it quits. Just like that? Don't care what everyone will say?"

Just like that? I spun around. "Yes," I stated clearly and placidly. "We've come to the end of the road . . . and what exactly *are* people going to say?"

He shrugged. "Oh, you know . . . divorce is a bad thing . . . you must have done something really horrible for me to divorce you . . . they might pick on your, you know . . . your father's family." He had the grace to blush.

I stared incredulously at him as I shook my head. "I can't believe you're speaking such shit. *I* must have done something bad? It's all because I'm a mixed breed?"

He sighed and shook his head. "No, no, I'm just pointing out how it can get . . . this is not a small decision. You're not returning a pair of shoes you don't like, you know?"

The man was unbelievable. "Getting married was not a small decision either," I growled, "but you haven't exactly upheld your end of the bargain now, have you? I cannot believe our entire marriage has been a lie . . ." I gulped. "And by the way, I have your phone, with all those *lovely* incriminating messages on it. Messages that I will *definitely* spread around Slumurbia should you even *think* of fucking me over!"

He held up a hand weakly. "Calm down, calm down, I said I think your demands are fair." He flapped the sheet of paper feebly. "I was just pointing out what might happen . . ."

Discussion over, Sameer flicked through a magazine while I opened one of my books and prepared for a healthy dose of escapism. I glanced at the title and managed a small smile as I entered *The Llama Parlour.*

The Patel posse burst into the room to find me giggling at my book while Sameer lay dozing.

"Ey, Maha! You laughing also!" Dada barked without preamble and jabbed at my book with his walking stick. Behind him Sameer jerked awake and Mummy and Foi immediately fussed around him.

"You saali, sitting here reading chopras?" the old man continued, knocking the book off my lap. "You know my wife marhoom?" he yelled. "So-so much she suffered. When we was young, your age, we was battling-battling, but she made sabar! Now you girls must also learn to make sabar, never mind what and what happens!"

I listened with my gaze appropriately downcast.

"So, now you just *sitting*?" he shouted. "Where your *beeg* mouth now? You got nothing to say? Just now I heard you had big bhen-chodh mouth for talking talaaq-balaaq!" he spat, prodding my foot with his cane.

I swung my feet under the chair, hoping that they would be out of reach. What did he expect me to say? Jee, Dada, you are right. I do have a big sister-fucking mouth, will make sabar and remain Mrs Maha "Poes" Patel?

I'd rather endure whatever he could throw at me than sully my mouth with such kak. In fact, I thought, I'd rather drink the warm spit out of his spittoon!

He swung around to address his cowering grandson. "And you! You sleep here like one weak bhenchodh bhailo!" He was puce with rage as he jabbed at the metal legs of the bed. "You are the maadar-chodh, man! You can't show who is boss? Divorce? Khabbaddaar!" he roared and shook his stick in the air.

I stood up. "I'm going to get a coffee," I said as calmly as I could. "Would anyone else like anything?"

Everyone glared.

"You think anyone can swallow anything, even!" Mummy snapped.

I grabbed my bag and made my way out.

❧

"Yes? Can I help you?" a nurse asked politely as I approached the nurses' station.

"I'm wondering if Mr Khan is around?" I responded.

She glanced at her watch. "He's due in five minutes. If you'd like to wait . . ." she said, waving towards a row of chairs that stood against the wall. I took a seat and resumed reading.

"Salaams, Mrs Patel," the good doctor greeted me politely some twenty minutes later as I stood up to shake his hand.

"So, tell me," I began, "how long will he need to stay in hospital?"

He scratched his head distractedly. "Not too long – he should be able to go home in a few days. Of course, it will take a few *weeks* of rest before he's back on his feet!"

Damn! I had bargained for a few weeks *in* hospital – a couple, at least.

"He's lucky he's fit and strong," the doctor continued. "He's healing very nicely."

Yah, the man's *got* to be fit to fuck two-two women at the same time.

The doctor peered at me. "Are you okay?" he asked, seeing the sour look on my face. "I promise you that he'll be as good as new before you know it."

123

I smiled politely. "Thanks, Mr Khan," I said, trying to dispel some of the tension as he picked up a pile of folders and set off purposefully. "I'm sure I'll see you later."

⁂

I took my coffee to a distant corner of the parking lot and lit a fag. Music filtered out of someone's car and I glanced around impassively, sipping slowly at my coffee. Dada Patel's yell of khabbaddaar had me on edge, and as I took a deep drag I wondered what *he* would think of my requests. Probably deem me a greedy, thieving bosri.

My phone bleeped and I clicked open the message apprehensively. Zeenat! I exhaled with relief.

Slmz. Big kak!! Dada called Nana! Stopped N from hotfooting to hospital. Promised I'd give u akkals! C u soon! X

Smoking in the parking lot, I typed in response. *Will wait for you here.*

I sent the message, let out a sigh and leant back against the cold concrete of the wall. Would Dada and Daddy try and prevent me from getting all I'd requested? I wondered. I'd offered to give up most of the Patel treasures, apart from my engagement ring. I'd also asked to keep my car and other personal effects and requested one of Sameer's flats. *One,* nogal!

Dada Patel had bought Sameer a flat for his eighteenth birthday. Not to be upstaged, Mummy and Daddy had then bought him a penthouse in Umhlanga for his twenty-first. I took a deep drag and grimaced. I'd pushed the boat out and asked for the Umhlanga penthouse. The size of it was obviously attractive, but the location

124

was what really appealed to me – the northernmost boundary of the city felt like a safe distance from Slumurbia. I stubbed out the stompie, wrapped my arms around my knees and stared at nothing while I waited.

Zeenat arrived twenty minutes later, all hot and bothered. "Bloody hell!" she said as she collapsed next to me and lit a fag. "What a bitch of a Saturday! First client at eight and nonstop since. And then Naani calls and insists I cancel the rest and rush over immediately to the Mahal!" She inhaled greedily and blew out a large plume of smoke.

"Sorry," I offered. "So what did Naani say?"

"She said," Zeenat paused, "mus tell you, 'You see this kaans?'" She balanced her fag beside her and held onto her ears for effect. "'See how they stuck to head? Yah, same like wife . . . She stuck to mathero . . . Only janaaza mus come out from husband's house, beti.'"

"No way!" I cried. "*Why* can't she just accept it, and say 'Allah knows best'?"

"*Not* possible," Zeenat said. "Can you imagine the shame? What face they gonna have and other such bull . . . Anyhow, I think they're meeting with the Patels later!"

I made a sound of exasperation. "I *give* up. Will it *ever* end? I mean, will people ever stop thinking about 'hu kehe'?" I asked, shaking my head dolefully.

Zeenat shrugged. "Well, honey, the shit has truly hit the fan now . . . So, it's going to be raining crap all over you. I hope you're prepared!" She gazed at me curiously. "You sure look composed!"

I flashed a brief smile. "Sameer reckons I've turned into a heart-less bitch, but really I'm just moving on." I sniggered lamely. "That's the one thing I have to give the Palace credit for . . . They taught me how to show good face!"

Zeenat sighed.

"Anyway," I continued, "I asked the doctor and he told me that Sameer only has a few more days in hospital, so this kak needs to be mopped up by then . . ."

"And what then?" Zeenat asked. "Back to the Mahal?" She frowned.

"Yah, I suppose . . . Well, for *now* anyway. I don't think Nana would *cope* if I chose not to spend my iddat there! Can you imagine the *double shame*?"

Zeenat grinned. "Gorinani is going to be in her element . . ." She laughed. "Be prepared for endless mentions of your fabulous Boesman jaath!"

"Oh, don't worry," I drawled drolly, "it's already made an appearance. Foi pointed it out earlier."

⁂

By the time we made our way back to the private ward, Katy was forking morsels of chicken and vegetables into Sammy's whoring mouth. I made salaam, led Zeenat to the extra bed and offered her a snack. I unwrapped a mini Dairy Milk and took a bite.

Katy threw me a dirty look.

Was I not allowed to enjoy chocolate just because *she* couldn't swallow anything? I turned to Zeenat irately and muttered sotto voce, "Am I supposed to commit sati on the pyre of my marriage?"

She raised her eyebrows. "You mean, are you supposed to kill yourself?" she whispered. "*Yes*, of course! Glad you get the picture already. You should basically behave as though your *life* is over!"

"Isn't that a *bit* extreme?" I stared wide-eyed.

"Are you nuts? A divorced woman should not be so shameless as to show her merry face everywhere . . ." she clucked as I sucked the chocolate stains off my fingers.

⁂

Naani insisted on lunch as soon as I set foot in the Mahal. Zeenat made a quick getaway, and I had no choice but to follow her to the kitchen. There was no sign of Nana, and I breathed a small sigh of relief.

"Make chur for *me* also," she ordered curtly as she took a seat and launched in. "Nana sit, worry-worry and cry and make dua . . . Now sor tired, he sleep way . . . Can't eat! Handu gurroo ma stuck thay jaai," Naani said, clutching her throat for emphasis. "Mus *use* akkals also! Allah give you big-big brains too! Dorn show aari jaath and charrbees! What *Sameer* say?"

I took my seat and sipped my tea. "Naani, Sameer and I are getting divorced," I said levelly.

"Chup reh!" she snapped, banging her hand down on the table with hitherto unknown ferocity. "Ai handu gaandu-gaandu rawa-dhe aweh . . ." she shouted.

I sighed. "Yes, Naani, I understand that you are upset, but for many years Sameer has been seeing another woman." I met her horrified gaze. "You know, sleeping with her . . ." I exhaled slowly.

Naani shook her head dolefully. "Arreh, Maha, what to do . . . Some-time mens do like that. You knor Stanger Sarah-Khaala," she low-ered her tone, "her son should do like that . . ." She reached out and grabbed my hand earnestly. "But he still coming by you?" she asked.

I managed a brief nod and she exhaled with relief. "Shukar, al-

127

hamdulillah!" she exclaimed. *"See* he still come by you, jus now he come right, leave that one too. Mus make sabar, beti."

I finished my tea mutely, scraped back my chair and prepared to leave. What had I expected? I asked myself. Had I really thought that she would encourage me to ditch the cheating sod?

"Gaan," I muttered as I locked my bedroom door behind me.

I dialled Zeenat's number after yet another restless night.

"Salaams! Howzit, you busy?" I babbled as soon as she picked up the phone.

"Wa 'alaikum salaam," she responded. "Actually I'm having a cup of tea and fag . . . My client just called to say she's going to be half an hour late. Good timing, my dear!"

I sighed with relief. "Client on a Sunday?"

"Yah, I know. She's vaaing on holiday tomorrow so she's desperate and I'm doing her a favour 'cos she's a regular," she explained. "So, how's it vaaing?"

"Don't ask! I *can't* understand Naani's bloody-mindedness! I told her everything and though she seemed to feel sorry for me, she chooned *exactly* what you said she would: mens do like that sometimes, must make sabar and he'll freaking come right!"

Zeenat snorted. "Arreh, what to understand, beti? One-one shames on your head too! You dornor divorcées are also super jux?"

"What do you mean?" I asked.

"Well, a woman who was married, and therefore bonking regularly, is going to be ready to jump on anything that comes her way if her husband suddenly disappears. *No* man is safe!"

I snorted. "So, what you're saying is that I'm going to be viewed as a bitch on heat?" I asked.

"Not only that, but you're fair game as well! Jy sal Slumurbia se gat sien!"

"Gaanbaals and all," I responded dryly.

"To add to that wonderful picture," she cackled, "be prepared for all the nunus to come crawling out of the woodwork!"

"Grim!" I swatted the image.

"Hey, you're like the Slumurban Diana," Zeenat said. "Kicked out of the Palace, shaming the royals, nogal!"

"Hilarious! But thank goodness *we* don't have the added complication of children."

"Oh, yah, absolutely," Zeenat concurred. "Then you would be shunned as a stupid, beyond-shameless bosri who couldn't even do it for the sake of the kids!"

"Such bullshit! Surely a happy woman makes a better mother?"

Zeenat barely suppressed her shriek. "Are you nuts? Who cares if a woman is happy or not? As long as she has what is necessary in life, she must put up and shut up. Thu hu gaandu-gaandu waath karech'?" she mocked.

"Hey, that's exactly what Naani said! Mad-mad waath I must forget about, apparently. So happiness falls under the realm of insanity?" I griped.

Zeenat snorted. "Listen, I'd love to choon, but I'd better get off my arse and prepare for this client now . . . Can't have my fag-breath all over her," Zeenat said, deftly changing tack.

"Okay, then," I said, "thanks for chatting."

I threw down the phone and collapsed onto my bed.

I awoke to Naani pounding on the door.

"Hawa, Maha, take . . ." she said as soon as I turned the handle, thrusting the phone in my direction. "Cape Town Ouma."

I grabbed the phone and made salaam as Naani waddled away down the corridor.

"Salaams, kleintjie, I hear things is not so goed. Are youse okay?" she asked, her concern instantly curdling my insides.

I gulped.

"I'm not too bad, Ouma, considering . . . I suppose Naani has filled you in."

"Ja, Maha, she mos told me what happened. What do you say?"

I pulled a chair, sat with a sigh and gave her my version of the story. At the end of my monologue Ouma sighed deeply. There was no love lost between Ouma and Sameer – the last time we'd spoken she'd had no plans to forgive him for walking out on her daawat.

"Ag, Maha, this is too sad, too sad . . . But Allah knows best and sometimes a marriage has to end mos. In the end of the day, kleintjie, youse just must be happy, nè? That is all we wants."

I sniffed and nodded. "Yah, Ouma, I know that. Please make dua for me."

"Don't worry about that," she replied. "I make duas every day mos."

"Thanks, Ouma, and thanks for calling," I replied.

"Nee, I never called, Maha. Your naani called me. I too was mos shocked. I thought, my goodness, what has happened to Maha!"

I sighed. Somehow it made me feel worse to know that Naani had hoped Ouma would knock some sense into me.

"Okay then, Ouma, take care. Salaams."

"Salaams, kleintjie, look after yourself now," she said and replaced her receiver with a loud click.

Slowly, I followed suit.

⁂

The few days that Mr Khan had said would be necessary for Sameer to recover enough to go home passed remarkably quickly and before I knew it D-day had dawned.

"What time Sameer get discharge?" Naani asked, wiping her hands agitatedly as I prepared for my final trip to the hospital.

"Around one, I think . . ." I replied.

She nodded. "When you take things? Now or afterwards?" she asked stubbornly.

I ignored her and sipped my tea. My phone beeped:

Salaams, Maha. Don't bother coming to the hospital today. You've made it very clear that you don't want to be married to me any more, so consider yourself divorced. Sameer

I froze. He was divorcing me by SMS! I dialled Sameer's number as a wave of hysteria slammed into me.

"Maha! What the fuck do *you* want?" Naseem barked into my ear.

I flinched. "Can I speak to Sameer, please?" I ventured quietly.

Naani's eyes met mine and I looked away.

"For what you want to speak to Sameer?" Naseem said, leaping down my throat. "You're divorced now, so you can leave him alone. And in case you're wondering whether it is allowed to send talaaq by SMS, Molwi Ameen said it is perfectly valid . . ."

"Yah, yah, tell her, Naseem!" Mummy's voice maundered in the background.

"Sameer has nothing to say to you, Maha. Patels don't beg!" Naseem snarled and cut the connection.

"Hu thayyu?" Naani demanded. "Who that forn? What they say? He got discharge?"

I shuddered. "No, he's getting discharged at one o'clock," I choked. "That was Naseem. Sameer won't speak to me . . ."

Naani clutched onto her chest breathlessly. "Thu hu kech'?" she gasped.

What was I saying? That was definitely a rhetorical question. Her eyes darted wildly across the room before she pounced manically upon the handset of the cordless phone, jabbing desperately at the buttons.

Self-preservation dictated that I should flee up to my room and perhaps lock the door behind me, but I was rooted to my chair. I couldn't move. Sameer had divorced me by SMS!

Meanwhile Naani had broken into a stream of incoherent Gujarati. "Seeeeet! Dorn gor nowhere!" she finally shouted at me as she grabbed my car keys, thrust them down her bosom and scurried out of the kitchen.

Two minutes later Gorinani burst wildly into the kitchen sans orhni – her oiled grey plait barely contained by the triangular scrap of voile usually hidden underneath it – Naani in tow. The cavalry had arrived!

"Seeeeee what you do? Saali raan!" Gorinani shrieked, gesturing wildly towards Naani. Flecks of spittle sprayed and settled invisibly. "You give your naani heart attacks too! Why you never just stay way by Sameer? You gaandi? Noooor akkals too!" She gave me a shove and I teetered on the chair.

Naani clutched her chest. "*Hu* dhukh, Maha! *What* we do? Nana sooo upset. He coming way . . ."

What exactly was he going to come and do? I wondered as my heart began to beat wildly.

Gorinani jabbed in the air. "What they tell hunda loko?" she demanded with juddering jowls.

I shrugged.

"Now see! Mus ask-ask and see what they tell peoples also!" She harrumphed melodramatically.

Naani glared fiercely. "*We* teach to make sabar, Maha! Why you dorn learn? So much sawaab too."

"Samiha, Nabiha, coming way also," Gorinani declared. "You wait." She turned to Naani. "Thumme be," she pointed accusingly, "say Zeenat to give akkal!" She sneered. "What that luchee knor? What akkals sheeee give?"

I watched, mesmerised, as the Goat butted wildly.

"Gor, chur banao!" she snapped.

I was only halfway through the tea preparations when the crunch of tyres on gravel turned my insides to jelly.

Nana strode in wordlessly, took hold of my arm and set off without a backward glance. I stumbled along behind him, wondering where he was heading and deciding that the safest option would be to follow submissively. He led me out through the main doors and pushed me towards the car.

"Get in!" he commanded curtly.

I obeyed.

He took off with the uncharacteristic sound of screeching tyres as I clutched onto the armrest, trying to control my breathing. He turned left out of the Mahal and I knew immediately that he was heading for the Palace. The bile rose in my throat. I wondered if I should mention that I'd already been sent a divorce by SMS, but in the end I decided that it was better to keep my own counsel.

Ten minutes later Nana drew the car up outside the main entrance of the Palace.

"Wait here!" Nana barked, but he had barely laid his hand on the seatbelt when Dada, Daddy and Dr Forjee stepped outside with folded arms like the fucking Triad.

They confronted each other solemnly on the stairway, but that was as much as I saw. I was too cowardly to even look in their direction, so I just studied my limp hands for what seemed like an eternity.

***

The trip to the Palace was sedate compared to the journey back to the Mahal. Nana glowered at the road and hung tautly onto the steering wheel. I nibbled compulsively on my hangnails, wondering whether he'd stop if I threatened to throw up.

Back at the Mahal Nana flung open his door, leapt out of the car and before I even had myself released from the seatbelt he was wrenching my arm brutally. "Get out!" he bellowed.

I climbed out of the car jerkily, completely unprepared for the explosive slap that landed on my face as soon as I had found my feet. I fell against the car and clutched my face instinctively as a sob escaped.

Naani and Gorinani were promptly on the scene.

"Ha! Ha!" the Goat bleated. "Ené maar!"

Hit her? As though Nana needed any encouragement. His face

transmuted to an angry shade of purple, his hand beat down upon me once again. "Saali bhenchodh!" he raged. "Make me look like stupid. Don't even say he gave talaaq also?"

Naani fell upon me with furious sobs and slapped my head. "Talaaq?" she shrieked hysterically. "He give talaaq also? What you do? Why he do like this?"

The Goat stamped about impatiently while Nana explained what had happened in Gujarati. I wiped my nose on my sleeve and prepared to flee into the house. It's now or never, I told myself before taking a deep breath and bolting for the kitchen door.

"Yah, gor saali," the Goat screeched after my departing form. "You in iddat now, can't gor norwhere!"

I paused for breath only when I had locked my door and stuck a chair under the handle. Then, without further ado, I strode into the bathroom, stripped off and, avoiding my reflection, stumbled sobbing into the shower.

Things to do in Durban
When You're Dead

I was in iddat – the period of mourning entered into by the wife after divorce or the death of her beloved. Unless she needs to work, this stretch of time is spent at home recovering from the trauma of losing her man – making it a bona fide occasion for behwa. It is also considered sufficient time to establish whether the vrou is pregnant, in which case iddat lasts until the birth of the poor child. Post-funeral it all made perfect sense. Post-divorce, however, being forced to welcome guests and bear the brunt of their disapproval and pity was torture of Yakuza proportions.

Much to Naani's alarm, I refused to spend any time with the mourners, and disappeared immediately after a perfunctory salaam. Meanwhile, Naani herself remained mute and wept at any opportunity – consistent with the grandparents' general approach, which could be readily summed up as unrelenting tight-lipped anger.

I holed up in my room for the first month – bent on short bursts of private scourging followed by longer bouts of sleep. Communication with the outside world was at an all-time low. No one called. No one visited. The only post was from Sabah – a "Congratulations on your divorce" card and, much to my astonishment, something she called a breakthrough in female pleasure. I stuffed it into a suitcase under my bed with all the lingerie I owned and tried not to think too hard about what Sabah was trying to tell me.

Some time during the second month I started managing longer periods of wakefulness that I filled with movies – everything from Bollywood to the latest blockbuster – and walks in the subdued winter garden. My flashy set of Patel wheels was finally exchanged at a dealership for a smaller car and a wad of cash – which I placed reverentially in the top drawer of my desk along with a set of keys to the Umhlanga penthouse that Sameer had posted to me. The spoils of war. My booty! I also succeeded in summoning up enough courage to open the box of books I had brought back with me from Cape Town and read my way through what remained of my parents' eclectic library, although the shoebox Ouma Galiema had given me remained untouched at the bottom of my closet.

The third month got off to a slow start. Zeenat brought over her tools and tried to spruce me up, but I remained pathetically unmoved. At least I'd be starting as a substitute teacher soon, I thought – at least that would give my day a different structure. I would be out of the house. A brief respite!

⁂

The phone rang and I reached for it lazily.

"I'm phoning on behalf of the Head of Islamia College," a nasal voice intoned. "It turns out we won't be needing a substitute teacher next month after all."

She cut the call abruptly, leaving me staring at the phone and listening to the dial tone. I stood for a few seconds before the enormity crashed down on me. *No* escape! Was this Dada Patel's revenge? The Head of Islamia College was Dr Forjee Vanker's brother, after all! Or maybe it was part of Nana's ploy to keep me stuck in the Mahal?

I made my way downstairs broodingly. Shit! I could hear Gorinani in the kitchen, exclaiming in dismay about some dreadful crime. She ignored me, waiting until I sat down with my tea before pouncing.

"Ey, Maha. Like raani you stay by your naani. Look the time! Must come kitchen early help your naani . . . old she . . . nor thaakat to do everything . . ."

I sipped my tea silently.

"Yah," she continued, nonplussed, "what this rubbish Naani say? You gor *work*? In school? Enough kaam by the house! What you need money for? Your nana-naani give everything. You got clothe. You got khawaanu."

I nodded. Acquiescence was the path of least resistance.

Naani gazed mournfully. "That Bibi-Khaala got rob last week? She told *all* loko came behwa, say, yah, that one-one stories too. That Sameer *sor* nice boy he want to fix. He talk with Aapa's brother too! Thu saali," she spat, pointing her finger viciously, "you make rush-rush finish . . . bechaaro in hospital and *you* say *must* give *one* time talaaq!"

138

Death, divorce and dhukh – all fitting reasons for behwa, chur-bur and catch-up on the latest gossip.

Gorinani clucked. *"Now* see? What *people* say? *You* wanted talaaq! Isn't? Isn't?"

"Haa!" Naani continued miserably. "And *what* what too they say. Patel family big, lort kaams that's why you run! You saali khottee!"

I was too lazy to deal with the Palace responsibilities? I got up po-faced, but the Goat wasn't done.

"Your naani never teach *naam* ni waalu . . . *kaam* waalu?" she asked. "Aaj kaal dorternlaws dorn like mus do *any* kaam!"

My decision to keep schtum about Sameer's infidelity was patently not doing me any favours, I thought as I carried my half-empty mug to the sink and sloshed out the remains. Even Naani appeared to have conveniently forgotten my reasons for demanding the divorce. No doubt the rest of Slumurbia would also have urged me to shut up, put up and pretend that all was hunky-fucking-dory. I grabbed my bag and keys and made for the door.

"Thu ka' jaach'?" Naani shouted.

"Pavilion," I replied automatically, though in reality I had no idea where I was going. I just knew that I *had* to get away from the Mahal.

I headed east and parked outside Milky Lane. The beachfront was pleasantly calm – a far cry from the chaos and over-crowding I associated with weekends and school holidays. I crossed the promenade, slipped off my sandals and sank into the grainy sand. It was low tide and gentle waves glinted in the midmorning sun as I glared at the ocean. I needed to send my CVs to the governing bodies of *other* schools, I decided. That was the only solution to Islamia College and their cowardly position.

139

On a Friday morning as I sat clutching my tea mug – watching footage of the Taliban capture Kabul and execute Najibullah – Mary's old school called, offering me a position for a few weeks in October. I would save the announcement for after the weekend and defer combat, which I reckoned was a wise battle plan.

That evening, after my final prayer for the day, I congratulated myself on surviving another week intact. "I'm in the shower!" I shouted to the Mahal, before locking my door behind me. I had planned on smoking a few drags of a massive joint Farah had bestowed upon me on the completion of my iddat. I'd been waiting for the right moment, and now, after being offered my first proper job, I had decided that I deserved a small treat.

A *few* drags, I warned myself. It was still early evening and the day was far from over: anyone could suddenly appear. I took a greedy fourth drag, stubbed the joint out carefully and stepped into the steaming shower.

Twenty minutes later I slipped into a pair of comfy pyjamas and flopped onto my bed with a silly grin. Perhaps I'd watch a comedy? I glanced lazily at my stack of videos, but the sudden rise in volume from downstairs distracted me. I unlocked my door gingerly and padded quietly onto the landing.

"Maha!" Naani's sudden bellow jolted me out of my zone.

I walked to the top of the stairs. "Jee?"

"You got visitor. You come down?"

"Send her up!" I shouted. If I was lucky it would be Zeenat or Farah and we could watch a video together. I walked back to my room and sat cross-legged on my bed in anticipation.

"Asalaam 'alaikum, Maha!" Aapa Abeda, madrassah teacher from days of my fair youth, said as she swished in to my room.

"Aapa *Abeda*! Wa 'alaikum salaam!" I stood up and accepted her embrace politely. "Sit, sit," I said, waving towards my bed. "Wow, I haven't seen you in years! What brings you here?"

She sat and gave me a pitiful smile. "Now, you know *I* don't drive and all. I wanted to come for *so* long and see you, but . . ." She sighed and patted my arm. "*So* sorry to hear about your divorce and all. Shame."

"Thanks . . . It's not that bad, alhamdulillah. But, yah, you must make dua for me."

"Yah no, inshallah. Allah must bless you with a good partner and fulfil *all* your pious desires."

Pious desires? I squeaked at the idea.

"You okay?" Aapa Abeda asked, flashing me a look of mild concern. "If you feel like crying, then you must cry and make dua, ask for forgiveness and all . . ."

"I'm okay," I said. "Just tired."

"Okay, well, this won't take long." She cleared her throat. "Yah, as I'm sure you know your ex-husband Sameer comes to talk to Moulana practically *every* night."

I shook my head. I had no idea that Sameer was being counselled by her brother.

"Lucky he *got* Moulana. But *shame*, I thought, you need *someone* to talk to and all. To give proper advice and moral supports."

So is this the plan? Ameen choons with Sameer, *you* choon with me, and together the brother-sister duo orchestrate our happily ever after?

"So, what you doing now your iddat finished?" Aapa Abeda asked.

"Well, I've got a temporary teaching post for now, and I've sent my CV to a few schools. So, next year is another year . . ." I shrugged. "I'm taking it one step at a time."

She nodded grimly. "But you don't need to work . . . You got everything you need. You know some women have to work." She sighed. "You must try and get married quickly also. If you get any good proposal just take it!"

"Why?" I couldn't prevent the word from popping out.

"*How!* Then you don't go round causing all kinds of fitnahs too. And also, *who* wants to marry a divorcée?" Aapa Abeda flashed one of her special frowns. "You're smiling too? You'll see all *dohas* will come and propose and all. What you think? Nice-nice proposals going to line up like before?"

Outside the room Naani's voice drew closer. I swallowed my retort and pasted on a benign smile. She appeared at the doorway and hovered. "Maha," she growled, "maathu dhurmp!" She jabbed her finger at my bare head. "Moulana want to talk."

Great. Ameen had conned Naani into bringing him into my presence. I stood still stubbornly, refusing to cover up in honour of the good Molwi.

Naani glowered. "Wear orhni, gaandi!" she whispered irately. Clearly she believed that my madness would benefit from the good Molwi's akkals.

Ameen waited for Naani to leave, keeping his gaze purposefully lowered. Then and only then did he cast a furtive glance around my bedroom.

"Go sit there!" his sister instructed, pointing to the armchair near the window.

Ameen obeyed silently, took his seat and proceeded to stroke his tshebe – his eyes still piously downcast.

"Moulana wants to talk to you, so you *must* listen!" Aapa Abeda said bossily, standing up. "I'm just going to the bathroom."

I swallowed my snort. I couldn't believe she was leaving luchee Maha, sans scarf, alone with her brother! I rested my chin in my hands and gazed at him boldly.

"You're looking well, Maha," he finally said in an undertone, looking up briefly. "Your iddat is over now?"

"Yes, it's been over for a few weeks . . ."

"Good, good," he twisted the long bristles on his chin. "It will be hard for you to remarry . . . You know that?"

I shrugged. "I pray that when the time is right I am blessed with my Mr Right."

He rubbed his hands together. "It's better if you don't have all that trouble, you know?"

Which means I should follow you meekly as you lead me back to Sameer? I barely blinked, gazing steadily as he shifted about uncomfortably in his seat before he resumed rubbing his beard.

"You must understand that I am only trying to *help* you . . ." he finally said, looking up earnestly.

Here it comes!

"Yah, so we were thinking, it will be a good idea if *you and me* make nikah!"

What? A fucking bombshell! Was I more stoned than I thought? I dropped my hands and sat bolt upright.

143

"You mean –" I began.

He nodded, cutting me off with a wave of his hand. "Yah. My *second* wife." He sat back, pleased as punch.

Abeda rushed out of the bathroom excitedly.

"So, so you said yes?" she squeaked. "Such a good idea isn't? You liked him when you was younger, *before* you got married," she reminded me.

I blanched. Liked him? Long ago, he'd been hormonally challenged and I'd taken advantage. It wasn't something I was proud of.

"One time then also you will be a Moulana's wife," she continued blithely, "wearing cloak and all, and then you'll see the izzat too will come away!"

They were *serious*, I suddenly realised. They believed they were *saving* me!

"Thanks, but I'm not ready to remarry right now," I responded grimly.

Abeda waved her arms about in agitation. "Oh, what ready? Your iddat's finished, so now you're *ready* to get married. Who you waiting for? Prince Charming?"

"No," Ameen interjected snidely, "she said that she's waiting for *Mr Right*!"

Abeda gave me a scornful look. "*Mr Right*? Ey, *Maha*! You think you can just get *everything* you want? Just now you wait-wait and go and do haraam everywhere also. You *good* for *that* also!"

I stuck my hands under me, before they sought out Aapa Abeda's skinny neck. "Well, if this is why you came, then thanks, but no thanks," I said brusquely. "You may leave now!"

Abeda gestured to her brother. He looked at me thoughtfully.

"Well, if you change your mind . . ." he offered.

Abeda yanked his arm roughly. "Ey, just leave her, man. She'll see how hard it is, then she'll come running." And so saying she flounced out of my room.

Ameen lingered. Had he really thought my jux levels would go through the roof and fling me into *his* expectant arms?

I remained seated until he sighed resignedly and headed after his clearly deranged sister, then I locked the door and concluded that I deserved a few more blasts of Farah's present. The nunus were well and truly crawling out of the woodwork!

⁂

For the rest of the year, post-iddat, I was blessed with silent hostility from all around me. My levels of saram – straight from iddat to work – had no doubt rendered them all speechless. Everyone's demeanour declared that I'd committed a major sin and nothing short of a public flogging would suffice as penance.

As soon as schools were out, Naani ensured that the hot, sultry December days were occupied with Ramadan preparations, and I spent most of my time slaving away in the kitchen. I was determined to remain optimistic. It was either that or curl up and die, I thought as I rolled out the pastry and sliced it into neat rectangles.

I eventually got to visit my apartment on the fifth day of Christmas. I stood at the end of the main room, gazing in awe at the floor-to-ceiling windows. "On the fifth day of Christmas, my true love gave to me," I muttered wryly.

Everything apart from the bed and fitted wardrobes could go, I decided instantly. The entire place stank of Palace, leaving me queasy for the rest of the otherwise pleasant Saturday.

⁂

"I saw the Umhlanga flat yesterday," I mentioned over Sunday breakfast. It was difficult to avoid the grandparents on a Sunday, unless I went out – which was bound to hail unnecessary grief from Gorinani.

They ignored me and continued to chomp on their toast and eggs. I glanced at the papers and bided my time. More violence in Cape Town between Pagad and the police. I sighed and looked up resolutely.

"I'll be spending my weekends there in the new year, to redecorate it," I continued and sipped my tea slowly.

Naani paused mid-chew and swallowed hurriedly. Nana gave me a death look.

"What redecorate? What's wrong with the decorations?" he snapped.

I shrugged. "I don't really like it. It's a –"

"You don't like it?" he bellowed, interrupting me. "That's what *you* good for! You don't like something, you just throw it out one time!"

"What you do alone-alone, Maha?" Naani asked, cutting in.

Find myself, perhaps? Just be? Gaze out at the great deep and get deep with myself? I craved the physical *and* personal space it offered.

Nana remained Mr Freeze – the indomitable monster that had long ago prevented him from having any contact with his only child.

"I was going to ask Zeenat to help me," I said. "I've already sold the furniture. It will be taken away this week. And Philip's son said he'd do the painting. He's been doing part-time work for some paint-ers and decorators." My spoils of war were being put to good use, I reckoned.

Nana glowered and I sipped my tea daintily, sanguine at the pros-pect of peaceful weekends.

Naani continued to look aghast. "Hunda hu kehe? Gorinani say you gor Pavilion like parwaarthi every time!" she complained. "Now? All people say 'See, she stay eklee-eklee!'"

I suppressed the shrug and looked away. I didn't care about Gori-nani or hunda loko and what they said.

"You got forn there?" Naani asked eventually.

I nodded.

"Yah, must give number . . . write big and leave by forn." She harrumphed and stood up, preparing to take to her musallah – making a huge palaver of turning to her Lord in torment. She paused at the door, re-adjusted her large prayer orhni and frowned. "Or, and after holiday Gorinani say mus take by Haribhai and Makro! Or, and after that we gor see Samiha mothernlaw, she sick too!"

Great! So, the new plan was to ensure all my forays out into the world would be accompanied by suitable elders – thus preventing the tongues from wagging. Such was my lot!

⚜

In the first weekend in January – ironically, what would have been the weekend of our *five*-year anniversary – I drove up north, crossing the Umgeni River.

"Eish, Maha!" Sipho enthused as he began laying out his tools. "Nice place you got here! Little furnitures, but is very nice!"

147

I dumped my packages around the apartment – milk and other essentials in the kitchen; clothes in the bedroom; the suitcase with Sabah's X-rated offering under my bed – and then dragged my boxes of books into the smaller room, which I'd planned to convert into a study. I'd already had a bookcase and a simple pine desk delivered. I unpacked my parents' collection tenderly, smiling as I deliberately set Erich Segal's *Love Story* next to *Carrie*. I left the brown-paper covers on the once outlawed books – Marx and Malcolm X – and placed them lovingly on the smooth pine shelves.

"Your new home," I whispered as I ran my hands along the gentle curve of their spines.

⁂

I locked the door behind Sipho and sighed into the soothing silence, watching as the city lights slowly illuminated the encroaching darkness.

I raised the temperature on the control panel and the central air conditioning ground to a halt. Deeper silence. I slid open the doors and stepped out onto the shaded balcony. The warm air swept inwards and the salty humidity clung to my skin as the muffled hum of the ocean rose up from the beach below.

A loud ring shattered my bubble and I lurched inside and searched blindly for the light switch before lunging for the phone.

"Asalaam 'alaikum, Maha! *So* long you take to answer. What you do?"

"Wa 'alaikum salaam, Naani. Nothing much. How are you?"

"That Sipho finish paint? You come now? Dark now!"

"He's got one room left, Naani! And, yah, it's dark, so I'll sleep over

148

tonight. And, anyway," I continued cheerfully, "Sipho's coming back to finish up tomorrow, so it saves me a double trip!"

I knew that whatever Naani thought, Nana would definitely approve of my petrol-saving decision.

"Or, okay . . . Lock door, read duas and sleep way early, orrite?"

"Okay, Naani, don't worry, I'll call you in the morning, okay?"

"Yah, must forn . . . Asalaam 'alaikum."

So, what to do on my wedding anniversary? Mope and mourn? Get drunk and abuse Sameer and Rozi over the phone? Well, for starters I needed music, I decided. What had they played on Capital Radio 604 all those years ago? "Everything I do I do it for you"? I snorted.

"Sisters are doing for themselves," I sang crazily as I shuffled through CDs and cassettes that still lay in one of the boxes. I pondered my selection before settling on a cassette of eighties classics.

I sang along at the top of my voice – I was all by myself in my very own home and the freedom was dizzying. I grinned out at the dark waters, flicking on light switches as I pirouetted in and out of the rooms.

Sipho had thankfully returned my room to its pre-decorated normality, but the smell of fresh paint lingered and I threw open the windows to purge the air. I yanked the suitcase out from under the bed and opened it with a flourish. "Take your passion and make it happen," I sang as I pulled out streams of silks and laces. I had a fair collection of sexy boudoir-wear, I noted with a small degree of awe. I piled the garments in the middle of the super-sized bed, pushed the case aside, and collapsed into it.

"You poor, neglected things," I murmured. I'd worn something different every night right up until our first democratic elections. After that milestone, Mr Patel would switch off the lights and wait for me to get into bed before demanding that I got naked. I sat up and stared at the contents of my bed. "Perhaps you should start loving yourself a little, Maha Jacobs Maal," I smiled encouragingly, "you're not *so* bad!"

The incessant shrill of the phone dragged me out of sleep and I reached out to my bedside table without opening my eyes.

"Hello?" I croaked.

Naani's voice echoed in my ear and I squinted through half-opened eyes at the clock. Nine thirty!

"Your nana already told Sipho to come way and finish," she prattled. "Wake *now*. He come way just now!"

I flipped onto my back with a sigh, rubbing my eyes tiredly as fat rays of sunshine bounced off the bright white walls.

Talk about a wake-up call. I grinned wryly as I surveyed the chaos – lingerie still littered the bed, I was barely dressed and my duvet appeared to have spent the night on the floor.

I uncrossed my legs and stretched languidly, grinning widely as my body recalled the unexpected delights I'd shown it. I let out a deep breath, stretching my legs with a foreign sense of satisfaction.

Truro High called while we were at Samiha's – causing Naani's frown to deepen as I stepped out of the room to take the call. I struggled to place the school – Reservoir Hills? Isipingo? Parlock?

"Can you come in for a brief interview?" the secretary asked. "We're really busy . . . New year and all." She sounded friendly enough.

"Yah, sure, when would you like me to come in?"

"The sooner the better . . . This afternoon?" she asked hopefully.

I glanced at my watch. "Is after three too late?" I asked.

"No, that's perfect," she sighed with relief. "Shall we say four?"

"That's fine." I scrawled the details on my hand. "I'll see you then."

I stared at the phone for a few seconds – another school had just called me! I couldn't believe it.

I made my way back to the living room, where Samiha's mother-in-law sat in her armchair, a blanket draped over her lap and a special trolley at her disposal.

"Ey, Maha!" she called as I re-entered. "What you making panchaath-banchaath on forn? Come sit and talk by us,' she ordered. "You came to visit sick people or make panchaath on forn?" she demanded as I took my seat quietly.

Samiha glared. "Now, see! You upset my mothernlaw and she's *so* sick also!"

Naani sat silently, as was befitting the grandmother of a besaram divorcée. Samiha turned her attention to her and shook a jar of sweets under her nose. Naani dismissed her demurely and fluttered her fingers. Can't be seen consuming in public – how *could* a soupçon be swallowed during these traumatic times?

⁂

The secretary was a short, plump woman in a sari, who beamed up from her desk.

"Please take a seat, he'll be with you just now," she said.

I chose a chair and flopped down.

"So, how come you're not teaching in some private Moslem school?" she asked when I had made myself comfortable.

I smiled. "They won't have me!"

She raised her eyebrows. "Oh, why? What did you do? Fall pregnant?"

I laughed and shook my head. "No, I *was* married, but I got divorced."

Her eyes widened. "Oh, big one that! Me? I still get nonsense from my old aunties because I never married at all! So many nice proposals I had, but no, I was too busy studying!" She grinned. "Poor you! I can imagine all the nonsense you're getting . . ."

Her phone rang and she gestured to me before picking it up.

"Hello? Yes, yes, okay." She looked up and pointed to the door behind her. "You can go in now."

A nervous tremor took hold of my legs for the first few steps. I took a few calming breaths and knocked politely before turning the handle and stepping into the head teacher's office.

Mr Pillay was a short, energetic man who hopped out from behind his desk to shake my hand vigorously and repeatedly offer me a seat.

"Thank you," I said.

"Jolly good, jolly good." He rubbed his hands and sat on the edge of his desk. "So Miss Maal, tell me about your teaching experience . . ." He waved his arms expansively.

I came to the end of my recounting rather quickly – ah well, it was the truth.

"So, you've never taught in a school like ours before?" he asked.

"You did your teaching practice in a private school, and then some filling-in at a Model C? Do you have *any* idea how different we are?"

I shrugged. "Sure, you have more black kids, so there's a second-language problem . . . You're probably over-crowded and under-resourced?"

He grunted. "Yes, yes, everyone knows that, but how does it translate in the classroom? How does it impinge upon the teacher's day-to-day teaching? The bottom line is that it's damn difficult. So, the million rand question, my dear, is will you cope?"

"How do the rest of your staff cope?" I asked.

"My dear, most of my staff have been at this school for well over ten years . . . Not only that, but they were mostly active participants in the struggle for democracy. They have their sacrifices behind them, so they are not about to look around at the chaos and run . . . No! They are absolutely determined to make it work. Their sacrifices cannot be in vain!" He dabbed at the corners of his mouth with a handkerchief. "So, Miss Maal, does that answer your question? Trust me, I'm not trying to dissuade you – I *need* teachers – but I would rather have teachers who know what to expect and are committed to making a difference!"

I listened quietly. "Do you think it would be possible for me to chat to a few of the other teachers?"

"That, my dear, is a brilliant idea." Mr Pillay grinned, a sudden flash of white against his dark skin. "I will escort you to the staff room where you can find out all you want . . . And then, go and think about it. But let me know soon. We need you, now you need to decide whether you need us!" And with that he adjusted his suit, put on his spectacles and led the way to the staff room.

Storm clouds were gathering and the day turned sullen as I negotiated my way back to the Mahal through the rush-hour traffic. I was nervous of the challenges that lay ahead, but the alternative – withering away at the Mahal – scared me witless!

Zeenat was waiting at the Mahal, all fired up. "Hey, Maha! Salaams! Howzit?"

I gave her a quick hug. "Wa 'alaikum salaam. I'm fine, just sweaty and tired . . ." I said as I led the way into the house and up the stairs.

"So, did you get the job?" she asked as she locked the door and pulled out her fags.

I threw myself on my bed and started unbuttoning my jacket, pulling off my headscarf at the same time. "Yeah, but he says I must think about it and accept it with my eyes wide open, so I'm going to sleep on it and then see how I feel."

"Do you know what I have been thinking . . .?" She paused to pass me the pack.

"What?" I pulled out a cigarette greedily and lit up.

Zeenat nodded. "Chances are no one is going to like the idea of you having a proper full-time job at a state school . . ."

I frowned. "Why should that be a problem? Are you saying Nana won't even think about it?"

She shook her head. "I can't see him giving in. And if he does, I'm sure there will be a few annoying conditions."

I smoked silently.

"So, I was thinking, what's stopping you from packing your bags, moving into your flat and doing as you please?" she asked.

I scowled. "If only life were that simple! I can't do that. Not after everything that's happened. Can you imagine how they would feel . . .?" I trailed off uncertainly, my excitement completely extinguished.

She shook her head angrily. "Well, Nana Maal is stubborn, man . . . You know that!"

I nodded resignedly.

❧

Dinner was the usual grim affair.

"Maha had a job interview today," Zeenat blurted out suddenly.

Nana paused to glare. "Thuro maathu!" he snapped and turned to Zeenat. My *head*! "She has *no* need for job-bob. She got everything she needs. She must help her granny. Ramzan starting too and Naani can't manage *everything* herself."

Zeenat nodded. "Yah, but it's *teaching*, so she'll be home early *and* have long holidays!"

He emitted a peculiar sound, pushed aside his plate and stood up abruptly.

Naani grabbed the opportunity to burst into tears. "Jor aweh. Nana upset. Can't eat too," she sobbed. "*Look* what you do, Maha? When you come heedee?" And, blowing her nose loudly, she huffed off behind Nana.

I sat back and sighed, mock-slapping my head. "Heedee?" I turned to Zeenat. "As opposed to waanku?"

Zeenat frowned. "You need to think straight and *come right*!" She sighed and started stacking plates. "Guess I might as well clear up, and as for you, Miss Maal, right now I advise you to shut your mouth and go to your room!"

155

"With pleasure, my dear!" I said, gesturing obscenely in her direction.

⚜

Fuck everything *and* everyone! Upstairs in my room I lit up and puffed furiously. Why was it that something as *basic* as a bloody job was such a major sodding issue in *my* miserable life? Stop being pathetic, I countered. Think of the girls being dragged to the woods for circumcision, or the wives beaten for bearing daughters or burning a curry. Think of the women who are arrested for being raped! What freedom of choice do those poor women have?

Zeenat shuffled in and flopped tiredly onto my bed. "I hate doing battle with the oldies . . . too exhausting . . ." She gave the pillow a quick pummel.

"Hah! Do you *blame* me for going nuts? It feels like the only thing that can fix this mess is going *back* to the *Palace.* Which *ain't* going to happen. Which *means,*" I drawled, "I am doomed!" I paced around the room, too wound up to sit.

"Well, you *do* have a few choices, you know . . ." Zeenat said.

"Oh, really, like what?" I snarled.

"Well, for one, you can do as *they* say, stay put and put up with the crap, and perhaps it'll get better as the days go by . . ."

"*Not* an option," I growled. "I would definitely lose my sanity!"

"*Or,* you could go off to work, give them something *else* to be angry about and endure the shit for the few hours you *have* to spend with them each day . . ."

"Sounds like a fabulous choice," I retorted.

"Hey, honey, I didn't say it was *perfect,* but at *least* it's a choice."

The following morning found me moping around listlessly, contemplating my fate. The phone shrieked through my torpor.

"Hello?" I mumbled.

"Is that Miss Maal?" a vaguely familiar nasal voice asked.

"Yes."

"This is Mrs Vahed from Islamia College," she began. "Mr Vanker, the *headmaster* . . ." She paused to allow the importance of the call to sink in, or maybe just to allow me to remember the man she was talking about – as if I *would be able to forget* the saintly brother of Dr Forjee Vanker. "He asked me to call and inform you that we have a position for a part-time librarian. From ten till two, Mondays to Fridays."

Another job! And this time an offer from Islamia, nogal!

"Oh, well, thank you for the offer," I drawled. "Can you post me the details of the contract and I'll consider it?"

"*Oh!*" she exclaimed – obviously I was *so jux* that I was supposed to jump at any and every opportunity.

"My address is on my CV. I'll look forward to receiving it. Salaams." I replaced the receiver and shook my head in disbelief.

Naani barged through the doors. "Who forn sor early?" she demanded excitedly.

"Oh, it was Islamia College offering me a part-time job," I replied calmly.

"Oh, hah, Islamia College haaru, near also. Part-time *bau* haaru . . . Mus take!" she gabbled frenetically, jabbing the air for emphasis.

I nodded. "I told them to send their contract, so I can see what they're offering."

157

"Hu contract-bontract? Mus give jawaab. Arreh, Maha! Thu bau gorni!"

Naani had modified her decree of dementia to one of dim-wittedness – was this progress? She shook her head as she busied herself with emptying the recently cleaned fridge. Her over-enthusiasm was a stark contrast to the antagonistic response to Truro High. Something smelled dodgy. Was it actually possible that they had engineered this job in order to provide me with one that met with *their* approval?

I picked up the newspaper and made my way back to my boudoir – I could do with the peace. Besides – I flung the paper onto the bed and grabbed my phone – I needed to call Sameer and give him the legal ultimatum.

"Salaams, Sameer, it's Maha. Everything okay?" I asked.

"Yah, not too bad. I hear you're starting work at Islamia," he said.

"*What?* Where did you hear that?"

"Oh, why? Is it a rumour?"

"They've *just* offered me a job, literally a few minutes ago. Where did *you* hear it?"

"Mummy said that Foi mentioned something . . ."

Which meant that Dr Forjee Vanker had *something* to do with it! It certainly seemed as though Nana was playing puppeteer.

"Isn't it ironic?" I hummed.

"What?"

"Nothing, just humming. Listen, I called about the legal proceedings . . ." And with that I launched into the real purpose of the call, pushing Nana's obvious cunning to the back of my mind. Eventually

I bullied Sameer into giving me a rough estimate on how long it would take him to begin formalising our divorce.

"Okay, but it's seven months and counting, so if nothing's done by then I'm going to get my own lawyer to start proceedings on my behalf," I threatened.

He acquiesced. "So, have you found an ou yet?" he asked, changing the subject.

None of your damn business! "So, are *you* still seeing Rozi?" I retaliated.

He coughed. "Listen, I have to go . . ." he said. "You should get the papers by next week. Take care." He coughed again. "Salaams."

So, from Slumurban Mahal to Slumurban School – it seemed Truro High was not even an option! It stank of frying pans and fucking fires but Farah and Zeenat both agreed that if I was given only *one* escape route to work, then I may well have to simply concede defeat – it didn't matter if I gagged as the pseudo-job was forced down my throat. It was only *one* battle after all, and I was all for winning the sodding war.

Reservoir Dog

Work proved to be another version of the daily drudgery I had experienced in the Palace kitchen, though my new domain was smaller and poorly equipped by comparison. The majority of the staff ignored me – avoiding the library at all costs in case whatever I had was catching – and it was only a few weeks into term that two brave souls eventually made their way to the library, ostensibly to avoid the photocopying queues in the main staff room. It soon became clear that they too were misfits – wrong race, wrong faith – and our brief chats provided the comic relief to the otherwise tedious daily grind.

A few weeks after starting the job I bumped into Dr Vanker – not *my* forjee any longer – as I paused at a petrol station after work to stock up on fags. He acknowledged me with a gruff nod and lowered his gaze – his usual staid and slimy act.

"Salaams. How are you?" I enquired politely, picking up a newspaper and packets of gum – purchasing contraband in the presence of the good doctor would definitely be a bad idea.

He grinned wolfishly. "Wa 'alaikum salaam, Maha. Alhamdulillah, we are *all* very well, shukar." He placed his purchases on the counter. "You know you have *me* to thank for your job," he said, reaching for his wallet and glancing at me over his proud protuberance.

I managed a small smile. "Oh? I didn't know . . ." And *such* a fabulously boring job at that!

He pulled out a fifty-rand note and slapped it on the counter before turning slowly and looking up. "What you mean *you* didn't know?" He stepped forward, leering. "How *else* you going to get a job *there*? What example you setting to all the young-young girls? That's why they never put you in the classroom!"

Saliva speckled his lips and I lowered my gaze instinctively. He was inches away, the blend of sweat and over-sweet itar coming off him nauseatingly.

"*Your nana* called *me*!" he continued, jabbing a finger in my face. "You make an old man cry with so much worry. Just now you go work in a state school and get all Nasaarah ideas!"

Christian ideas, nogal! I felt queasy – the upshot of his words and proximity – and struggled to control my breath as the next few seconds unfolded bizarrely.

He lurched towards me. "*I* did *your* nana a *big* favour, my *dear*!" he said, waving his hands about and brushing them swiftly across my breasts.

I flinched. Fucking favour se *moer*!

"*I* convinced my brother to give you a job, so that maybe you could be saved." He licked the spittle off his lips, turned to the counter and collected his change and shopping bag airily.

I paid for the items, turned to make my exit and walked straight into a long arm that was blocking my path – my tits smacking against this sudden boom-gate! I recoiled instantly as Dr Vanker's face appeared before me, and clutched onto my bag. Surely twice was *too* much of a coincidence?

"Not *so* fast, my dear. You not *even* going to say 'thank you' to me for organising this good job for you?" He shook his head dolefully. "That I will definitely *have* to tell your nana!"

"Jazakallah for the job," I managed to force through my clenched jaw.

He grunted. "You *must* come for a check-up, Maha," he said, his eyes on the curve of my breasts under my T-shirt. "You don't have to come to the surgery. You can come to Reservoir Hills one evening. Hmm . . ." He leered salaciously. "You look a bit *pale* also. Maybe you're dehydrated after fasting in this heat, or maybe you're anaemic . . ."

I nodded unhappily. "Jazakallah," I muttered as Dr Vanker finally turned away.

Back in the car my hands trembled as I struggled with the seat belt and ignition all at once. Deep breaths – calm down – *one* thing at a time. *First*, breathe! I inhaled deeply and closed my eyes for a few seconds. Strap yourself in, turn the key! The car roared to life and I forced focus on manoeuvring it onto the road.

I flicked the button for the window and allowed it to wind itself down. The cooler air gusted through and I breathed again. What the *hell* was *that*? I needed to throw up! Breathe! Breathe! Music! I fumbled desperately with the switch until the CD player whirred to life and mindless, almost wordless, Robert Miles thumped out. I increased the volume to indecent levels in a bid to drown *everything* as I drove automatically down the back roads to Slumurbia.

I headed straight for my room, stripped off my clothes and threw myself into a scalding shower.

⚜

I had one new message, I noted as I kicked my grubby clothes out of sight. I flumped on the bed with a sigh and opened it.

Slmz. Back frm UK. Have books 4u. Call when ur free.

Shahzad! I dialled his number and lay back as the call connected.

"Salaams, Maha! Howzit vaaing?" he answered.

"Hey, Shahzad, thanks for getting me books," I responded tiredly. "How was London?"

"Okay, you know . . . So, anyhow, what's new?"

"Oh, not much apart from protests, TRC hearings and corruption charges . . ." I sighed theatrically.

He laughed. "So how are things with you?" he asked.

"Surviving," I muttered.

"Still tough, then?"

"Oh, ups and downs, war and peace, friends and arseholes . . ." I trailed off.

"You sound tired," Shahzad said.

"Yah, I guess so, it's this heat. Anyhow, I'll let you know when I can pick up the books, if that's okay?"

"Yah, sure. Just call or SMS . . . Maybe we could meet up for coffee?"

I yawned. "Oh, okay, I'll let you know . . ."

I dropped the phone onto the bed. Coffee with Shahzad! Now that would be risky – unless we met up at some arb place off the beaten track, and even then. I closed my eyes. One day at a time, Maha, I told myself. One day at a time.

❊

I drove home after yet another day of the same old kak, weaving listlessly through the school-rush traffic. Back at the Mahal I dumped my bag at the foot of the stairs and yanked off my jacket and scarf before heading for the fridge.

"Sameer's foi forn now!" Naani said in what had become her usual surly tone as I poured myself a glass of water.

I felt a faint stirring of discomfort. "Oh, why? What happened?"

"Nor, nor problem, Dr Forjee say you look *so* sick and all. What loko say? You mus gor Reservoir Hill for looi test!"

I blanched, gulped down the water gracelessly and wiped my mouth with the back of my hand.

"Mus gor, Maha. That Sameer uncle got sor nice kaam for you also. You knor Gorinani say, hunda mota-mota families gor your school! Samiha, Nabiha too send!"

So because of this grand favour, of working at a school filled with the kids of the local big shots, I was to subject myself to his pricks and prods. I shuddered at the image that popped up unbidden and swallowed the bile that rose in my throat.

"I'll go to Farah if you think I need a blood test, Naani," I said firmly, picking up my glass.

She lunged for my arm as I prepared to make my getaway. "Nor!"

164

she barked. "Gorinani check sugar too. Nana take after Magh-rib."

So I had *no* choice – *again*! I blinked back sudden tears and extri-cated my arm carefully from her clutches, before turning and flee-ing to my sanctuary.

I scrabbled around my drawers for chocolate and crammed a chunk into my mouth. Oh, sweetness, overwhelm me, I begged, stripping off my clothes and throwing myself onto my bed. *Fuck* them all, I thought viciously as I kicked my legs wildly.

Naani rapped on my door before Maghrib. "Maha, read namaaz, get ready!"

"Leave me alone," I mumbled into my pillow.

"Just now Nana take by doctor. Kay dhungh waaru perr je!" She banged on the door a few more times, setting off only after I'd shout-ed that I was ready to pray *and* dressed decently.

For the first time since I could remember I was numbed beyond belief. I knew I *had* to pray, and reckoned I would attempt to make them up – but right now, I was deadened by dread. I remained under the safe cocoon of my godhru and rocked back and forth. I would simply refuse to go and pay the price, I decided.

"Hu che, Maha?" Naani shouted, pounding irately on my door some time later. "Gorinani waiting, jus now Nana come way."

I grunted and remained still. The bed, I surmised, was a safe dis-tance from the door. My phone beeped and I pulled it out to read the message. Zeenat. I squinted irately.

Call me when you're free. Scorching news! X

I threw the phone onto the godhru. I couldn't have cared less.

Two minutes later Naani was back, this time pummelling wildly. "Open door!" she bellowed. "Nana came way. He get cross. Jaldi kar!"

"Tell him to carry on," I replied. "I'm not going."

"Saali suvar!" she shrieked.

"Stupid pig" was probably as lewd as she'd get, I reckoned as I clutched onto my godhru. Finally, I heard her thunder down the stairs and ventured out of bed tentatively, peering through the window to watch Nana's car ease slowly out of the driveway. Gorinani would no doubt be waxing lyrical about my shameless insubordinate behaviour, but who cared. I locked myself in the bathroom and lit a fag, unable to dwell on what exactly I'd just evaded.

⁂

The sound of screeching tyres, followed by banging doors and loud voices cut through the inane chatter on my TV. I flicked the switch mechanically and braced myself. Footsteps thudded up the stairs and along the passage before stopping at my door. I took a deep breath and waited.

The door shook violently as Nana pounded. *"Maha! Get* out now! Dr Vanker was *so* worried he came *here* to see you! Now open!" he yelled.

If Maha didn't go to the good doctor, the maadar would come to Maha? I shook my head in disbelief and made my way slowly to the door.

Nana and Dr Vanker were both scowling. I greeted them perfunctorily and waited.

"See, Maha! Dr Vanker came all the way from Reservoir Hills to check you," Nana said pointedly, evidently expecting polite gratitude.

I grunted and Nana bristled.

"No problem, Maal Mota," the Vanker cut in smoothly, "u enè akkal dewa!"

So, he was *going to give me brains*! With no other option I stumbled back as he pushed his way into my room.

"If you lie down on your bed, I'll be able to examine you properly," he said, shutting the door behind him.

He hadn't locked the door. Surely he would have done so if he had evil intentions? I took a petrified seat on my bed.

"You know, Maha," he spoke loudly as he opened his bag slowly and removed his stethoscope, "you must learn to show respect to your elders!" He strode purposefully towards me and sat down heavily, simultaneously shoving me down flat on the bed. "You can't see how much dhukh you're giving your grandparents? So *much* they do for you!"

He raised one hand towards my face and I flinched instinctively as the hand weighed down over my mouth and his malodorous blend of sweat and cloying itar filled my nostrils. "Gave you everything," he continued. "Found you a *perfect* husband . . ."

He shook with what I took to be anger as he lifted the stethoscope, snaked his hand under my T-shirt and felt his way around. "Breathe! Breathe!" he barked as he gave my nipple a sudden savage squeeze.

My scream twisted reflexively through my body and shuddered up my throat only to be smothered by his meaty paw. I slammed my eyes on his sanctimonious face.

"And you throw it all in their faces," Dr Vanker panted, intent on finishing his monologue. "You don't *listen* to them, just want to live your life like one luchee! Staying alone by the flat also!" He tightened the pincers around my nipple – stethoscope long abandoned. "*What* nonsense you get up to? *Who* you bring there to naach?"

The tears leaked through my lashes and trickled onto my face.

"So?" He shouted without warning. "What have you got to say for yourself? What's that? Was it 'sorry'? Louder!" he shrieked triumphantly.

I squeezed my eyes shut and held my breath, anticipating a blow as his hands moved off my body. I sensed him looming above for a few seconds before he swooped down and yanked my hair. "You listen to me," he enunciated hoarsely. "You learn to shut your mouth and behave or I will find *other* ways of shutting your mouth, you understand?"

I nodded the best I could.

"Good!" he spat, picked up his bag and stepped out of my room.

Nana's apologies for the takleef – for being a burden – filtered through as though from a distant galaxy. I lay pinned to my bed, every muscle constricted in agony as their voices receded and doors slammed.

⁂

I was still stuck to my bed when the sound of re-approaching footfalls echoed through my door and Nana and Gorinani thundered into my room.

"I hope you opened your ears, and heard nicely what that man said!" Nana barked.

Gorinani jabbed at my head with one of her fat fingers as I attempted to sit up and wipe away the tears. "Ha, ha, hambarr!"

I began to shudder as the thought of the good doctor resuscitated the urge to hurl.

"You knor doctor told you got *no* looi also," Gorinani continued. "He give tablet. Never take money too!" The saint!

"*Tell* her the *news,* maybe her maathu will open . . ." Nana interrupted with a growl. "Tell Maha what *else* he said. *Tell* her! *Tell* her!" he insisted, his voice rising in pitch with each syllable.

I forced myself to focus on Gorinani, who was shifting about wheezing excitedly, hoping that I could keep the bile down. Perhaps, I thought, if I didn't move at all, I would be able to blot out the memory of the bastard's paws on my flesh.

"Ha! Hambru?" she questioned officiously. "Doctor kayyu . . . How must say Naani? Just now she get heart attack! Sameer nu nikah che . . . ai Juma!"

Sameer getting married this Friday – so *that's* the big deal? I *almost* laughed.

"Oh, to who?" I asked eventually.

She harrumphed and settled into a seat. "Chohan girl . . ." She shrugged.

"Not from Durban," Nana muttered.

So what about Rozi? Perhaps *this* had been the sizzling story that Zeenat had wanted to share? Whatever! The legal proceedings were definitely going to speed up if Sameer was settling down again, and that could only be a good thing as far as I was concerned.

"Her father is Doctor Vanker's cousin also," Nana offered.

All in the fucked-up family! I remained silent. Disappointed at my reaction, Gorinani leapt out of her seat – agile as a goat – and sped off in search of Naani, suddenly unconcerned about heart attacks. Nana, meanwhile, hovered around expectantly.

"I'm sorry, Nana," I managed eventually.

He grunted and turned to leave. "Oh, yah." He searched his pocket. "Here's your iron tablets," he muttered.

I took the little bag and threw it casually onto my bedside table. "I think I'll go and spend a couple of days at the flat," I called after him as he made his way out of the room. "I don't feel too well, so I won't be going to work tomorrow. I'll just stay until the weekend."

"Alone?" he barked, turning to glare at me.

I shrugged. "I'll tell Farah to come and stay. But you saw the place," I wheedled, "it's quiet *and* safe."

Maybe it was the horror of Sameer's impending nikah and the need to prevent Naani's paroxysms every time she caught sight of me, but he managed a gruff nod. "Just stay there and rest . . . Don't go any-where!" he lectured.

I nodded, muttering a quick salaam, and bolted to my car before he could change his mind.

⁂

Slmz. Need to breathe. I typed to Zeenat as soon as I made it to the car. *Meet me at my pad! Urgent!*

Then I turned the key and dashed off into the night at top speed.

I slowed at an intersection, turned up the air conditioning and burst into loud howls as the car hit the motorway. My foot flattened the accelerator and the speedometer rose along with my wails. I drove wildly, sobbing. I wanted to scream. I wanted to tear my hair out.

Suddenly sati seemed the perfect solution. *Where* was a fucking pyre when you needed one? I careened down the off ramp and screeched to a halt at a stop sign. Nothing short of setting myself alight felt like a viable option.

The sudden glare of a filling station startled me as I negotiated the last few turns before the flat, and before I knew what I was doing I found myself making the turn and parking. I grabbed my bag, went into the little shop and filled a basket methodically.

Having paid for my purchases I watched impassively as Pious – according to his nametag – loaded the charcoal, firelighters, matches and other essentials into my car. The makings of a pyre!

On the back seat ten bottles of Bacardi Breezer lay alluringly alongside the milk and bread I had bought. How was getting drunk going to *fix* me? Who cared? If becoming pideli could bring on temporary oblivion, then I would drink now and repent later, I reasoned.

⁂

The flat was quietly welcoming, but my uneven breath boomed in the silence. I lit a cigarette to calm my nerves and then promptly stubbed it out.

First, unpack! I ordered when my hands had stopped shaking. Moving towards the shopping, I emptied the bags methodically – lining the Bacardi Breezers up neatly in the fridge – and then pulled out a bin liner. Stripping off in the lounge, I threw every item of clothing I had been wearing during my examination by Dr Wanker into the sack. The urge to puke returned with a vengeance as I looked at the pile at the bottom of the bag and I fled to the bathroom, falling to my knees and heaving convulsively over the toilet, before eventually sprawling on the cool tiles in agony.

After some time I moved to my bedroom and cocooned myself in my dressing gown. My phone beeped just as I was about to get into bed. Zeenat! I thought. Finally!

Slmz. Just got your msg. Was in movie! R u at flat? X

But the thought of telling her what had happened was just too much. I felt the bile rise in my throat once again.

At flat. I finally typed. *Going to sleep. Choon tomorrow. X*

But sleep was a distant dream. Fat chance of getting any, unless of course I drank myself silly! Two minutes later I found myself carrying the ten coloured bottles into the lounge on a tray. Opening one, I slowly poured myself a glass of daaru, mesmerised by the look of the foreign drink. I left it to settle and moved across to the stereo. REM? *No,* far too mild. I grimaced. *Murder Ballads* would be perfect.

I walked back to take my first sip of forbidden fruit-flavoured drink. Taking a hearty swig, I paused to savour the taste. Odd, but not totally horrible, I concluded, as I sat back with a sigh, raising my glass to Nick Cave while he sang about poor Crow Jane: "Horrors in her head, that her tongue dare not name . . ."

I took another huge gulp of Bacardi Breezer. "Thu daaru piyech'!" I screeched out loud, à la Gorinani, and rummaged around for a fag.

In no time I had downed the first bottle, guzzled the second and was busy opening the third. Doctor *fucking* Vanker Forjee with his caring home visits! I thought as I squinted at the remaining bottles. The sleazy skanky scumbag son of a bitch! The fucking chuth-cunt-bitch-arse-maadarchodh-fucking-gaanbaal *se moer*! Gaanfaced trustee of the big city mosque!

172

I swilled the daaru around in my glass and glared glassy eyed out at the endless ocean. If only I could turn into a whale, dive into the ocean and spend the rest of my days out at sea, coming up occasionally for air.

I sniggered. "You're drunk *and* you're crazy, Maha," I slurred, heaving myself up slowly. "The only question is which came first: the madness or the drink? Are you crazy because you are drunk? Or drunk because you are crazy?"

I poured the blue liquid down my throat. I am drinking the ocean, I decided, quaffing the remainder before crawling across the floor to the CD player. "Kill it, Nick! I need to tjank!" I slurred as I stopped the CD and reached for a new one – causing the pile of discs to collapse with a clatter. "Hey, Celine!" I pushed the felled discs aside and wiped the dust off her cover. "Haven't listened to your sap in ages."

I hit play, collapsed against the nearest chair and promptly burst into tears.

⁂

The sun roused me with its deep glow. I squinted blearily at what was sure to be a stunning sight and felt my insides swirl. Oh, *hell*, I needed to pee. I raised myself to my knees, cringing as the crick in my neck straightened itself out, and crawled across the carpet. Grabbing onto a table for support I heaved myself up and wobbled towards the bathroom.

My tongue was stuck to the roof of my mouth, my head felt like a ditch-digging crew was making its way through my cranium and my face was caked with coagulated snot and trane. I flumped onto the bog, supported my head with both hands and peed with a huge sigh of relief.

"To piss and be pissed!" I enunciated into the empty bathroom, my croaky voice echoing weirdly off the newly painted walls. I stared blankly at my reflection, watching my mouth contort as I attempted a smile.

Finally, I stood up slowly, turned on the tap and managed to flick a few droplets onto my face before my head fell against the cool spout. I parted my lips and tried a few sips. My brain rocked wildly as the water hit my stomach! *More* sleep! Immediately!

I shuffled towards my bedroom and heaved my body onto the bed.

⁂

I awoke a few hours later and began to methodically remove every trace of my night of depravity. My body felt like a battleground. I knew what I had done was wrong, but surely, I thought, He would understand that I'd completely lost it and needed to drown my sorrows? And of course I *would* ask for forgiveness. I sighed as I threw the evidence into yet another black sack.

Finally, I flicked on the kettle, stacked the dirty dishes into the sink and squirted Sunlight washing-up liquid onto them, my insides whirling as I turned on the hot water and allowed it to run for a while. Then I carried my tea to the lounge and lit a fag while picking up the phone and dialling Zeenat's number.

"Salaams, Miss Maal! Why the *hell* haven't you been answering your phone?" she asked as soon as I made my salaam.

"I told you . . . I was sleeping. Trying to escape my Slumurban hell!" I retorted. "I only woke up a little while ago!"

174

"Lazy cow!" she pronounced. "So, what's the fuss? Didn't think you'd be so traumatised by Sameer's nikah?"

I inhaled slowly and let out a plume of smoke before replying. "You ought to know me better than that!"

She snorted. "The story around town is that you've gone to Cape Town to see your ailing ouma, but of course everyone knows that the *real* reason is that you were so upset when you heard about the wedding that Dr Vanker had to come to the Mahal and give you one injection for shock!"

"As if! I'm in Umhlanga for heaven's sake, and I'd rather not talk about Dr Vanker. Anyways, I need a good therapist!" I snapped.

"So, you've finally come to the realisation that you're totally bonkers?" Zeenat said. "What rocked your boat?"

"More like who rocked my boat . . ." I muttered forebodingly.

"Oh?" she responded. "Wait!" she instructed. "Before you continue, I just need to say that I can only join you tomorrow. I'm working mad hours these days. In fact, can you believe that Sameer Patel's future vrou and her entire entourage are coming to *me* for their pre-wedding treatments?"

I coughed and spluttered. "That's hectic!"

"I *know*! I was totally rocked when I found out. One of my regulars asked me quite casually to do her niece, and I'd already agreed before I knew *whom* she was marrying. Sorry, sweets, but hey, you could always come along and help get Ms Chohan ready!"

I snorted. "Now, why the hell would I want to do that?"

She laughed. "Well, just don't say I didn't offer. Oh, by the way, guess what her freaking name is? You couldn't make it up if you tried!"

"Just choon, bitch! I'm not in the mood!" I snarled.

"Calm down, woman! You're going to love this! It's *Sabera* Chohan," she crowed triumphantly.

"Brilliant, *Patience* Patel! You're right, it's *too* mad to be true . . ."

"So, choon what happened," Zeenat said, switching subjects calmly. "Naani gave me the chapter and verse on how your stubborn arse refused to vaai to Reservoir Hills. She said the saintly doctor actually came to the Mahal and 'Never charge even!'"

"Yah, well, guess what hazrat doctor did? He groped my tits!" I spat vehemently. "Can you believe the maadarchodh? And then he kindly threatened to use other methods to shut me up if I didn't behave myself!"

"Fucking hell and high waters!" Zeenat yelled. "You *can't* be serious?"

"So, now I'm hallucinating dirty old men?" I snarled. "What are you trying to say, woman?"

Zeenat gasped and for once was silent.

"Are you going to say anything?" she finally asked, her tone suitably subdued.

"To whom?" I snapped.

She sighed. "Dunno . . . Advice desk for abused women?" she mumbled.

"Fucking hell! Can you imagine the shit-storm if I go down *that* path. They will insist that I out the guy and deal bravely in court with the trauma of trying to prove he molested me!" My stomach churned as I spoke and I leaned my head against the cool wall. "And you know what the sickest thing is? If it had happened to someone else, *I'd* find it difficult to believe the poor girl!"

Zeenat sighed. "You know, even *I* can barely bring myself to believe you. Fucking doctor-holier-than-thou looking down his fat nose at everyone. And you're right, if you say anything they'll paint *you* in other undesirable shades."

I grunted. "Yah, remember that Molwi from Pietersburg?"

He had hit on a student, she'd complained to her parents and they'd immediately taken it up with the mosque trustees. The poor girl was told to shut her mouth and the good Molwi was relocated to the bundus, but she still became known around town as a slag.

Zeenat grunted. "What a fucked-up story!"

"And you know what pisses me off the most?" I said angrily. "The fear of being vilified means that chuths like him get away with doing whatever they want!"

"So, tell me once and for all that you're quite sure you're not going to go off on a one-woman crusade on this." Zeenat sounded seriously concerned. "You know it's one of those things that's really hard to prove this way or that . . ."

"I may be mad, but I'm not stupid," I reassured her. "I've given the grandparents enough grief for the decade, don't you think?"

"Okay. . ." She huffed. "Listen, I can't choon much longer, I've got a client coming in a few minutes. Will you be okay until tomorrow? Shall I ask Farah to stay with you?"

"Nah, I'm *gatvol*. I just need to be alone for now, and you know what, flying down to Cape Town might actually be a brilliant idea."

"Well, let me know if you're going to do that," Zeenat said. "Will you go to Ouma's?"

I drained my mug of tea with a long slurp. "Probably . . ."

"And you're serious about the therapy . . ." she trailed off worriedly.

"Definitely! If I can't name and shame the maadar, it's my only option."

❦

Time to shed the shit, Maha, I told myself and kicked the bin liner of soiled clothes towards the entrance. I had spent most of the day in bed, trying not to think about the events of the previous evening, but as I had drifted in and out of sleep I realised that I had to do *something* to take back control of my life. I switched on a few lights, grabbed a jacket and made my way down to the parking lot, bin liner in tow.

Driving along the coastal road, I headed for the widest part of the beach, parked a short distance from the nearest braai-stove and turned off the engine.

The sun had begun to set as I lugged the big bag of charcoal down into the braai area and began to make a fire. "You can't start a fire, you can't start a fire without a spark," I muttered as I crumbled the firelighters over the charcoal like feta over a salad.

I struck a match and held it against the white crumbs, watching as the flames leapt ebulliently. Taking a deep breath, I stepped back, opened the black sack and threw the first item onto the fire – my soiled T-shirt. It caught alight with a sudden roar and I was forced to draw even further away as black smoke filled the air.

Across the beach the ocean droned gently, while up above a few gulls cried out to each other as the day disappeared. I tore the bag apart and fed the fire with the remainder – watching dispassionately as it all went up in flames.

Maybe I *should* drag myself off to Cape Town, I thought as I

178

watched the last of it burn. Now seemed like a good time to make such a move – after all, the rumour had already been fed into the system – and it would be easy to put my pseudo-job on hold (I was lucky if I saw three kids in the library all week!).

I found an old braaing fork someone had left behind and impassively poked the charred remains of my clothes. I drew the line at scattering the ashes over Slumurbia, I thought, and snorted disparagingly.

You're crazy *and* a coward. You're running away and taking the easy way out. But then, what better way to try and move on than to put some distance between myself and my Slumurban hell? I argued. One thousand eight hundred kilometres between Dr Gaanbaal Wanker and me. It sure was tempting.

⁂

I headed back to the car, still warm and flushed from the roaring fire. I wiped my sweaty brow, unlocked the car and climbed in with some relief. Strapping myself in, I turned the key. The car choked, spluttered and died. I switched off the lights and tried again. Shit, double shit and crap. *Now* what?

I grabbed my bag and pulled out my phone. Shahzad. He *had* said to call if I ever needed help. Well, this was a *real* emergency, I reckoned as I searched for his number and clicked on dial.

"Maha?" He sounded surprised.

"Salaams, Shahzad. Look, I'm sorry to bug you. Are you busy?"

"It doesn't matter. What's wrong?"

Was it that obvious? I sighed. "I'm in Umhlanga . . . Do you know the bit of the beach where you can have a braai?"

"Yah . . ." he drawled. "Do you need me to pick you up?"

"No, no . . . I mean I *do* need you to come out if you can. My car won't start!"

"Oh, shit! Okay, now listen to me! *Stay* in your car, do up the windows and keep your phone in your hand, okay?"

"Okay. Thanks, Shahzad," I whispered, swallowing the fresh lump in my throat.

"Stay calm. I'm on my way!"

❦

Shahzad burned rubber as he drew to a sharp halt beside me, leapt out of his car and ran over to my door. I fumbled with the lock, struggling to release myself while he waited patiently until he could help me out of the car.

"Maha, are you okay?" he gazed down at me, his eyes searching mine. "It's okay, I'll sort it out and if I can't then I'll take you home and get a garage to pick up the car."

I nodded dumbly, unable to stop myself from mutating into an unsightly snivelling wreck.

"Hey, Maha, come now, it's okay . . ." he murmured soothingly as I whimpered on his shoulder.

I was in his arms, I realised with zero sense of alarm – the flood of tears had been too overpowering for anything else to matter.

Shahzad patted my back patiently as I soaked his shirt with my slobbery sobs until they petered out into painful hiccups.

"I'm sorry," I gasped.

He patted my arm and shrugged. "Listen, I'm going to try boosting your car now," he said. "It's getting dark."

I nodded and reached for a tissue while he connected cables to both engines and then instructed me to start up. The car stuttered weakly before dying out.

"Try again," he called from behind the wheel.

I nodded and turned the key. The car spluttered – like Dada Patel having a session with his spittoon – before finally roaring back to life.

"Yay!" I clapped, gratified by the comforting purr of the engine.

Shahzad left his engine running and leaned against my door. "Let it run for a bit and then I'll follow you home . . . just to make sure. Are you staying at the flat?"

I nodded. "Thanks *so* much for coming out . . ."

"Don't be daft!" He smiled.

"Still, thanks, I appreciate it! Hope I didn't interrupt a hot date!" I managed a brief smile.

He laughed. "Trust me, I wouldn't know one of those if it came and bit me on the arse!"

"Yah, right, Mr Moosa, whatever you say!" I looked away, overcome by the sudden sense of deliverance.

He patted the roof of my car. "Okay then, I think we can move along now. So lead the way and I'll follow you."

"Stalker!" I shouted with relief as he disconnected the cables.

⁂

I drove carefully along the dark roads with Shahzad watching my back right until I parked in my bay, overwhelmed, exhausted and on the brink of fresh tears.

"Thanks a million . . . And sorry about your shirt." I pointed with an embarrassed blush to the soggy patch across one side of his chest.

He smiled. "I'll send you the dry-cleaning bill! Oh, yah," he fumbled around and stuck a foreign bag out of his window, "here are your books. I forgot I had them in the car."

"Oh, thanks so much. Do you want to come up for coffee or something?" I offered unthinkingly. "Sorry!" I rushed out, suddenly mortified. "Please don't feel obliged or anything. I'm okay, really. Please go back to whatever it was you were doing." Maha, you're babbling! Are you afraid Shahzad is going to think you're a jux slag? Shut the fuck up, gaandi!

"Thanks," Shahzad said, switching off his engine. "Coffee sounds good."

I exhaled slowly and walked towards the lift. Maybe he was just being polite. Maybe he really did feel like some coffee. What difference did it make?

"So, you're staying here for a bit?" he asked as we stepped into the elevator.

I nodded. "Actually, I'm supposed to be in Cape Town," I offered cryptically.

He smiled. "Missed your flight because you were stuck on the beach?"

I still hadn't decided about Cape Town, I realised. "I may go. I'm not sure. I haven't packed or anything," I said as I opened my front door and headed to the kitchen. "Just make yourself comfortable," I called out as I filled the kettle and hit the switch before pausing to survey the area. Everything was in order, thank goodness. No sign of my recent breakdown.

Shahzad was flicking through my CDs when I brought the coffees into the lounge.

"I see you've been listening to Nick Cave," he said.

"Yeah, thanks for getting me that. It was perfect for last night," I uttered drolly.

"I can drop you off at the airport if you still want to go," he offered as he settled into the armchair across from me.

"Are you sure?" I frowned. "Haven't I imposed enough? Aren't you busy tonight?"

He shook his head. "Stop it with the imposition kak. I'm *not* busy and I can wait while you pack. But have your coffee first, chill and then decide what you want to do."

"So, are you invited to the wedding?" I asked a few seconds later, grimacing at the thought.

He shrugged. "Yah, I'll probably go to the nikah, and try and avoid the reception. Do you know her?"

I shook my head. "Nope. She's from out of town, I hear." I paused. "So is it over between the two chuths, or is Sam just messing up someone else's life?"

He wrapped his hands around the mug. "I have no idea. We haven't exactly been spending too much time together recently."

I raised my eyebrows. "Oh, really?"

He nodded and took a sip. "It's no big deal . . ."

I stared thoughtfully at the great outdoors.

"Are you upset because of the wedding?"

I snorted. "Give me a break. I was *happy* to leave that lying maadar! I'm just envious that it's been so easy for him to move on."

183

Shahzad sipped his coffee slowly as I leaned back against the sofa. He smiled. Shit, the guy was gorgeous.

"So?" he asked. "Made any decisions about Cape Town yet?"

"I'm not the most decisive person, you know." I gulped my coffee. "I think I'll sort out a flight for tomorrow, I'm too tired to fly across the country tonight."

He nodded. "Well, then I won't keep you up – you should be in bed!" He stood up.

I clunked my mug onto the table and followed suit. Gaan! I wouldn't mind a bit more distraction.

"Thanks for everything," I whispered as I kissed his cheek, this time allowing myself to savour the sensation of his body's proximity to mine. "You're very kind, sir." Somehow my arms found their way around him, and I allowed myself a few seconds of stolen pleasure.

Finally, I exhaled slowly and loosened my arms until I was gazing up at him again. I smiled sweetly, leaned forward and pressed my lips against his.

My unanticipated action jerked us apart violently. My body was aflame and cheeks burnt as I bit hard on my lip. "I'm sorry," I mumbled.

He shifted his feet, which were all I could focus on, and put his arms back around me. "When we are upset," he sighed against my hair, "we often do things we don't understand. It's not an issue, and I won't read anything into it, okay?"

My body leaned naturally towards his and I felt my loins stir. Was it wishful thinking or was *his* body stirring in response? The sensation advanced slowly, but he released me before I could complete my analysis.

184

"I'd better be going," he blurted, looking away. "Let me know if you need a lift to the airport, okay?"

I nodded my head, my body warm and fuzzy from the contact, my brain still buzzing wildly. I was probably beet-red! I produced a small smile.

"Well, if you're free, then I'll book a flight for around three in the afternoon . . ." I finally said. "If that's okay with you?"

He nodded. "Fine, I'll see you tomorrow around one o'clock," he said and turned to let himself out of my flat.

Fine. *Whatever.* I remained standing there. A part of me was obviously not completely functional – why couldn't I ask Farah or Zeenat to drop me off at the airport? Why torture myself by being in the presence of Shahzad? Shahzad . . . had he deliberately and decisively cast me off because I repulsed him? Stop winding yourself up, Maha! I steadied my breath. Why had I discarded all that daaru?

Shut up. *Do not* think. Move *directly* to bed, *do not* pass urine, and *do not* collect yourself. I hit the sack.

Deconstructing Maha

Farah made arrangements for me to see Professor Parker in Cape Town, an old friend of her late father.

"He doesn't see patients any more, he's retired from therapy," she explained between shifts. "But he *does* make exceptions now and then."

"Thanks, Farah, I appreciate it. So, how long will I need to go? A couple of weeks?" I asked.

She laughed. "No one can predict that. The average crisis intervention is usually about six weeks. But why don't you just go slow for once?"

I sighed. "Okay, whatever!" I wrote the details into my diary and flicked it shut. "As long as it helps!"

"If you go in with the right attitude, it will."

"Yah, baas, whatever you say. So, what's new?"

"Fuck-all apart from work and more work. And when I'm not working, I'm asleep. Fabulous life I have right now!" she remarked drolly. "How's Cape Town?"

"Not sure. I've just been sleeping and watching movies that dear Tante Gabiba dropped off . . . along with a car!"

"Well, then you should definitely shift your arse and enjoy some long, scenic drives!"

"Oh, don't nag! I'll get out eventually. At least Ouma just lets me be!"

Ouma was content to confine fussing to mealtimes, when she filled my plate and then insisted on second helpings.

Farah grunted. "Good for you. Just make sure you take it easy, okay?"

I promised without difficulty, curled up and prepared for more shuteye.

<hr/>

I took a taxi the first time I ventured out – in spite of Tante Gabiba's spare car parked in Ouma's yard – shying away from the stress of driving on foreign roads. The driver played Mariah Carey all the way through the city and by the time I got to where I was going I was ready to strangle someone. Alan Boesak would be a good choice, I decided after taking in the headlines at the final four-way stop.

Prof Parker stood up as I entered his office, pushing his spectacles in Alice-band fashion over the silvery cascade that swung down from his head to lie across his broad shoulders. He shook my hand effusively, his face creasing into a warm smile as I politely accepted the proffered seat.

"So, Maha Maal, friend of Farah Osman, get comfortable and tell me why you're here," he said as soon as I had settled myself down.

"Because I need help," I volunteered.

Prof Parker adjusted the collar of his loose ethnic shirt – very Madiba-esque – and scrambled about in the pocket of his jeans before producing a pen with a flourish and scrawling something onto the notepad in front of him.

"Help with?" he finally asked.

I sighed. "I don't know . . . How to cope. How to feel human. I don't know who I am any more."

"Good, that's a good start. Therapy is not a miracle cure, you know – it's more like help with polishing the mirror, so that *you* can see yourself clearly."

"What if I don't like what I see?" I retorted.

"Well, if you had let me finish," he smiled, "I was *about* to say, it's a way to learn about yourself *without* judging yourself." He chewed the end of his pen thoughtfully. "And if there are things you don't like, then we can try what the Greek philosopher Epictetus suggested: first say to yourself what you would be, then do what you have to do!"

I nodded – as long as the man had a plan, I had hope.

⁂

By the time we lurched out of the madness of March and into the relative sanity of April I was firmly settled in Cape Town. Zeenat had spread the story back east that I was playing nurse to Ouma. She believed it would be better if no one (not even Nana and Naani)

188

heard about Prof Parker – and that suited me just fine. Shrinks were associated with insanity, and a woman in need of one had a bleak future in Slumurbia.

I couldn't care less. Right now, for once in my whole entire life, it was mostly about me.

The therapy was gut-wrenchingly protracted, but a lifetime of kak was not discarded easily and such was the price I had to pay if I was going to attempt to live authentically. Ouma, meanwhile, remained nonplussed by my ups and downs and paid no heed to my loud music, endless tea drinking, chain-smoking and back-to-back movie watching, concerning herself instead with Eid and hajj – or *gajj,* as she pronounced it. Apparently many of her friends had finally set off on the epic odyssey.

One morning I awoke to find her in the kitchen, clanging dishes and banging pots.

"Ek gaan with Tante Gabiba to the karamat in Macassar . . ." she said to me without looking up. "Oh, and Nadima and thems is climbing up the mountain after Eids one of the Saturdays. They invited youse to join."

I walked over to her with concern. "Is everything okay, Ouma? You look upset."

Eventually she glanced up at me, her eyes brimming with tears. "You know all the gajjis is mos in Mina now? Tante Gabiba says there was a big fire there. She don't know how many hundreds of people just died . . ." She yanked at a piece of Carlton paper and blew her nose wildly.

"Were your friends there?" I asked. "Have you called their families?"

"Ja, we mos phoned everyone, but they know nothing. The old ladies don't have cellphones, and they can't gets through to the agent, so we have to mos wait. So I say to Gabiba, let's go and sit in Macassar for a while. Maybe I feel better." She sat down with a heavy sigh.

The first time I'd returned to Cape Town, with Sameer, Dada Patel had warned us against going to the karamats. "All kinds of nonsense people do there!" he'd expounded. "Worshipping holy men! *We* don't do that! It's haraam!"

Sameer had nodded obediently, and as no one had offered to take me to any such place before, the matter had never required any thought.

I sat opposite her and stroked her hand. "Who's buried there, Ouma?"

She looked up in shock. "Ag, sies, Maha! Sheikh Yusuf." She stood up suddenly and busied herself with the kettle. "You know, the Dutch did bring him here because he was making troubles there by Indonesia. So they stuck him in the middle of the bush mos, just so's he wouldn't give ideas to all the slaves. But no, algamdoelillah, they made a small farm and that was a great place of learning. People should come there from far." She took a calming breath.

I went over to hug her. "Relax, Ouma, remember the doctor said you shouldn't get over-excited."

She shooed me away. "Well, decide if you're coming. She is mos coming to fetch in half an hour."

I nodded. "Yah, okay, I'd love to come with . . ."

I couldn't see the harm of visiting an area of great historical importance – or spending time in what was sure to be a beautiful shrine to a great man who stood for peace, justice, freedom and learning!

⚜

The actual mazaar lay on the peak of a gentle slope – a small, evidently historic building. Ouma and Tante Gabiba stopped to greet the woman standing outside. I paused and took in the sparse surroundings: animals grazing on large tracts of land dotted with small homesteads, and in the distance the bustle of the township.

The woman unlocked the door and we entered reverently. The air was cool and fresh as we lowered ourselves and sat on the worn prayer mats that lay around the gaily coloured tomb. Sweet perfume pervaded the air and serenity appeared to wrap itself around me, seeping through to my very core. I released a slow sigh of relief, and for once my mind was quiet and my body calm.

Ouma sat with her head bowed and her eyes shut. I smiled and followed suit, floating while my lips moved in tranquil invocation.

I remained in this blissful state, unconscious to everything until Ouma whispered, "Come, Maha, times to go . . ."

My eyes opened placidly, I let out a restful breath of air, stood up and drifted towards the door.

On the way home Tante Gabiba invited Ouma and me over for dinner. "Nothing fancy, just bredie we having tonight . . ."

Ouma looked at me and I nodded. I knew she would rather be with Tante Gabiba while she tried to get information on the fate of their friends in Mina. I sighed as I stared out at the setting sun and said another little prayer for all the hajjis.

Prof Parker handed me the twentieth tissue – I'd been sobbing and raging for the past half an hour. He waited until I'd blown my nose and wiped my face.

"It doesn't make you a coward to acknowledge that in the *real* world we sometimes have to find the balance between two bad things," he said, uncapping his pen. "There's no definitive way to deal with abuse and in some cases, outing the perpetrator is the best option, even though the victim does require bravery and endurance to go through with it."

I grunted. "I can't help feeling like a complete wuss . . . Even Mary, who's a teenager, had the good sense to knock over a glass of water when Naseem attempted to touch her!"

"Reacting in the moment doesn't *always* go according to plan," Prof Parker continued. "From what you are telling me, the doctor sounds like a typical bully who will defend his position no matter what. So there's really no point in beating yourself up over what you *didn't* do. It is important that you chose to deal with the experience and not simply sit back and suffer while it fermented in your subconscious. Give yourself credit for that, Maha."

I nodded.

"But," Prof Parker continued gently, "it will be extremely beneficial if you were to go up to the man, and say very firmly that you are not afraid of him, and should he attempt any such thing again, even if it is with someone else, then you will have no qualms about speaking up and dealing with the societal judgement!"

"What?" I squeaked.

Prof Parker nodded. "It's important for you to confront him.

That's really the best way of dealing with a bully. *Think* about it at least."

"Would it be okay if I confronted him in a letter?" I asked. "Or does that just prove my wussiness?"

He shook his head slowly and his silver mane swished hypnotically. "Writing a letter does not confirm your lack of courage. It's better than nothing. But I don't expect you to get up and go and do anything this instant. Just think about it, and in the meantime why don't you accept your cousins' invitation to climb that mountain?"

❦

The Saturday after Eid was perfect for climbing – cloudless skies and only the hint of a breeze. We walked past the mile-long queue of tourists waiting for their cable-car tickets and paused near the fleet of tour buses.

Nadima smiled. "We're taking this route," she said, gesturing towards a signposted path. "It's the easiest one."

I nodded, clearly relieved.

"Platteklip," Nadima said as we eased along the gentle incline that speared to lead directly under the cableway. "You know, Afrikaans for 'flat stone' . . . See, this bit is quite easy."

I nodded and focused on my footing.

Nadima paused after a while and waited for me to catch up. "Look . . ." She pointed. "That's Platteklip Gorge . . . Hope you've been using the stepper at the gym!" She giggled at my look of horror.

I took refuge in silence as I avoided the prickly fynbos and followed Nadima onward and upward. The climb was more arduous than I had expected and I found myself pausing to catch my breath more and more frequently as the path grew steeper and the sun higher.

"You okay?" Nadima asked half an hour later. "Do you want to stop for a drink?"

I nodded. "Scared to stop," I managed to gasp, "in case I can't start again."

My throat was parched, I was pouring with sweat and if I didn't have some water soon I'd probably collapse – but what would happen to me if I sat down and couldn't get up again?

Nadima laughed. "Ag, *no*, you shouldn't think like *that*. You *have* to stop and rest. You can't climb a mountain without stopping! It's impossible!" She laughed again. "Okay, listen, there's a good place to stop just up ahead. Just a little further and we'll have a rest. Okay?"

I nodded, pulling out my water bottle and taking a deep slug as I urged my leaden legs forward, placing them stoically in front of each other. "Damn you, Professor," I muttered as I clutched onto a rock to steady myself.

I had cried copious tears over the casualties of my life in the sanctuary of Professor Parker's office, but he had calmly mopped them up, promising all along that we would get to the bottom of the well together. At least he'd helped me acknowledge that *I* had nothing to be ashamed of – I was not wearing a sign on my forehead that asked every arsehole to kindly abuse me!

I scrambled upward, squeezing my eyes shut, refusing to look up or down, focusing steadily on where I was and inching forward. I *would* get to the top, I told myself resolutely, and I *would* confront Dr Vanker – though fast-mailing a missive was as brave as I would get. So, perhaps not head-on, but damn close!

By now the rest of the gang were distant blobs, much closer to the summit – only Nadima lagged behind, obviously bringing up the rear. We continued climbing, the only sounds my grunts and gasps.

"Fuck this, I can do it," I griped as I struggled to hoist myself higher.

"We can stop *here*," Nadima called out from a nearby outcrop of rocks. "We're almost there now, and there are great views from here." She patted the flat boulder.

I huffed over, collapsed beside her and slowly raised my gaze to the city sprawled below.

"Wow! What an amazing view!" I exclaimed.

"Look," she pointed to the tiny cars lined up below us, "our car's there somewhere. Can you believe you've come this far?"

I smiled out at the city and shook my head, too overwhelmed to speak.

"What a blerrie shitty few months. Ag, Maha, life can suck," Nadima sighed, "but you can't complain on a day like this." She smiled.

I squinted at the light and offered a fleeting smile. I had come far indeed! I had almost conquered this maadar!

"Oor ons ewige gebergtes," I sang to my amazement.

"Waar die kranse antwoord gee . . ." Nadima joined in with a giggle.

I smiled. "How does the last verse go?" I asked. "It's that new bit in English – do you know it?"

She shook her head. "Nope, *who* goes round singing the anthem nowadays? Back in the day we was singing 'Die Stem' at school and 'Nkosi Sikelel'' at all the rallies." She turned to me curiously. "When was the last time *you* sang the new anthem?" she asked.

195

I sipped my water thoughtfully. "Oh, it was when I was doing substitute teaching last year. I was there for the concert and we all sang it then . . . It feels like another lifetime now." I wiped my mouth and stuck the bottle into my backpack.

Nadima smiled. "Don't even want to *think* of the last time *we* joined a protest. Ag, it all became so ugly afterwards." She shook her head glumly.

"Are you talking about Pagad?"

She nodded. "Boeta Miley and Braim," she jerked her head towards the summit, "they lost two or three friends to drugs. Ag, shame." She shook her head and sipped her energy drink thoughtfully.

"Yah," I mused aloud, "Pagad started off with good intentions, I suppose."

She nodded. "Exactly, and then it all turned to kak. Come, let's go . . ." She stood up and dusted herself down before helping me to my feet.

I lumbered uphill staunchly. The end was in sight, and with one final burst of energy I found myself atop the mount. I managed a little jig before slumping in an exhausted heap against the nearest rock.

Nadima laughed. "It's a great feeling, nè? I bet the others have already walked to the other side." She scanned the peak before throwing her hands up in frustration. "I bet they're eating at the restaurant. Come, let's go find them."

"Umm, you carry on," I panted. "Let me just catch my breath first."

She smiled. "No problem, it's straight that way . . . You take your time," she said and set off across the mountain top.

I leaned against the rock and gazed up at the sapphire sky – exhausted, but elated. Finally, as my strength returned, I unzipped my bag, found my water and took a greedy gulp. Down below me the seemingly calm waters sparkled, stretching out endlessly towards the horizon.

I had no idea when I'd be going back to Durban, I thought as I hauled myself to my feet. Prof Parker reckoned I just needed to start what he called "active, conscious, true living" again, but I didn't see why I couldn't just stay exactly where I was. He had told me that he thought that I was living passively, too afraid to be myself, but standing on top of Table Mountain, grinning out at the gorgeous Cape of Good Hope, I felt anything but passive.

❊

"So, what happened on the night of the bonfire?" Prof Parker asked on a wintry morning, West Coast style.

I had made my way happily up to Prof's domain in my new boots, coat, hat and scarf – revelling in the foreign winter attire – but now I felt myself flush as his question burnt up my good spirits.

"I left my car lights on 'cos it was getting dark . . ." I began in a resigned monotone. "So, by the time I was done with the fire my battery was dead. I called Shahzad and he came to the rescue."

"This is the same friend who drove you to the airport to catch your flight to Cape Town?" he confirmed, scribbling away as usual. Today's shirt was black with purple and royal-blue paisleys.

I nodded. "So he followed me back to the flat and I invited him up for coffee." I paused. "I was grateful for his help . . . It meant a lot to me."

"He accepted your invitation?" he asked.

I nodded. "I made the coffee, then we sat and chatted a bit . . ."

He nodded and made another note.

"Finally, he stood up to go and I thanked him again, with a hug and kiss," I continued. "I mean, we'd hugged and kissed before . . . It just felt different that time."

"Hmm, so you've never thought of Shahzad as a potential partner?" He held up his hand before I could interrupt. "Not necessarily an actual boyfriend, but a sexual playmate."

My flush was now crimson. "You know, I *have* sometimes wondered *what* it would be like . . ." I tucked my clammy hands under my thigh. "But I think most women who meet him must do that. He's like a Johnny Depp or something . . ." I offered earnestly. Well, it *was* bloody true.

He scribbled furiously. "So what happened after you hugged him?" Prof asked.

I took a deep breath. "I kissed him on the lips, and we both sprang apart like fucking repelling magnets!"

"Now, now, *such* language from a lady!" He shook his head in mock disapproval. "So, the shock was too much?" He smiled.

I shrugged. "He came over and gave me a gentle hug and said that when people are in shock they do crazy things, and that he didn't think any less of me . . . And then we spoke about my arrangements and he left."

"Have you seen him since?"

"He drove me to the airport, obviously," I said. "I tried to bring up what had happened and apologise, but he just waved it away and said we didn't have to discuss it . . . End of story."

"So, why *isn't* it end of story?" Prof asked.

I felt myself stiffen. "Well . . ." I sighed. "When he hugged me, my body sort of just moulded to his, and I thought I felt him respond . . ." I trailed off helplessly, unable to articulate that which twisted my innards.

"Yet, he stepped back and went home. And you felt rejected?" He gazed at me thoughtfully.

I shifted about uncomfortably and eventually nodded.

"Why do you think you felt this way?" he asked.

I shrugged. "Dunno . . . 'Cos he's a man?"

"So, what you're saying is that you've been conditioned to believe that a sexually aroused man will go forth and take what he can," Prof paused for breath, "and because he didn't, you feel rejected?"

I shook my head. "I don't know *why* I feel so bad, but a part of me just wants to hate him for making me feel like this!"

"Like what?"

I was ablaze. "Like . . ." I twisted my fingers agitatedly, "I *wanted* to be with him . . . He *knew* I was turned on by him and yet he chose not to . . . to . . . Perhaps because it would give him no pleasure?"

"Or perhaps because he didn't want to take advantage of your fragile state?" The professor tapped his pen thoughtfully.

I glanced up with a frown. "What do you mean?"

"Only moments earlier you had been sobbing in his arms, so he knew you were emotionally vulnerable, but he did the gentlemanly thing. He didn't take advantage of you. You see it differently *because* you were emotionally vulnerable at the time. Quite often we cope with trauma by seeking sexual comfort."

I stared at him in shocked silence.

"Well, when you *do* meet up with him again, let me know how you get along," Prof said with finality in his tone. "He sounds like a nice guy."

I nodded. "He is," I conceded grudgingly. "Are you getting rid of me?"

"I think you're ready to go back, don't you?"

"Go back to what? And why do I *have* to go back? Ouma's health is deteriorating. It would be good if I stayed with her, you know?"

He shrugged. "Be that as it may, you *should* start thinking about it. You'll be fine. If you decide to stick around, I'll see you once every three weeks, and if you go, well, you can stay in touch via e-mail . . ."

I nodded uncertainly. "Well, anyway, thanks for today," I said, standing up to shake his hand politely.

"Think about it, Maha." He patted my arm paternally. "You've climbed a mountain and you've clarified your position with Dr Vanker. You can do *anything*!"

⚜

I snuggled under one of Ouma's home-made blankets, lost in the hopelessness of *A Fine Balance* – one of Shahzad's offerings – as I struggled through my first true Cape winter. My phone shrilled suddenly.

"Salaams, Maha. Howzit?" Zeenat greeted me.

"Salaams, Zeenat . . . What's up?" I asked her.

"Umm, actually, high drama. Naani's in hospital . . ."

"Oh, *shit*! What happened?" I squeaked, sitting bolt upright immediately.

Ouma shot me a concerned glance.

"She was fine this morning, but apparently she told Gorinani she was feeling dizzy earlier this afternoon. Anyhow, she collapsed when she went to read Maghrib, so they've rushed her into hospital. She's stable now."

"Bloody hell! Do they know why?"

"Well, they're doing tests and stuff . . . Thing is . . . it's . . ."

"I know," I interrupted with a sigh, "expected that I be *there*. Is it okay if I fly up tomorrow?"

Zeenat sighed. "The sooner the better," she said. "Though she's not exactly *critical*, so I suppose tomorrow should be fine . . . Make it in the morning, though, okay?"

Matters were now firmly out of my hands. I was being hauled back east.

"Yah," I muttered, "okay then. I'll speak to you in the morning . . ."

"Yah, I better go and see to the hordes that have descended upon the freaking hospital . . . You'd think Slumurbia had relocated!" she snorted.

"Go and be dutiful and duryi now . . . Keep izzat and all," I teased.

"Yah, what izzat to keep, sor shameless you not even here!" she retaliated.

"Give Naani my salaams, and tell her I'm making dua," I said as Zeenat hung up.

Ouma looked at me quizzically as I dropped the phone back into my lap. Slowly, I explained the situation.

❧

I walked down the badly lit road that led to the cemetery, flanked by Ouma and Tante Gabiba. My parents! I recited a few verses of the Qur'aan and sent it off to them with a teary smile.

"Just now *I'll* be joining them . . ." Ouma mumbled as we made our way into the cemetery.

"Ag, Ouma, why do you like to speak like that?" I scolded her gently.

"Maha, I is mos old now! How long can I live?"

Tante Gabiba cackled. "You'll probably live until you're completely toothless . . . Like *your* ouma!"

Ouma grinned. "It's true . . . My ouma, she lived until she was one hundred and two!"

"See, Ouma, you'll be around for a while longer!" I wagged my finger as we approached the graves.

"Ja, but she must sell that place mos and buy a small flat, or otherwise get someone to stay with her . . ." Tante Gabiba said pointedly.

Ouma nodded. "Ja, ja, moenie worry nie, I already decided to do that. Having Maha here has made me realise what you've been telling me all these years is the truth."

I shuffled closer and rested my head on her chest, allowing her to wrap her arms around me. "I'm glad I was of some use, Ouma," I said as I drank in her sweet baby-powder scent.

Ouma squeezed me gently. "Ag, Maha, kleintjie, now it's time to mos go back and look after your other granny . . ."

I nodded sombrely as I made ready to bid my parents farewell.

⁂

I felt a creepy sense of déjà vu as I strode down the by-now-familiar corridors of Durban's premier infirmary.

Naani lay pale and woebegone against a pile of pillows while

Gorinani fussed around her, adjusting sheets and rattling on about how *she* had heaved poor Naani off the floor.

"You looking *sor* well, Maha!" Beema, Raeesa's grandmother, pronounced reproachfully as I moved through the inevitable cluster of people gathered in Naani's room.

What was I supposed to look like? I wondered.

"Salaams, Naani, how are you feeling?" I asked as I kissed her cheek and gave her a hug.

"What *how* feeling?" Gorinani snapped, barely pausing in her ministrations. "Thu *aweh* aawee? *Now* you come way too? Sor late? If your naani die Janaaza too finish!"

Well, she's not dead so I haven't missed her funeral.

Naani offered a wan smile. "How you, Maha? Doctor say heart weak . . ."

"Haa! See, Maha!" Gorinani continued. "You give sor much dhukh heart too come way weak."

I ignored her, concentrating on Naani instead.

"You see Sarah-Khaala?" Naani uttered hoarsely in my general direction.

"Do you want some water?" I offered, but before she could respond Gorinani had already grabbed the jug and sloshed out a glass.

Naani sipped and thanked her profusely.

Sarah-Khaala – my mother's hirsute aunt from Stanger – burst in and fussed over Naani for a few minutes before turning to me.

"Ey, Maha! Found one *nice* boy for you and all," she blared. "Nice *doctor* too . . . Never get married, sor nor chirrens, nothing. Forty-two he is. You knor my neighbour, Bilkis Bhen? Yah, *her* nephew. He stay near Stanger. You knor Shaka's Kraal? Yah, from there he . . ."

Fabulous! A forty-two-year-old *boy*, nogal! Now that Sameer was settled, it appeared that the family had decided that time had come for me to also venture back into holy matrimony. I glanced away from Sarah-Khaala only to catch Naani looking up at me pleadingly from her prone position.

"Yah, Maha, dorn worry," Sarah-Khaala continued, unruffled by my silence, "*after* Naani gor home, I bring and come way by the house . . . Then you can see make panchaath everything . . ."

Surely I was old enough to arrange my own date somewhere decent and make my decision in peace? I exhaled quietly and decided I'd deal with it all when the time came – right now the only doctors that mattered were those treating my naani.

Sarah-Khaala shuffled off, evidently satisfied that she'd fulfilled her part of the bargain – it was pretty obvious that the old aunties had plotted this all a while ago.

"You come straight from airport?" Naani asked with a small smile.

I nodded. "Yah, oh, I got you something . . ." I opened my handbag and pulled out a small box of dried Cape fruit, which Gorinani immediately yanked out of my hand and placed on the table alongside the other snacks.

"Gor bath, change, Maha . . ." Naani suggested weakly.

Gorinani nodded. "Ha, yah, bring Sarafina in house . . . She can clean, make nice, just now Naani come way then all visitor come too."

I nodded. I could do with some time to catch my breath – I leaned over and kissed Naani goodbye before grabbing my handbag and heading out to find Zeenat.

Zeenat had been cornered by Chotanana and Beema and looked relieved at my approach.

"I need you to take me home," I said.

"Or, you going already, Maha?" Beema scolded. "You just came sor quickly. Thu jaach'?"

"I need a shower and Sarafina needs to clean the house . . ." I responded curtly, trotting off after Zeenat who was already striding down the hall, hellbent on escape and probably in dire need of nicotine.

"Hey, Zee! Wait up! What's the hurry?" I called out after her as I hurried along behind her. "Did you think Beema was going to grow tentacles and haul you back?"

"She makes me *want* to bhema!" she muttered, her pace remaining brisk.

I followed quietly. Zeenat unlocked the car and leaned tiredly against it.

"Oh, for goodness sake, woman!" I clucked, shaking my head. "Why don't you hand over your keys and let me drive? You look like shit!"

She threw them at me and let out a huge yawn. "Wow, so nice of you to say so. Guess the up-all-night look doesn't suit me?" And with that she pushed her seat back and closed her eyes.

Back at the Mahal Zeenat continued her snooze in the guest bedroom – which meant I could clatter about in the rest of the house without any qualms. I stepped gingerly into my bedroom. This was my first time back since that night with the *good* doctor – over four months earlier! I let out a sigh of relief and threw open the windows. What exactly had I been terrified of finding?

My phone chirped. Farah.

Slmz, love. Hear you're back. R u free this weekend? X

I dialled her number immediately.

"So, what's new in Durbs?" I asked.

"Same old, honey, you haven't missed much in four months." She paused. "So, you sound pretty unfreaked to me. I'm assuming the therapy helped?"

"Yah, I went back to my roots," I muttered cryptically.

Farah snorted. "So does this mean that you're completely back to normal?" she asked.

I nodded. "I'm good. For the first time ever in my life I was free to just do as I pleased."

"I'm glad, girlfriend . . ." Farah responded happily. "Hey, I bumped into Shahzad last night!"

"You mean you *weren't* working?" I gasped in pseudo-shock even as I felt my insides clench at the sound of his name.

"Actually, I'm on an okay shift at the moment, so you may as well make the most of me while you can . . ." she warned.

"So, what was Shahzad up to?" I asked as airily as I could.

"He was at the movies . . . *Alone*, nogal . . . So we watched something together and then he drove me home." She paused. "He played that wretched Eric Clapton song over and over like some lovesick fool . . . I thought I was going to go nuts!"

"So, what did he choon?" I asked.

"Well, let's see . . ." She paused thoughtfully. "He spoke of the weather, Maha, sport, Maha, the movie, Maha . . ." She burst out laughing.

"*What* about me?" I squeaked.

She giggled. "*Why?* What's going on? Is he pining for *you*? Does he want to *change the world for you*?"

"Oh, don't be daft!" I snapped as I felt the blush rise against my will. "Speaking of movies," I continued, changing the subject as fast as I could, "I thought of you often in Cape Town . . ."

"Oh, really?" Farah parried.

"My pa's cousin dropped over a ton of movies, including some eighties classics: *Pretty in Pink, Streets of Fire* . . ."

"Oh, wow!" she exclaimed. "Whatever happened to Diane Lane and Andrew McCarthy?"

I sniffed. "Who knows? But I felt completely ancient watching them! Oh, for the days of blissful adolescent ignorance and ideal-ism!"

Farah giggled. "Yeah, can't believe we thought we knew every-thing! Speaking of know-it-alls, I have fab news . . ." She paused. "Sabah's coming down in December! Can you believe it?"

I squealed excitedly – that was certainly something to look forward to.

❦

As Durban segued from its pseudo-winter to summer, barely ac-knowledging spring, Farah resumed her crazy hours and Zeenat got busier and busier – warmer weather meant more waxing. No one mentioned Islamia College and this didn't bother me in the least as

I had no plans to continue in my dead-end job, even when it would be possible for me to resume work again. Naani was finally discharged, although she was still very frail, and the extensive extended family soon relocated to Maal Mahal, where my days revolved around nursing Naani in between preparing seemingly endless meals and high teas.

"Maha!" Nana called as he pounded on my door for Fajr.

I opened the door, shaking off the sleep.

"What?" My thoughts immediately flashed to Naani – she *had* been stable when I had checked on her before going to bed.

"That Princess Diana, she died!"

"What?" Suddenly I was wide-awake. *Dead! Di?*

"That boyfriend also . . . He too died . . ."

"What?" I reiterated dumbly. "Dodi *and* Diana?"

He nodded sombrely and set off towards Naani's room. Bloody hell! She had been much loved – even by Nana it would seem.

I washed and prayed, sitting sombrely for a while post-prayer, unable to believe the sad, sad turn of events.

It was all over the news, loop after loop of the same montages of Diana as she smiled her way through her life. How was it, I wondered mournfully, that *entire* villages of people could be obliterated and the world blinked and moved on, and yet *one* woman's death could dominate the news so completely? I switched off the TV and headed gloomily down for tea.

Gorinani arrived earlier than usual. "Samiha not coming today!" she babbled. "*Too* upset . . . You knor *sor much* she like that Diana." She sat down with a huge sigh. "Yah, *she* too . . . For what mus get divorce? Then she gor naach everywhere . . . Now see?"

"When it's your time to go it doesn't matter whether you're sitting at home or out naaching," I offered, my melancholy temporarily subsumed by irritation.

She glared and harrumphed, unable to dispute the facts of death. I ignored her scowl. My life was definitely too short to waste on worrying what the Goat thought!

Sleepless in Slumurbia

❧

Schools were out and the city embraced the long summery days by extending shopping hours, preparing for holiday-makers and decking the streets with tinsel.

"Nana . . ." I ventured over breakfast one soggy morning, "I'm going to spend a few days at my flat . . . It must be filthy!" I was beyond exhausted and in dire need of some time out.

He nodded curtly. "Don't go Christmas time . . . Too many visitors to see Naani, but also Ramadan starting after New Year."

I nodded. Great! No argument!

"Zeenat will stay with you?" he asked suddenly.

I shrugged. "I'll ask her, but Sabah is around, so she and Farah will be there."

He made a disgruntled face and returned to his newspaper.

The thought of escape sustained me through the tedium of the seemingly never-ending holidays – with their added cheer of extra visitors from across the Vaal. Gritting my teeth, I stuck on a demure smile and served tea and endless tubs of home-made ice cream.

⚜

Sarah-Khaala pitched up between Vaalie guests on Christmas Day with the Suitable Boy from Shaka's Kraal and his mother in tow – the idea being to call on Naani and check out the divorcée in one practical, cost-effective visit.

Dr Bassa was a dumpy, dour man with a comb-over. But he was also single and thus complication free, so I ought to thank my lucky stars!

Nana shook his hand heartily and immediately launched into panchaath while leading him towards the main lounge where he usually entertained male guests.

"No! No! Baboo will sit with me!" Mrs Bassa called after her son as she followed Sarah-Khaala into Naani's room, flicking her heavily hennaed seventies-style bangs as she went.

Nana twitched like he had been brought up short on a leash, then with a small smile he turned and led my suitor after his mother.

I waited for everyone to take their seats and poured the tea primly, refusing to make eye contact with the strangers. Then, placing the tray on the side table, I prepared to leave.

"Ey, Maha, where you running way?" Sarah-Khaala bellowed. "Gor sit by visitors." She waved me towards the guests.

I grabbed a cup, took my seat and sipped daintily, grateful for something to do while the conversation faltered.

"So, Maha, how old are you exactly?" Mrs Bassa asked.

211

Great! The interrogation had begun.

I smiled politely. "I'll be twenty-six in a few months," I said.

Baboo stirred but remained mute.

"Oh, *nice*! You must be got married young. *Lucky!*" she declared. "Baboo here is forty-two. Never mind," she jabbered, "he's *so* nice and settled with his practice and all. Finish pay for the house, too!"

I stifled a snort.

"What *you* think, Baboo?" Mrs Bassa asked, turning to address her beloved.

Babs looked me up and down brazenly, patted his comb-over and turned to his mother. "Can she cook properly?" he asked. "Dhal dheewar and all?"

All he cared about was whether I could cook lentils and pulses? I quelled my irritation.

"Ey, *what* you talking?" Sarah-Khaala boomed. "She can cook *all* kind things. Her naani teach her *properly* in kitchen."

Naani nodded in agreement.

Surely Naani knew that Babs wouldn't fit the bill? I thought. Was she really this desperate to see me married again?

Dr and Mrs Bassa appeared to be pleased. "*You* made these biscuits, Maha?" she quizzed as she dunked one into her tea, took a hearty bite and chewed merrily with her mouth agape.

"Umm, yah . . ." I managed, mesmerised by the churning gloop in her mouth.

Babs slurped loudly on his tea and finally turned to me. "You're a teacher, isn't?"

I lowered my gaze, sipped staidly and nodded.

"I know the headmaster of the Shaka's Kraal high school, so don't worry about jobs," he offered magnanimously.

Sarah-Khaala beamed, oblivious to my torment.

Finally, with the examination over, I stood up abruptly and busied myself with the dishes. Mrs Bassa ignored me and proceeded to chat to Naani and Sarah-Khaala while I grabbed the tray and fled to the kitchen, only to walk straight into the Bovine Bitches.

"So, what you think of *Doctor* Bassa?" Samiha pestered.

Nabiha stood behind her nodding. "Yah, we heard that he was engaged three times but every time, *just before* the wedding, *he* changed his mind!"

"So, you think he'll propose to you?" the Calf asked, irritated by my silence.

I shrugged.

"Or, your nana said you going to stay by your flat for New Year," Samiha said, switching course. "I hope you don't invite boys there and all! You know *one-one* things too everyone says about you."

I couldn't help but laugh – much to her annoyance – before flouncing off to my bedroom and locking myself in.

The proposal came the next day – via a delighted Sarah-Khaala – and Gorinani was despatched to inform me, perhaps in the hope that I wouldn't dare respond with anything untoward if the Goat delivered the news.

"Sor, now mus make Istikara, then after, Nana give jawaab," she ordered.

I shook my head. "I don't need to make Istikara," I said firmly.

She staggered with outrage. "Thu gaandi *ne* gorni! You think nice-nice maangus come way now? Ey, what mus tell Naani?" she demanded before charging towards Naani's room, eager to share my latest impudence.

"Neither mad nor stupid," I muttered. I didn't *need* to consult with the Lord on Babs.

My refusal to even consider the sodding maangu had everyone in a lather by the concluding weekend of 1997. I ignored the drama and focused on getting through what remained of the year. The end is nigh, I consoled myself.

⁂

I dusted, swept and scrubbed my apartment to perfection. I arranged candles and fairy lights around the room and stood back to survey my handiwork, smiling at the sparkling light. I loaded a CD into the player and opened the windows to the sultry midsummer night.

Sabah arrived first, bearing pizza, drinks and gifts.

"Maha, you gorgeous thing, you're looking absolutely fabulous, darling!" she crowed, putting on her poshest British accent.

"Ayyo, Sabah," I drawled Chaar-style, "I see you went way overseas and all and came way one coconut too!"

She laughed and hugged me fiercely. "Been worried about you, you know . . . You don't *e-mail* regularly enough! Farah and I have had enough of your technophobia. From now on we expect two emails a week!"

The intercom buzzed. "Speak of the devil!" I grinned.

"Ai, what kind, Maha? Mus choon she'll live long!" Sabah countered.

A minute later Farah staggered in under the weight of what looked like even more food.

"I got us some burgers . . . But I think it was a mistake to order food while *thinking* about fasting," she giggled as she dropped her bags.

We carried the things outside and settled down.

"So how's England, Sabah?" Farah asked.

She nodded and swallowed. "It's brilliant! Completely different . . . Everything's just so old!"

Farah bounced around. "Hey! What do you reckon New Year's Eve would be like *in* Ramadan? A completely different experience . . ."

I nodded. "Well, it has to be different, doofus . . . 'tis the time to focus on the spiritual." I smiled.

Sabah nodded. "To be honest, I'm happy we have this yearly time out from normal life . . . Even if you run around like a loon all year, you're forced to slow down and smell the roses in Ramadan."

"Wow, Sabah, your sadhu levels have soared since you went way overseas also!" Farah teased.

"Yah," she grinned, "it's called growing up, darlings!"

⚜

We changed into bathing suits and headed up to the sun deck – where we could chill in the hot tub.

"I think Maha's got the hots for Shahzad, but she's keeping schtum about it . . ." Farah said to Sabah with a broad wink, as we stepped into the warm, swirling waters.

I stuck out my tongue.

"Isn't that Sameer's friend?" Sabah asked.

I nodded.

"So, have you *always* had the hots for him?" Sabah giggled.

"Don't be daft! I never looked at any man *that* way while I was married."

Sabah snorted. "Seriously?"

I bobbed my head as I lit a fag. "It's not like I ignored men . . ." I said. "I think it's pretty normal to go *wow* if you see someone cute. But that's all. Hey, *I* took my vows seriously. Marriage is something you are supposed to make an effort at."

"So, tell me about this dude . . ." Sabah said. "What's he like? Does he know how you feel?"

I blushed. "There's nothing to tell."

Farah giggled and splashed about. "*Leave* her. She's incapable of speaking his name without going all Jane Austen! Apart from being one hot dude, he's actually a good guy! Sensible, balanced . . . He's a *good* soul!"

Sabah looked at me with amusement. "Endorsed by Dr Osman, nogal! You should tell him how you feel, girlfriend. Life's too short . . ." she instructed sagely.

"Hey, the fireworks will be going off soon," I said, changing the subject as I stood up, stepped out of the hot tub and reached for a comfortable towelling robe.

Sabah and Farah followed suit and we made our way back down into the flat and positioned ourselves behind the huge windows, looking out across the sea. "A whole New Year, a new fantastic point of view," I hummed, smiling to myself as Sabah shrieked with delight at the explosions of colour that suddenly blossomed above the city.

My phone rang and I answered it automatically.

"Happy New Year, gorgeous! Are you busy? Can you speak?"

Shahzad! I gasped and instinctively moved away to the furthest spot in the room. I caught my breath and steadied myself.

"Hey, Shahzad," I managed in an unflustered tone. "Happy New Year! I'm not too busy . . ."

He laughed. "Great! Are you in Umhlanga?"

"Yah, the view is fab . . ." I blurted as Farah moved towards the CD player and began to go through a pile of discs.

"I hear that you've been a *busy* girl," Shahzad continued, "what with your grandmother and everything."

"Yah, it's been a hectic few months," I conceded as Farah selected a CD.

"Hey, Shaz, my bra . . . leave your stekkie and come check what Rozi's brought . . ." a familiar voice chimed in the background.

My body froze for a split second before relaxing. Not *my* concern, I realised gratefully as Shahzad placed his hands over the mouthpiece and mumbled something to Sameer.

Shahzad cleared his throat. "Sorry about that, I *should* have warned you that Sameer and Rozi were around."

I stifled my giggle. "Nah, I'm cool, I just feel sorry for his vrou, poor thing. Anyhow, you'd better go and join your party," I suggested.

"Listen, before I go, we need to talk. Would you mind meeting me for coffee sometime?"

"Can't we just chat on the phone? I mean, is it that serious that it has to be said in person?"

He sighed. "I think it's better if I can discuss it in person. So, can I take you out?" His words came out in a sudden rush.

I turned my back on Farah – this was serious stuff! I gulped but dived in nonetheless. "Like a date?" I asked. There, I'd said it!

"Erm, yah . . ." he replied.

"Okay," I said.

"Okay?" He laughed. "You'll go out with me? Great! That's the best news of the year!"

I laughed, refusing to dwell on his evident joy. "So, I guess you'd better go back to your jol . . ."

"Yah, I suppose I should . . . I'll call you later, okay?"

I grunted. "Have fun . . ."

"Salaams, then . . ."

"Salaams," I replied as he cut the connection.

I turned around to find Farah grinning at me. "He said we need to talk," I told her. "He's going to call me later . . . and he asked me out!" I squeaked, holding up my phone and twirling around.

"The marvellous Mr Moosa just called her and asked her out!" Farah yelled to Sabah over the pulsating rhythms of the music.

Sabah twirled in excitement, increasing the tempo of her movements. "Wow!"

"He's calling her later to make arrangements, apparently . . ." Farah shouted, ignoring me completely.

"That's brilliant!" Sabah pronounced. "He must smaak you, my china!"

I gave her the finger. "We shall see . . . I'm *not* getting my hopes up . . ."

Yah right, Maha, as if you could control the great big leap your heart took at the sound of his voice.

Sabah raised her eyebrows, waved her arms about and wriggled her hips. Farah shook her shoulders and swung her hair about in mad rocker style. I was content to simply shimmy along.

218

As the music wound down Farah flopped on the nearest chair. Sabah soon followed. "Bloody knackered! We're getting old!" she declared.

"What do you guys want to do? Just chill?" I asked.

"I think it will be brilliant to sleep upstairs . . . 'underneath the stars' . . ." Sabah sang.

"Oy, Sabah! *You* singing soppy sap! What happened to your grungy rocky hardcore music? Died along with Nirvana?" Farah teased. "Bet you Maha has some Mariah!"

I stuck out my tongue. "Course I do . . . I have quite an amazing CD collection . . . thanks to . . . ummm . . . *Shahzad* . . ." I blushed slightly.

"Really?" Sabah looked interested. "Anything cool?"

I nodded. "Oasis, Blur, REM, Beautiful South, Nirvana . . ." I grinned. "Smashing Pumpkins . . ." I counted off on my fingers. "Oh, and Nick Cave and the Bad Seeds! Don't you just *love* that name?" I giggled.

"*You* have *Smashing Pumpkins* and *Nick Cave*! Un-fucking-believable," she declared with a grin. "I will have to *see* this to believe it!"

I shrugged. "He travels a lot and so always brings back new CDs."

"Ooh!" Sabah raised her brows. "And Sameer never minded?"

I shook my head. "He brings stuff for everyone."

"Got her a serious stack of books a while ago," Farah chipped in.

"Yah, that *was* brilliant," I agreed and leaned over to the pile of music. "How about this?" I held up Abba Gold. "Come on, you know you can't resist!"

They nodded simultaneously.

Sabah bobbed about in time to the music. "I'm glad you've bounced back, Maha. The whole ordeal must have been quite nightmarish, especially the moerse kak afterwards!"

I made a face. "Bit of an understatement . . . but, yah . . . with a little help from my friends . . . time . . . therapy . . . climbing mountains, etcetera." I sighed. "I was saying to Farah a while ago how I couldn't help but think of the blissful ignorance of youth – you know, when everything is so cut and dried."

Sabah grinned. "Yah, black and white . . . partner cheats, you boot his bum pronto, without blinking!"

" 'Young and sweet only seventeen' . . ." I sang along disparagingly. "Yah, and if any man bullies you and behaves in a savage manner, you'll knee his balls!"

Farah nodded and bounced along to the song.

"But you *are* okay now?" Sabah persisted.

"Yah, I feel much more . . . *alive!*"

"Zombie was *never* going to work for you, sweetie," she declared. "Have you seen the slag since?"

I shook my head. "Not since she came to the hospital to see Sameer . . ."

"Do you reckon they are still together?" Farah asked curiously.

I snorted and filled them in on the tail end of my conversation.

"Ooh!" Sabah squealed. "Let's crash their party and hurl abuse at her!"

Farah jumped with excitement. "Yah, yah . . . we can stop and buy some eggs and tomatoes on the way!"

I laughed. "Thanks, gals, but I think I'm okay just chilling here. Besides, month of patience coming up and all . . . I'd rather have some hot chocolate and sing along to Abba!"

I gave my phone the umpteenth glare, as it lay stubbornly silent. How the heck was I supposed to relax? What time was Shahzad going to call? Surely not now, at one thirty in the morning? He was probably still partying! Whatever, I thought with resignation, as I carried a laden tray up to the sun deck.

My phone rang and I jumped, almost dropping the assembled bottles and glasses. Steady now, Maha! I lectured myself as I found somewhere to lodge the tray and fumbled for my phone.

"Hello?" I gasped, ignoring Sabah's questioning gaze.

"Good morning, gorgeous! Are you still up and about?" Shahzad asked chirpily.

"Yes, yes, I'm awake!" Calm down, Maha!

"Well, can you come down for a few minutes? I'm outside!"

"Okay . . ." I cut the call and glanced across at Sabah and Farah. "He's downstairs in the car park and wants to see me for a few minutes!" I couldn't help but squeal. "Can you *believe*? Do I look okay?"

Sabah nodded. "Chill out, woman, you look fine . . ." she said with a cheeky grin.

Farah laughed. "Yah, Maha, relax! It's only Shahzad, the most eligible Memon in the city!" she teased.

❦

Shahzad was leaning against his car smoking a fag, ostensibly stargazing.

I walked towards him, tingling with nervous anticipation.

"Hey, Maha! Howzit vaaing?" he called out with a grin. "Sorry to take you away from your mates."

I smiled. "Not a problem . . . So, what's so urgent?" I asked, immediately fussing around for a cigarette, in desperate need of distraction.

He laughed and leaned forward to light my fag.

"Thanks," I said and took a puff, ignoring the mad drumming in my chest.

"Well, I know it stinks of desperation, but seeing as you've already agreed to go out with me sometime, I thought I could perhaps get you to seal your promise with a small kiss," he said, his eyes sparkling impishly.

I burst out laughing. "You voor thing! But sure, my word is my bond."

I kissed my fingers and placed them gently over his sensuous mouth. What's boiled your brain, Maha, you jux woman? I chided myself.

He held my hand against his mouth and very slowly placed a soft kiss on my fingertips. I looked away and stepped back as desire poured through my body.

"Hey, are you okay?" He peered at me worriedly, puckering his brow. "Am I coming on too strong?"

I took a slow breath and shook my head.

"So," I swallowed, "did you have a nice time at the party?"

He shook his head. "It was okay up until the time I called you . . . Things got a bit weird after that . . ." He shrugged. "What about you?"

I nodded. "We partied upstairs." I pointed a finger towards the building. "It was brilliant. The fireworks were awesome from up there . . . So what exactly do you need to choon about?"

"It's nothing, actually," he raised his hand. "I just needed an excuse to ask you out, and the only way I could think to get you to take me seriously was if I had something important to tell you." He grinned sheepishly.

The heat worked its way through my body as my heart abandoned the drums and took up a song and dance routine.

"I know, I know . . ." Shahzad nodded. "You're shocked *and* horrified, but there you go – Shahzad Moosa smaaks you!" His eyes twinkled merrily.

My mouth smiled of its own accord.

"Have I actually managed to shock you into *silence*?" he asked.

I tore my gaze away and blinked out at the darkness.

He sighed. "I know it *sounds* crazy and sudden, but believe me when I say that I've been struggling with this for years. Actually, it started while you were still married, though at the time I told myself it wasn't *you* per se, more what you guys seemed to have . . ." He made a self-deprecating snort. "You know the song . . . You meet the woman of your dreams – and her *perfect* husband!"

I looked up at him, completely hypnotised by his words.

"Are you going to speak *at all*?" he asked with mock-petulance.

I was still smiling, I realised; speech was impossible.

Shahzad moved closer and as he did so my body leaned towards his automatically until my head fell happily onto his shoulder. I smiled peacefully.

"Can I assume that you're *not* pissed off?" he asked quietly.

I nodded against his shoulder, rubbing my cheek on his shirt and sighing with gratification.

"Can I also assume that you're actually a *little* happy?"

I nodded again.

He raised his arm slowly and wrapped it around my body – suddenly I was floating, sailing, soaring. I swallowed and looked up at him.

He returned my gaze, smiling gently. "You can't just stand there like a mute . . . You have to tell me how you feel."

I pouted. What could I say? I hadn't even articulated my feelings to myself. In fact, I had no idea what they really were. Lust? Love? A combination?

"I'm sorry, I shouldn't force you to say something just for the sake of it," he said.

I shook my head. "It's not that . . ." I cleared my throat noisily; suddenly it felt as though the words were vying to gush out. "It's just that I haven't admitted anything to *myself* properly . . . So it's kind of hard to voice my feelings right now. All I know is that I can't *stop* thinking about you and when I *do* think about you . . ." I trailed off, unable to continue with my line of thinking.

He smiled, reached up and played with a curl of my hair.

"So what are your plans for today?" I asked, changing tack.

"No plans, sweetheart . . . My only plan was to get my one and only new year's resolution done and dusted."

"What was that?" I asked.

"To tell you how I feel. I decided that I needed to do it as soon as possible . . ."

He shook his head, grinned and ran his hand through my hair – a completely asexual stroke that managed to set me alight. I exhaled loudly as my body melted against his and I felt his hands run up my back and down my arms – previously neutral zones that had suddenly jumped on the erogenous bandwagon.

"I guess I'd better get back to my guests . . ." I finally said.

He smiled. "Yah, well, I suppose you have to. But what about my kiss?" he asked, puckering his lips melodramatically. "A real one this time."

I grinned. "Sure . . ." I leaned over and smacked my lips soundly against his.

He slid his hand behind my head before I could move away. I closed my eyes as his mouth pressed gently onto mine.

"Are you happy?" I whispered.

"Mmmm," he murmured against my mouth, "truly, madly, deeply!"

Gorinani and Samiha stood at the entrance to Maal Mahal, their arms folded accusingly. I psyched myself up as I grabbed my bag and locked the car, but despite my best efforts the look on Gorinani's face snuffed out my cheer at a good ten feet.

"Maha! *Sor* late you come. *Sor* long you gor," the Goat growled. "You knor nurse too take time for holiday. Sor much kaams and you gor naach? So many visitors too came way! Lucky Samiha here whole time."

And a happy New Year to you too, you churlish goat!

Samiha glared. "You even *know* what's happening?" she snapped as I tried to make my way inside.

I paused and shook my head – my insides grew taut. Had something happened to Naani?

"You can't even phone and say what time you coming too! Nana was talking to Chotanana on the phone and some burglars came away," Samiha continued.

"Where? Here?" I flicked a nervous glance around.

Samiha grunted and stepped aside. "No, stupid, at Chotanana's . . . Nana heard gunshots and shouting, so he quickly put down the phone and made me phone the police from my *cell* . . . Then he took my Baboo and drove there!"

"Oh! How's Naani?"

"Arreh baap reh baap, Maha!" Gorinani bleated, "Your naani *halgat* shock now . . . plus worry-worry too much." And with that she pushed past me, heading hastily into the house.

For once Gorinani's diagnosis of complete shock looked spot on. Naani lay on her bed wide-eyed and gasping for air. She tried to heave herself up as I walked towards her.

"*Naani*, please lie down . . . Rest . . . I'm sure everything will be okay. Samiha is phoning Baboo now to find out what's happening . . ."

"Toubah-toubah ai hu dhukh, Maha?" Naani said, shaking her head as I leaned over and kissed her tear-stained cheek. "Chotanana too got lort-lort paiha and *bandhuk* too . . . So long Nana tell him put by bank, but he dorn listen."

"Now you know the doctor said you mustn't get over-excited," I lectured. "So please calm down . . . Allah knows best, okay?"

So Chotanana kept cash *and* guns in his home – clearly a dangerous combination.

"Or, now you come way make Allah, Allah!" Gorinani snapped as she strode into Naani's room. "Police came way . . . Shootings and all . . . Chotanana too get shot . . ." she gabbled, struggling to get everything out at once. "Then they take by hospital . . . Beema halgat shock thaigi . . ."

Naani gasped at the news. "They catch?" she asked.

Had the thieves been caught? I gazed up curiously.

"Neeeeee puchu . . ." Gorinani squealed with dismay, and hurried off to instruct Samiha to get an unabridged report.

Naani mumbled and moaned as I sat beside her and awaited Gorinani's return. "Hu dhukh, Maha!" She sniffed. "Doctor say can't fast . . . Now Nana can't gor masjid too. Arreh, Allah, beeg days coming . . ." She shook her head dolefully.

"They caught two chorrs, Naani," Samiha said, bursting into the room excitedly. "One or two ran away . . . They don't know how many came . . . Beema only saw two, but she heard noise on the other side of the house also . . ."

"Where she?" Naani asked.

"Yah, they bringing her and coming way here now . . ." Samiha nodded.

<hr />

Chotanana and Beema convalesced at the Mahal, and Beema spent most of her waking moments crying or getting panicked and refused to leave the house at all. Escaping into the arms of my beloved was impossible as the hordes descended in seemingly greater numbers than ever before, despite the fact that it was the month of abstinence. For once, the Mahal fussed over breaking fast as the inconsiderate joined us for iftar and the added baking and frying took up the blistering afternoons. To add to my drain, Raeesa and Anwar were unavoidable regulars – Beema and Chotanana were their grandparents and *how it will look if own grandchildren not there?* Though at least Raeesa had ditched the hugs and kisses now that I was a besaram divorcée!

Post-Taraweeh, when all were in bed, I eschewed air condition-ing, threw open my windows to the balmy nights and chatted to Shahzad about everything and nothing until sehri. The endless sul-try nights made our solitude all the more bittersweet and true to self I aided and abetted the tone with love songs from my youth. Shahzad found it a tad annoying that he couldn't simply drive up to the Mahal and tell Nana Maal he was taking me out, but he accepted his African luck with fortitude.

African Patience

❦

Eid eventually rolled round, a sombre affair as it was Naani's first non-fasting Ramadan. She had nothing to celebrate, she reckoned, and spent most of the day in floods of tears.

I finally got to see Shahzad a few weeks later. Farah served as cover – no small responsibility as blowing it would probably give Naani a real heart attack and I would forever be notorious for sending my poor grandmother to an early grave.

I drove to his apartment with nervous excitement.

"Hey, Maha," his voice crackled through the intercom, "do you want to come up or shall I come down?"

"I'll come up," I replied instantly, driving through as soon as the ornate gates swung open. You're just keen to see his apartment, I told myself. No, you're not, you just want to jump his bones, jux luchee!

I clicked my alarm, walked briskly to the front door of the apartment block and pushed my way through.

The elevator announced its arrival and the doors opened to reveal Shahzad leaning against the inner wall. "Couldn't wait to see you," he said and smiled, stretching out his arms to me.

I squealed with delight – I didn't care if I appeared jux – and walked straight into his embrace.

"Oh, Shahzad," I sighed, looking up into his eyes, "I've missed you so damn much."

He nodded. "I know . . . It's been hell!" He leaned over my shoulder to select the floor, and placed his lips over mine as the doors closed and we soared to the top of the building.

⁂

Shahzad's apartment was tastefully masculine. His television alone took up an entire wall – almost!

"It must be like being at the movies," I said, gesturing towards it.

He grinned. "Yah . . . I guess I'm a boy who likes his toys."

"Well," I looked around, "these toys are *definitely* suitable."

"Come," he said, reaching out for my hand, "I'll show you around en route to my office."

I followed obediently, peering into the kitchen, dining area and bedrooms as we headed for the last room in the flat. Finally, Shahzad flung open the door on a small space littered with files, boxes and books.

My eyes gleamed at the chaos. "Oh, Shahzad, it's a Slumurban wet dream!" I giggled. "Have you shown me this so that I can sink my teeth into the task immediately?"

230

He grinned. "What? You call this a *mess*?"

I grinned back. "Well, what do *you* call it?"

"Organised chaos!" he stated as he rummaged around behind his desk before pulling out a bag of books with great flourish. "Here, I found this the other day." He poked around and pulled out a book. "I think I bought it for you ages ago, but for some reason it sat in this bag."

"Thanks," I said, pouncing on the Kathy Lette with glee. "You know," I chortled, "Zeenat reckons Ms Lette believes we're better off with dildos and girlfriends!"

Shahzad smiled. "So, do you still want to go out somewhere?" he asked. "Or shall we order takeaway?"

I shook my head. "Dunno . . . We can go out if you want to. But I'm happy to chill here."

"Okay, so can I get you something while we decide what to do?" he offered. "Water? Something stronger?"

"And w*hat* exactly would be stronger than water?" I asked.

Shahzad seemed unperturbed by my question. "Juice? Coke? Did you think I was offering you a dop?"

I made a face. "*Well,* I don't know whether you drink daaru at home as well, *do* I now?"

He grinned at me. "Haven't you sussed by now that the pain I needed to dull with daaru was all because of *you*?"

"Because of *me*?" I squeaked in horror.

He sighed melodramatically. "I met the woman of my dreams, only to find that she had already married my mate!"

I punched him gently on the arm.

"Hey, would you like to see the garden?" he asked.

I giggled and glanced around. "Garden? On the top floor of a building?"

"Come and see!" He led the way to the huge French doors and threw them open ostentatiously. "See! Shahzad don't speak lies, missy!"

I stepped out in wonder. It was indeed a rooftop garden, complete with paving stones, garden furniture and plants.

"Wow, Shahzad, you even have a mini lawn!" I clapped my hands excitedly. "It's amazing. It's gorgeous. I *love* it!"

He smiled happily. "I knew you would," he said. "Why don't you get comfortable and I'll get us some drinks? Any preferences?"

"I'll have whatever you're having. I'm assuming that's safe?" I called out as I kicked off my shoes and stepped onto the lawn, gazing up at the sparkling stars with delight.

He paused. "Honey, you picked me up and put me back on the wagon."

I smiled into the clear night, feeling the forgotten tickle of grass under my feet, curling my toes around the blades. I turned to find Shahzad leaning against the doorframe, watching me with a satisfied smile on his face.

"Need some help?" I asked lazily.

He shook his head. "I'm fine. The view from here was always good, but tonight it's awesome." He paused. "Do you want something to eat, as well?" he offered.

"You're so well mannered, Shahzad," I said as I sat down on the grass, revelling in its earthy fragrance. "It's freaky! Do you have *any* faults?"

"Of course I do! I'm human so don't get your hopes *too* high!"

"Well, I haven't seen anything that I reckon qualifies as a fault . . ." I teased.

"You've seen me drink . . . I've had sex outside of marriage. I've lied. I fart horrendously . . ."

I spluttered before erupting into howls of laughter as Shahzad turned away to fetch our drinks.

"So, do you ever see Melissa?" I asked as Shahzad plonked himself down beside me with a couple of cans of Coke and two glasses.

"I was wondering when you were going to ask about her . . ." He made a face and popped a can.

I shrugged. "So?"

"Well," he said, handing me a glass of Coke, "part of the deal was that she kept her distance from me."

I grinned. "That's a good thing, I reckon."

"You have no reason to be jealous," he said, popping the second can, "and anyway she's got an ou . . . but I do see her sometimes."

"Oh, where?" I asked as evenly as I could.

He raked a hand through his hair. "Adam . . . my son, spends a weekend a month with my folks. That's why I usually go up to Joburg once a month." He fumbled around his pockets and pulled out his wallet.

"Well, that's nice," I said and took a sip of Coke. "You are his father, after all . . ." Shit! He was a *father*!

"Here's a picture." He handed it over and shrugged. "If I'm there when she drops him off or fetches him, then I say hello . . . That's about it."

I gazed at the cute little boy in the photo. He bore a startling resemblance to his father. "Wow, he looks so much like you . . . How old is he now?"

"He's six in that photo," Shahzad smiled, "but he's eight now."

"I'm sorry it's taken us so long to talk about this," I said as he returned the photograph to his wallet.

"Hey, I understand . . ." He paused. "Do you know that Adam was the first person who knew I was in love with you?"

"How come?" I was suitably intrigued.

"Well, he confided in me about a lovely girl in his class who was too shy to speak to him . . . So I told him *I* was worse off: the woman I was in love with could never even know of my love!"

I shook my head and laughed. "He sounds like a sweet kid. I guess I'll meet him sometime."

"You don't have to," Shahzad said, "but it would be great if you did."

I smiled and lay back, staring up at the universe. Life was never as simple and straightforward as we imagined it would be. I edged closer to him, until my arm touched his shirt.

"I guess my baggage is a bit complicated . . ." he said, lowering his head and placing his mouth over mine.

My thoughts were instantly silenced as his hands began to move across my body. I was losing control, I realised as I ran my hand roughly down his chest. What was wrong with me? I had never felt so horny in my life. I broke away abruptly and greedily sucked in the night air.

"What's wrong?" Shahzad asked.

I shook my head. "I have to hold myself back . . ."

I peered shyly through my hands, flushed and flustered. Had *I* just voiced that?

"I want you to relax about crossing the line . . . I *won't* let that happen, I promise! Y*ou* set the boundaries and I'll stick to them." He raised his hand solemnly.

"Can a man really be trusted to stick to boundaries?" I asked.

Shahzad snorted. "*All* men are not wild beasts! We are perfectly capable of self-discipline . . . our dicks won't implode if we *don't* orgasm!" He stretched his arms out towards me. "So, tell me where exactly the line is."

I succumbed – burying my head in his shoulder and smothering the cry that threatened to escape. "No sex," I whispered.

"So, no sex . . ." he murmured gently, running his fingers down my neck and over my curves, sending shivers of desire coursing through my body once again. "But I *can* promise to satisfy you by *other* means?"

He slid his hand between my legs and I struggled to suppress the cry that came from somewhere deep inside me.

Could I simply loosen up, trust him – when I didn't trust *myself* – and enjoy? Trust him, I ordered myself sternly, finally yielding to my body's demands.

⁂

I hummed while making my early morning cup of tea, recalling the pleasures of the night before. It had undoubtedly been a hot *and* heavy February night like no other!

Gorinani stomped across the misty garden as I poured the boiling water.

"Ey, Maha, *sor* late you come," she said as soon as she had her head through the door. "Where you gor naaching-naaching?" She harrumphed and folded her arms militantly.

I shrugged. "It wasn't *too* late," I muttered, my grin disappearing almost instantly.

She clutched onto her cheeks dramatically. "Ey, jus now everyone say you gor eklee-eklee . . . ardi raathe!" she blustered belligerently.

It wasn't exactly *dancing*, woman, I thought, and I'm doing it again as soon as possible! I suppressed my yawn as I focused on my tea.

"Jor aweh! See now! Sor tired too! How you do all kaams?" Gorinani continued. "Just now visitors come way to see Naani . . ."

I sipped my tea slowly and averted my gaze from the vexed look on her face.

Gorinani eventually got fed up with my silences and disappeared to report my behaviour to Naani.

I started as my phone shrilled to life.

"Hey, babe, howzit vaaing?" Shahzad crooned.

"Surviving . . ." I spoke quietly, listening hard for the tell-tale sound of the Goat. "What are you up to?"

"Nothing much, just helping with some freight issues . . ."

"Freight issues?" I asked. "As in ships and containers?" I sipped at my tea, craving a fag and the view from my bedroom.

Shahzad laughed. "Yah, something like that."

"So, are you all packed?" I asked. He'd mentioned a business trip when we'd kissed goodbye.

"More or less . . ." he said. "Damn! I'm going to miss you so much . . . Will I be able to see you before I go?"

"When exactly are you leaving?"

"My flight to Paris is on Monday, but I'm leaving for Joburg the day before . . . So, Saturday night?" he asked.

"Umm . . . I'll check and let you know. Friday night may be easier . . . Let me see who I can get to granny-sit."

"Do that. I have to see you before I set off."

Zeenat kindly granny-sat while I pretended to spend another evening in Farah's company. Two days later Shahzad flew off to see his family and then on to Paris for business.

⚜

On a cold and uncharacteristically frosty morning in the bleak mid-winter, the pear-shaped sun rose over the east coast of southern Africa. The previous day had seen Naani struggle more than usual and by midmorning the doctor had deemed it necessary to admit her – yet again – to the good Saint Augustine.

Samiha headed over as soon as she got wind of the latest developments.

"I just heard now-now, Maha," she said. "How's she? She's gone already?"

I nodded. "Yah, they needed to take her by ambulance, so she left half an hour ago . . ." I paused. "Are you going to the hospital now? 'Cos if you are I won't rush. I'll let Sarafina sort out Naani's room first . . ." Whether it was merely to show face or not I *was* grateful that the Herd dropped everything during Naani crises – many hands eased the responsibilities.

Samiha nodded tersely. "Yah, yah, I'll go now and take Mummy with me . . . What time you'll finish?"

237

I shrugged. "Thanks, Samiha, I'll come as soon as I'm finished here . . . An hour or so? And no one needs to cook for Naani, the doctor said she's going to be on a drip for now."

"Oh, okay then . . . Where's Nana?" She glanced around.

"He went with Naani . . . Thanks, Samiha," I repeated, smiling and edging away, giving her no choice but to move as well. "I'll see you later then . . ."

⁂

The phone rang while I was pulling out Naani's suitcase. I reached for it automatically.

"Thank goodness you're still at home!" Zeenat exclaimed.

"Why? What's up?"

"Don't worry . . . It's nothing to do with Naani – she's stable," she said, hearing the worry in my voice.

"Alhamdulillah!" I uttered with relief. "So, choon then . . ." It was probably some new story about me and my wanton ways. Gorinani was convinced I "had somebody" – why else would I have said no to the wonderful Babs Bassa?

"I just wanted to prepare you for possible Patel sightings at the hospital," Zeenat said.

"Oh, something happened to the old fart?" I asked.

Zeenat sighed. "Actually it's a helluva hectic story . . . You know I have a client that's Patience Patel's aunt? Well, she was here this morning for a wax –"

"And who's in hospital?" I interrupted impatiently.

"Naseem," she blurted.

"Oh? How come?"

"Hectic shit!" she said. "I feel bad even speaking about it! It's *really* kak . . ."

"I wouldn't have expected otherwise," I muttered caustically. "Are you actually feeling sorry for him?"

I heard Zeenat light a fag on the other end of the line. "Well, listen to this and see how you feel. Patience's aunt reckons Naseem owed some Nigerian drug lord money, and tried to pay him back with cellphones . . ."

"Let me guess," I said chirpily, "the phones were stolen and therefore blocked?"

She groaned. "Guess he's tried that stunt before, then . . ." She paused. "Anyhow, the goons got hold of him and beat him to within an inch of his life. I'll spare you the gory details, but it was beyond bad."

I shuddered. Zeenat was right, I did feel sorry for the maadar. "I wonder what Katy Patel's spin is on this!" I said archly, pushing aside my revulsion.

Zeenat grunted. "Who knows? I just hope Naseem has learned his lesson . . ."

⁂

Later that day, while heading for a sneaky fag in the hospital parking lot, I did indeed catch sight of Katy and Fay walking down a corridor together. I ducked behind a pillar and watched as they sashayed past in their stylish ensembles, engrossed in a low-voiced chat.

I lit up as I approached my favourite wall. Oh, shit! I held my guilty hand behind me as I tried to ascertain whether it was an uncle or stranger hovering around my hideaway.

The dishevelled man looked up haggardly, sniffed and wiped away tears. Fucking hell! It was Sameer Patel looking like death warmed over.

"Salaams, Sam, you look like shit," I greeted him calmly.

He blew his nose loudly and stuffed the tissue into his pocket. "Ey, Maha, what are *you* doing here?" he rasped. "Who's in hospital? Your naani?"

I nodded. "I heard about Nas," I muttered. "Is he okay?"

Sameer rubbed his stubble. "It's been hectic . . . He's not stable yet."

"And you?" I asked. "Are *you* okay?"

He sighed. "Well," he fiddled with his rumpled shirt, "you can see how I look!"

I nodded, feeling a surprising surge of pity. "So, where's your vrou?" I asked.

"At her ma's . . . She can't get over-excited, she's umm . . . Not sure if you heard? She's pregnant."

"Oh, wow!" I was truly amazed. "Congratulations! When's she due?"

"Next month. I don't really know how I feel about it all, though . . ." he confided.

"If she's due soon, then do correct me if I'm wrong, but weren't you jolling with Rozi on New Year's Eve? Surely you *knew* she was pregnant then?"

Sameer turned crimson and nodded. "Yah, I knew about the baby then, and think I panicked. But I haven't been with *her* since then!" He looked up and met my gaze. "It's true. *Kassam!*" he swore.

I shrugged. "Good for you, Sameer Patel!"

"So, is it true?" he asked with a small smile. "About you and Ba?"

"*What* about me and Ba?" I smiled. "We've always been good friends!"

"Okay, so don't tell me . . .' He waved his hand dismissively.

I stubbed out my fag and popped some gum. "Want some?" I offered.

He took a stick and unwrapped it slowly.

"See you, Sameer," I said, hoisting my bag and heading back to Naani's room with a sigh.

Naani remained in hospital for what felt like an eternity. I barely saw Shaz, and when I did it was for a quick drink at the most convenient coffee shop.

I sent him a grumpy SMS.

Slmz love. Life sucks. Naani worse. Love u. XXX

I opened his response.

Slmz babe. Chill! Sounds like you need some loving. When shall we meet? X

I managed a small smile.

Will see what I can arrange. Will let you know. Holding thumbs. X

I clicked on send just as Samiha burst into the kitchen bumptiously – so puffed up she looked like she was about to erupt.

"Asalaam 'alaikum, Maha . . ." she sang smarmily. "You are in such *serious* trouble, you know?"

I resisted the urge to punch her pugnacious face. *Now* what?

"*Someone* saw you with that *Memon* boy!" she spat, looking at me with unconcealed contempt.

"Oh, really?" I offered.

With all our clandestine meetings, it had been bound to happen, I ruminated philosophically.

"What you were doing alone with him, Maha?" she cried. "You know it's haraam too! What people will say and all? No shame too you got! Ey, I give up with you. You don't learn even! Now imagine how sick your naani will get when she hears this?"

"So, don't tell her then." I smiled.

She looked aghast and drew in her breath sharply. "What? You mad? And then what if someone else tells her? Then what? Ey, Maha. You're just too stupid, man!"

I sipped my tea, choosing to ignore her diatribe.

"Well, you *know* what everyone will say?" she screeched apoplectically. "They'll say, 'Yah, he's Sameer's friend and yorl was carrying on from when *you* was *still* married . . . *that's why Sameer left you*'," she hissed.

"*We* got divorced. He did not just leave me," I muttered, glancing around for my phone.

Need to speak, I typed. *Urgent. Are you free? X*

Yes! X, Shahzad responded almost instantly.

"Oh, who you SMSing and all, Maha? That boy? Or Zeenat? That's half your problem, you know? Every time you go running by Zeenat! What she knows about good advice? Bladdy stupid never get married too . . . too busy with her business and clients and acting all professional and all . . ."

Bladdy? Such filth from your mouth, Samiha? Silence was my only solution, so I pursed my lips and typed.

Call you in 5. X

"Oh, *now* what you doing? *Where* you going? You going to phone *him* now, isn't?" She pointed accusingly at my cell.

"Don't jump to conclusions," I offered mildly as I stepped out of the kitchen, slammed the door and raced upstairs.

⁂

"So, your nana will demand to know what you're doing with me?" Shahzad asked, when I'd finally finished explaining the situation. "I reckon I have the solution, although I had great plans on how I was going to present this . . . Ah, well . . ." He sighed.

"What the hell are you talking about?" I lit a fag and dragged deeply.

"Oh, heck! Fine, I'll tell you the solution . . . and *then* I'll explain how I had hoped to show it to you. Okay?"

"Okay . . ." I drawled worriedly.

"Tell your grandfather that I have asked you to marry me. I *mean* it. I would love to spend the rest of my life with you. I had these elaborate plans about giving you this ring . . ."

Shahzad exhaled loudly, but my mind had frozen at the words "marry me".

"Perhaps it's a *good* thing I didn't get to make a fool of myself . . ." he finally continued, when it became clear that I wasn't going to respond. "But, hey, I wanted to ask you properly, you know . . . on bended knee with a ring in my hand."

"How much time have you spent thinking about this?" I blinked away my tears.

"*Too* long," Shahzad said. "You think I'm completely nuts, don't you?"

"I'm . . . I'm just overwhelmed . . ." I gasped as my brain finally began to thaw. "I mean, you've just asked me to be your vrou!"

"Is that a bad thing?" he asked.

"Of course it's *not* a bad thing . . ." I laughed, shaking my head. "It's *wonderful*!"

I felt a sudden rush of emotion.

"I love you," we whispered simultaneously.

"I am officially the happiest man in the city," Shahzad declared. "So, do I need to shave and get a haircut before I present myself at the Mahal?" he asked.

I blinked, swallowing hard. "Are you going to come with your folks?" I asked.

"If you want me to . . ."

I grunted. "Definitely the best option . . . If you come on your own Nana would reckon you're shameless *and* rude. Not a good way to start!" I smiled.

"Okay, I'll give my ma a call later. She'll be ecstatic, by the way – she's been nagging me for ages to propose to you."

"What?" I screeched. "Your ma knows about us?"

"My mother and my sisters . . ." he replied coolly.

"So, if your folks are so chilled, how come they made such a stink about Melissa?"

He snorted. "My grandparents made the stink, and my pa was working with his ballie at the time, so added complications, you know how it can be. And anyway, I reckon I was saved. Who knows, I may never have met you!"

I giggled. "Well, I shall look forward to meeting your folks . . . What about your sisters?"

"My sisters are due to come over in December – you'll get to meet them then. Besides, they live thousands of miles away, so they won't bother you," he teased.

"Funny, but seriously though, please let me know in advance . . . Don't just pitch up at the Mahal out of the blue and give my poor naani a heart attack, okay?" I warned him.

"Of course, woman, I know how to conduct myself!" He laughed.

"I'd better go and face the music . . ."

"Will you be okay?" he asked.

"Have no choice, but hey, *this* time I'm facing the music with a song!" I giggled.

⁂

Gorinani pounced as soon as my big toe hit the bottom step.

"Ey, Maha, you knor *all* the people talk about your dhandhas. Nor saram too you got!"

"Yah," Samiha said, sauntering in, "like mother, like daughter . . ."

"Don't bring my mother into this, please," I managed to state calmly. "What's wrong, Gorinani? Have you spoken to Nana?"

Gorinani glared at me, affronted by my impertinence. "*Had* to tell Nana. Just now somebody tell? Keewu lage? Yah, he forn and say, yah, he coming just now," she growled, shaking with rage.

"Well, he's coming with his parents one of these days . . ." I stated affably, suppressing a smile. Cordiality was my game plan.

Samiha's hands flew to her hips and she hooted sarcastically. "And *you* think Nana and Naani are going to just meet them *nicely* and make arrangements?" she asked. "Just like that?"

"I'm *not* sixteen, Samiha . . . I'm twenty-six going on twenty-*seven*,"

I continued placidly. Why couldn't Nana simply be happy for me – what was so wrong with that?

"Hah! *Thu bau moti!*" Gorinani screeched. "Too beeg for booooot! Sor nice boy we show from Shaka's Kraal. *Doctor* also. You say too old. *Maathu!*" She jabbed her finger in the direction of my head. "Now you gor find *Memror*! You see . . . Naani get more sick!"

My grin struggled to free itself, so I pushed past the Goat and the Calf and headed for the kitchen.

⁂

I watched Nana Maal lock his car and walk wearily to the front door. He looked pale and drawn and every one of his seventy-seven years as he shuffled forward, and I couldn't help but feel a twinge of guilt as I made my way towards him.

"Salaams, Nana," I greeted him bravely, planting a gentle kiss on his gaunt cheek.

"What your nana must say, hé?" Gorinani griped behind me. "Sor sick he look. Sor much dhukhs . . ."

Nana remained silent. I looked at him and my eyes filled with sudden tears. For once, I *was* going to speak up, regardless of snot and trane. I cleared my throat.

"Shahzad Moosa and his parents from Laudium will be coming here one of these days . . ." I said quietly.

"Ai hu?" Gorinani flapped about in agitation, literally stirring the air. "Beeg people mus speak. Ai hu thu handu arrange kare?" She shook her head in agony.

"His father will call you tomorrow, Nana," I continued, ignoring the Goat completely.

246

Nana looked up eventually. There were daggers in his eyes.

I sighed.

He jabbed his hand in my direction. "Besaram you are, Maha," he reproved angrily. "*Who* is this boy? *Who* are these people? Do we even *know* them?"

I shrugged. "Moosa, big Memon family in Laudium . . . I don't know if you know them, Nana, but if not, you can get to know them . . ."

Gorinani almost keeled over with shock. "Arreh baap reh, gaandi, gorni Maha! Aweh *hudd thayyu* . . . Jah! Jah!"

Somehow I managed to stand my ground in silence as Nana prodded me sharply. "*Go,* Maha, I don't want to see your face now . . ." he said and turned away.

I scurried upstairs as calmly as I could, only to burst into tears as soon as I was safe within my room.

⚜

"Went better than I expected," I sniffed down the phone to Shahzad ten minutes later.

"Really? Are you sure everything is okay? I mean, he's not going to come up to your room and beat you, is he?" he asked worriedly.

"I've locked myself in, and *if* I think something like that is possible, I'll jump out the window and drive off, okay?" I blew my nose loudly.

He sighed. "Well, I spoke to my folks and they're flying over in November. I know that it's still moons away, but it's all set from our side . . . You reckon it will be safe to come?"

"Don't be daft! You think Nana will dala with you?" I giggled.

Two Weddings and a Funeral

I was looking forward to meeting the Moosas, relieved that their visit was simply to rubber-stamp the proposal and not to check me out. It was a far cry from the grand Patel daawat many years earlier, when I had lain on a feast while they appraised me. I couldn't wait to see Shahzad either.

I smiled, slipped on my heels and waited for Zeenat to deal with the finer details of hair and make-up.

She arrived before Maghrib. "Sorry I'm so late, I hope you haven't been fretting?" she said as she set about unpacking her bags.

I nodded. "Yah, I'm okay . . . Just a little nervous about meeting the Moosas." I shrugged as Zeenat began to arrange her unguents neatly on my dressing table. "But that's normal, I guess."

Zeenat nodded. "Yah, you're meeting them for the *first* time, but you already know that they're happy."

"I know. I'm more concerned about Nana's never-ending sulk. He's been moping around for months now!"

Zeenat laughed as she daubed foundation onto my skin. "Naani's probably consoling him with 'at least he's Chaarou', plus rupaaro too . . . like one Memon jalebi!" She smacked her lips emphatically and grinned at my expression. "Ey, *you* too had to find Memror . . . *One-one* things everyone's chooning also: Maha likes to eat Memon mithai!" She chortled.

"I don't give a fuck . . ." I grunted. "*They* can choon ten-ten things if they wish. Right now all I care about is Nana. I just hope he behaves!"

⁂

Everything was quiet as Zeenat and I made our way downstairs. I giggled as I imagined Nana wheeling Naani furtively across the Mahal, escaping through the kitchen before the dreadful Mr Moosa made his appearance. Zeenat wagged a finger and led me into the formal lounge.

Nana snubbed me while Naani scrutinised my appearance from her makeshift bed with a disapproving frown. "Where your orhni?" she asked.

I shook my head, allowing my uncovered hair to swish about in all its waanku splendour. "I'm not wearing an orhni, Naani," I said gently. "I'm *in* the house and no one else is coming apart from Shahzad's parents . . ."

She sighed and pleated the bedcovers. "Nana not happy, but what can do? Have to make sabar . . ." she trailed off.

I managed a small smile before retreating with Zeenat to the kitchen. She filled the kettle and switched it on while I surveyed the trays of biscuits, sweetmeats and savouries that I had selected for the meeting. It was a simple but tasteful spread, I decided.

Suddenly Zeenat cocked her head and widened her eyes. "Is that a crunch of tyres I hear?" she gasped, clutching onto me theatrically.

"Could be anyone," I blustered, shaking her off and pretending to engage myself in counting the cups for the umpteenth time.

The doorbell chimed. Zeenat and I paused and exchanged looks. This really was it.

⁂

I found Nana muttering with resignation as he slid back the bolts and turned the key in the giant lock on the front door.

"Asalaam 'alaikum. Aawo, come, come inside," he said, stepping back to allow the Moosas in.

Shahzad, I noticed immediately, was looking delectable in a finely pinstriped suit. He stood aside politely, turning to the woman beside him. "Ma, this is Maha," he said. "Maha, this is my mother, Farhana Moosa."

I extended my hand and smiled shyly at the beautiful, immaculately attired woman.

She waved my hand away with a warm smile, and instead enveloped me in a fragrant embrace. Nana Maal stood by quietly, a muted shade of sour. I sighed. At least it was better than a fully blown paw-paw face.

Moosa Moosa, a large, bear-like man, pumped my hand effusively and kissed both cheeks soundly. "Lovely to meet you," he boomed. "I can see why my son is so enamoured."

I blushed and flicked a gaze towards Nana, who appeared to have taken on a greenish tinge. "Nana, this is Shahzad . . ." I said.

Shahzad smiled as Nana shook his proffered hand, then Moosa Moosa introduced himself, before Farhana offered a demure greeting. Finally, with the introductions complete, I led them into the formal lounge, where Naani was waiting patiently.

After everyone had been served and prodded to partake, Nana Maal cleared his throat. Mr Moosa paused and looked up.

"Well, down to business then." He beamed. "We all know *why* we're here. Our son, Shahzad, wants to marry your granddaughter, Maha. That lovely woman sitting there." He gestured in my direction and I blushed furiously.

Nana harrumphed and mumbled, but I could see that there were tears in Naani's eyes.

Farhana nodded politely. "Yes," she said, looking at Naani, "we understand Ramadan *and* Christmas are next month, so *whenever* it's convenient. Shahzad doesn't want a big wedding, but it would be nice if his sisters are around." She turned to me. "Are *you* happy with that, Maha?" she asked.

I nodded. Neither of us was comfortable with the waste and extravagance of lavish weddings.

"Better if is quick, we don't want them doing haraam and all," Nana declared decisively.

"I agree, Mr Maal. How about tonight?" Shahzad suggested affably.

What? *Tonight?* Was he completely deranged?

Nana glanced at his watch and nodded. "Good. We can all go for Esha after tea and then have the nikah."

Farhana Moosa looked aghast. "No, no, I don't think we should rush," she said, looking at her husband pleadingly. "Shahzad and Maha are *adults*. They can behave themselves . . ."

Naani intervened calmly. "Nice if *all* family come for nikah," she said quietly.

They turned to me.

I shrugged. "I think we should at least wait for your sisters," I said, addressing Shahzad.

He smiled broadly.

"Won't that be in Ramadan?" Nana interjected.

Moosa Moosa cleared his throat. "Well, that's no problem if we're having a small wedding. So, is that decided then? You kids happy with that?"

"That's fine," Shahzad said, while I nodded in agreement.

Farhana appeared relieved. "Well, now that we've settled that, why don't you give Maha the ring, Shahzad?"

Shahzad walked towards me and I stood up in anticipation, unable to contain my delight.

The gem glinted in the well-lit lounge, complementing its bright platinum band, and I caught my breath as Shahzad slipped it down my finger.

"Was that a flash of insanity?" I asked quietly.

He shook his head. "I thought it was a flash of inspiration! Thought your nana would appreciate me making an honest woman of you *sharp-sharp*!"

I grinned as Nana cleared his throat and Shahzad released my hand, stepped back decorously and returned to his seat.

The run-up to Ramadan – complicated by Naani's depression at the thought of another year unable to fast – meant exhaustion on all fronts.

Shahzad laughed at the irony. "It's hilarious! Now that Nana Maal will *allow* me to take you out, we just can't find the time to make it happen."

"Yah, right, it's a hoot!" I whinged, pulling out a Tupperware from the freezer as I prepared for dinner, the phone clenched between my ear and shoulder. "So, are you coming over for supper?"

"I'll come around later, if that's okay," he replied.

I grinned. "Of course that's okay."

"So, how's Naani doing?" Shahzad asked. "Is she still crying all the time?"

I sighed as I lowered the samoosas into the fryer. "Yep, there's no end in sight . . ."

"And what did the doc have to say this morning? Everything else okay?"

"Well . . ." I flipped the samoosas and adjusted the temperature. "Nothing works properly. He reckons it's all downhill from here. Poor Naani . . ." I trailed off morosely.

"Yah, that's old age," Shahzad said sadly. "It's not for the faint-hearted. All we can do is pray for her suffering to ease." He paused. "I was thinking, maybe we could stay with your grandparents after we get married. If you want to, I mean."

I yanked at a roll of Carlton paper, tore off a few sheets and slapped them onto a plate with a sigh.

"It's very kind of you to think of it," I said as I emptied the samoosas onto the plate and left them to drain. "I might just take you up on your offer."

"I think you should think about getting back to work, though," Shahzad went on.

"Oh, yah?" I leaned against the counter.

"Yah. Just because your naani is sick doesn't mean that you have to put every other part of your life on hold," he said. "You need to think about *you* as well."

"You have a point, Mr Moosa," I conceded.

"So, had any thoughts on New Year's Eve?"

"Haven't had time to think about that . . ." I sighed. "But do you *really* want to have the nikah and a big family jol *on* New Year's Eve? You know it will be in the middle of Ramadan?"

"Why does it have to be a big deal just because it's Ramadan?" he responded. "Besides, New Year's Eve is special for *us.* Plus, my sisters are *in* the country. We did agree to marry while they were around and I love the idea of a barbecue! Think about it, at least."

I grunted as I heaved two huge jugs of milkshake out of the fridge. "I will," I promised, "but it's a double horror of Ramadan and braai! Can you imagine the Goat's glee?"

"I'd better get changed and get my arse down to the mosque," Shahzad said, changing the subject. "I'll see you later, okay?"

"Yah, okay," I sighed. "Make dua . . . Love you. Salaams." I replaced the receiver and headed for the dining room.

"Ey, Maha!" Samiha yowled as I plonked the heavy jugs onto the table. "Why you never make chocolate milkshake? You know my Baboo don't like strawberry . . ."

Joy! But I forced out a small smile.

Ignoring my silence, Samiha took in the place settings shrewdly. "Shahzad is not coming for supper?" she asked.

I shook my head.

"Oh! *How* it will look? Better if he comes here for *some* suppers at least . . . You know, *what* his mother will think?"

I ignored her gripe and added cutlery to the table. "What's Naani up to?" I asked.

"She's reading Qur'aan now . . ."

"Hey, we're thinking of having the nikah and reception on New Year's Eve . . ." I offered.

The Cow flushed instantly. "What? Yorl mad or what?" she bubbled with indignation. "In Ramzan also! You should just have the nikah . . . For what you want *two-two* weddings and all?"

"Hu che?" Gorinani said, bursting into the room, her nose twitching at the scent of skande that hung in the air.

Samiha turned to her excitedly. "Maha and Shahzad want to have nikah and reception on New Year's Eve, Ma!" she squealed.

Gorinani growled. "Hu New Year's nu ma rech' . . . All gher khorm make New Year's . . ."

New Year's Eve was a *religious* matter?

"What Nana say, gaandi?" the Goat asked me. "Ramzan too! What all people say?"

I shrugged. "Well, we *did* all agree to have the nikah while his sisters were in town, and they'll only be around for a few more weeks . . ." I muttered as I edged towards the door. "Anyway, I'm going to check on Naani."

"Ey," the Goat shrieked, "dorn say Naani . . . Just now she get worserous . . ."

Shahzad arrived later, as promised, bearing a basket of fruit for the grandparents. Naani smiled shyly as he placed it on the table and offered to serve her.

"Nor, nor, you eat, bhai. I too upset . . ." she said tearfully. "Jus now Ramzan too doctor say again dorn fast . . . can't look the food also . . ."

Communicating with Sameer had been much simpler for her – he'd disarmed her with his fluent Gujarati – but Shahzad was not discouraged by the challenge.

"You mustn't worry, Naani," he consoled her. "You can't fast because you're sick. Allah is testing your patience in a *different* way."

"How your mother-father?" she asked him.

"Everyone's well," he replied. "And my parents will be in Durban soon."

"Or, nice, they stay by *you*?"

He shook his head. "No, they've got a flat in Umhlanga – they'll stay there."

Naani nodded as I gave Shahzad a questioning look.

He smiled. "We were thinking about having the nikah and a small reception while they're here," he offered.

Naani puckered her brow. "Jus now Ramzan too . . . Is hard . . ." she trailed off and gave me another frown.

I shrugged. "Well, it *will* be convenient, Naani, 'cos Shahzad's family will be around. His sisters are here from *overseas and* it's holidays, so no one will have to go to work the next day . . . umm . . . and we just want to have a small braai. Nothing too fancy."

Naani frowned. "Braai? Why dorn have biryani, Maha?" She

managed a small smile in my future husband's direction. "*Sor* far your bhen stay too . . ." She paused. "Must tell Maha's nana," she sighed. "Where your nana, Maha?"

"He's eating ice cream and watching cricket with Goranana . . ." I replied.

Shahzad turned to me. "Yah, it's the last day of the test today, and bad weather as usual." He grimaced.

"Why don't you go and watch some cricket with the ballies, and perhaps bandy your idea about . . ." I suggested.

Shahzad nodded. "Okay, Naani," he said, bending down to kiss her on the cheek, "I'm going to sit with Nana for a while. I'll see you later if you're still awake."

Naani patted my hand as soon as Shahzad was out of the door. "Nice poyro . . ." she murmured. "Rupaaro, too." She blushed.

Nice *and* handsome! I smiled. "He *is*," I said.

"Allah keep jorru salaamat . . ."

"Aameen," I said as I leaned over and kissed her – pleased with her prayer for a safe and peaceful union.

⁂

I sat with Naani until she dozed off, then I set off to recapture my fiancé.

Shahzad groaned along with Nana and Goranana as someone dropped a catch.

"Shahzad said yorl want to have the nikah and reception New Year's?" Nana said as I perched on the edge of the armchair. "It's *in* Ramzan, sor don't expect anyone to help. I warned him also." He glanced at Shahzad, who nodded in acknowledgment.

Nana refocused on the match for a few seconds before throwing his hands up in irritation at the pathetic play. "If *yorl* make all arrangements," he said, turning back to me. "Have simple also. His sisters are here from *overseas* . . ." he trailed off.

Goranana looked up at the mention of *overseas* and nodded approvingly.

Was that the go-ahead? Great! I grinned and nudged Shahzad.

⁂

I'd asked Zeenat *and* the Cows – the latter to appease Naani – to call the family and give the daawat.

"*Everyone* is saying *why* Blue Lagoon," Samiha prattled down the phone. "So far from the nikah mosque, and all the madraajees will be there with their daarus and loud music and all!"

"Don't worry, there'll be a few small gazebos, so you can sit in one," I suggested with a grin.

She sighed. "Anyway, I better go finish up in the kitchen. You know we're going to the beach tomorrow? *Before* Ramzan and all, plus shop is closed. The children want a beach picnic, so Nabiha and all of us . . . We taking Naani also!"

"Oh, that's nice . . . And what about Nana?" I asked. It would be great if I could have the house to myself for a while.

"Oh, no, he and my papa want to watch the cricket," Samiha said, dashing my hopes.

"Hmm . . . How will you all fit into your kombi?" I asked curiously.

"Yah, I don't know . . . Maybe *you* will have to come too. Naani will want you to look after her." She sighed – evidently my presence was far from welcome. "I'll phone you later." She paused. "What you

258

wearing for the Blue Lagoon braai?" she suddenly asked, changing tack. "You know *you* too, first you want to have two-two weddings, then you can't even have one *normal* wedding! *Everyone* is saying what kind to have a braai for reception and asking *who* is doing the braai? They must make salad and all?" She harrumphed.

"I told you already," I said, rolling my eyes, "it's not a normal braai, it's a Pakistani one. And it *is* a wedding, so the entire thing is catered. No one has to bring *anything* . . . just themselves." I sighed, fed up with repeating myself. The concept of "khaalee ath" – attending barbecue daawats empty-handed – was clearly unheard of in Slumurbia.

Samiha grunted. "*Which* Pakistanis going to cater?" she asked. "You sure they won't make it too thiku, then no one can eat also . . . You know these Memons, *they* eat sooo thiku your nose even leaks."

"Please don't worry," I managed to enunciate through gritted teeth, "I'm sure they will cater for all palates. Anyway, I have to go. Let me know about tomorrow, okay? Salaams."

"Wa 'alaikum salaam," she responded primly as I replaced the receiver with a grateful sigh.

⁂

"So, who else is with me?" I asked Baboo as he heaved Naani's wheelchair into the boot of my car.

"Only my mothernlaw, I think," he grunted.

"Okay," I grumbled. Having to listen to Gorinani all the way to the beach hadn't been part of my plan, but what could I do? "And where exactly are we going?"

"Just near Brighton beach," Baboo replied. "There are some nice beaches that side . . ."

I took my seat and waited for the Goat.

She huffed and puffed along eventually. "Ey, Maha, you knor where mus gor? Why you dorn follow kombi?" she instructed.

"Yah, I know where I'm going, and I can always call if we can't find them," I told her.

"Sor nice day . . ." Naani offered.

"Ha, ha," Gorinani nodded, "*sor* much loko from where-where . . . Town too full of traffics . . ."

I eased onto the motorway and headed south.

⁂

The Cows had already set up camp on a grassy knoll above the beach by the time we arrived. It was a good spot, I reckoned. At least this way the Cows didn't have to worry about getting sand in their shoes.

Nabiha's corpulent husband, Essop, ambled towards our car as I struggled out of the driver's side. "Don't worry," he called out, "I'll put your naani in the wheelchair and bring her. You take my mothernlaw and go there!" He pointed to where the rest of the clan had taken up their positions. "Oh, yah, and give your keys so I can lock up."

"Thanks," I replied, throwing them to him. "Come, Gorinani, it isn't too far to walk . . ."

Gorinani shuffled alongside. "Lucky they got nice spot too . . ." she huffed. "Lucky they came way early . . ."

I grunted and paused as a puppy gambolled into our path. "Hello, doggie," I said and smiled.

Gorinani froze, clutched onto my arm and took a step back. "Orma, orma," she squeaked in terror.

"Calm down, Gorinani, it's only a small dog," I said as the dog yapped and hopped about. "It won't bite you."

"Nor, nor," she panted, refusing to budge. "Is dog . . . Just now come way by me."

I sighed. "You go, Gorinani, and I'll distract the dog . . ." I said, finally managing to prise her fingers off my arm. "Hey, doggie . . ."

I watched Gorinani out of the corner of my eye as she edged away fearfully, keeping a beady eye on the animal who was now more interested in sniffing at my basket and bag.

⁂

Essop parked Naani under an umbrella, facing out to sea.

"Naai-naai, Essop, bring back," Gorinani told him. "Just now wheelchair gor down . . ."

He shook his head. "This thing got brakes, Ma," he grunted. "Don't worry."

Grumbling, Gorinani took her place beside Naani.

"Lovely view, hey, Naani?" I said as I gazed out at the sparkling sea and cavorting children.

She nodded. "See Baboo already gorn in water . . ." she observed.

"*Toooo much* he like to swim," Gorinani clucked indulgently.

"I'm going down to the beach to take a walk," I said, rolling up my jeans and slipping off my sandals. "I've got my phone if anyone needs me, okay?"

"Hachao je . . ." Naani called out.

I obeyed, stepping carefully to avoid the sharp rocks. I flashed her a grin, waved and leapt onto the warm sand.

My pockets, filled with shells, slapped heavily against my thighs as I headed back to the Herd. Squinting through the glare, I watched as the puppy I had petted earlier bounded after a ball. It bobbed merrily towards Gorinani, and I laughed as she squealed and leapt out of her chair, startled by the reappearance of the terrifying creature.

Gorinani waved wildly. "Jah, kuthru, jah!" she bellowed at the puppy.

Then, as I stood there giggling at the Goat's antics – the Cows equally terrified and incapable of shooing the little dog away – her bulky frame wobbled as she lost balance. The shells I was carrying fell through my fingers as I saw what was about to happen. The breath jammed in my throat as for one interminable moment everything slowed. Gorinani's weight landed on the edge of Naani's wheelchair, and the whole mess of flailing limbs and wheels succumbed to the force of gravity.

Gorinani yowled. "Orma! Orma! Orma!" she bellowed as the wheelchair hurtled down the bank and crashed into the sand below, turning over and spilling its occupants onto the beach.

I blinked, transfixed by what had just happened. Then, suddenly, I was running, scrambling across the sand towards the scene.

By the time I arrived Baboo and Essop had disentangled the old ladies – Gorinani was babbling, but, worryingly, Naani was silent.

I caught my breath as I reached her. "Naani! Naani!" I sobbed. "Are you okay?" But it was obvious that everything was far from well – a slow trickle of blood was oozing out of one of her ears.

"She must have hit her head on one stone," Essop mumbled. "She's unconscious . . ."

"Helicopter!" I sobbed, whipping out my phone and dialling Farah's number.

I gasped out the details. "Please arrange a chopper to take her to Saint Augustine's," I asked her. "You know her heart's not strong, and *who* knows how long the ambulance will take?"

Farah agreed to my request, told me to remain calm and cut the call.

I stabbed the buttons shakily. "Shahzad!" I shuddered. "Naani's hurt! We're taking her to hospital! Please come quickly!"

"What happened?" he asked.

"Don't ask what happened, just *come!"*

I shrieked out directions before cutting the call and turning back to Naani's prone form.

⁂

Shahzad screeched to a halt beside the kombi as the paramedics loaded Naani into the chopper on a stretcher. I ran into his arms the moment he climbed out of the car.

"It'll be okay," he whispered after I had explained what had happened. "I'll take you to the hospital right now."

I strapped myself in, watching as the whirring blades gathered momentum and the helicopter rose vertically from the beach.

"Are you okay?" Shahzad asked as he turned the key in the ignition. I shuddered as the chopper flew off into the wide blue yonder, my body beginning to convulse as the emotion poured out of me.

⁂

By the time we reached Saint Augustine's, Naani was already in surgery, but it didn't take them long to figure out that there was nothing they could do for her and she was quickly moved into the intensive care unit.

Later that same afternoon Nana stood beside her bed, reciting Qur'aan tearfully, as I sat numb and mute, clinging to Naani's limp hand, my mind a complete blank.

⁂

Nana and I kept an almost constant vigil at Naani's bedside. On Saturday evening, news of the new moon had filtered through to us – the month of patience dawned – and so Nana and I swallowed a few morsels in the early hours of Sunday morning, in preparation for the first fast.

I prayed and took up my position, leaning against the bed and hanging on to Naani's pale hand. Nana was exhausted yet continued with his stoic recitation. I closed my eyes, my lips moving slowly in supplication until I drifted off to sleep. Shortly after the dawn of the first fast, Naani passed on to the next plane of existence and somehow someone succeeded in separating our hands and removing our bodies.

⁂

The family descended upon the Mahal right away, and took on the sombre task of laying Naani to rest while I holed myself up in my bedroom, Shahzad offering whatever consolation he could.

At some point I was steered into the formal lounge, where Naani lay wrapped in her white calico. She appeared calm as I leaned forward and pressed my lips against her cold forehead. I choked as the funereal smell of camphor assaulted me, resurrecting the childhood memories I had spent so long carefully burying. Naani was gone forever! I began to sob uncontrollably as Zeenat stepped through the crowd of mourners and reached out to take my juddering body in her arms.

Nana entered as I wailed on Zeenat's shoulder – Essop, Baboo and Goranana shuffling behind him, Chotanana and his entourage bringing up the rear. As I watched, Nana took his place beside Naani and began to recite the traditional prayers through his tears. Then the mourners' chants amplified as the men lifted the janaaza and faced the exit. The buzzing subsumed me, and I fell heavily against Zeenat – unable to move, unable to stop crying.

"Come," she whispered, as the men headed off to bury Naani, "let me help you back to your room . . ."

⁂

Slumurbia drifted in and out of the Mahal for the next three days – gathering to recite the verses from the multiple copies of the Qur'aan Naani had lovingly covered and stacked in her special cupboard. The only noticeable absentee was the Goat, who lay sedated in bed next door, her leg encased in plaster.

On the fourth day, I sat in the kitchen shovelling spoonfuls of Manjra the caterer's kheer into my mouth – pondering the presence of kheer at funerals – when Farhana Moosa, my future mother-in-law, walked in.

"Salaams, Maha, how are you doing?" she asked.

I swallowed my mouthful of the thick rice pudding and nodded. "I'm okay . . ." I said, managing something like a half-smile.

"I've just come to tell you that we can cancel the braai if you want," she said, concern written across her face. "Everyone will understand, so don't feel bad . . ."

I shrugged. "I'm not sure," I said, looking up at her.

She took my hand and patted it gently. "Think about it, and speak to Shahzad, but don't feel obligated in any way."

I smiled – properly this time. "Thanks . . . ummm . . ." I realised suddenly that I had no idea what I was supposed to call her. "I really appreciate it . . ."

She hugged me and then stood up to leave. "Well, we're going back to Umhlanga now . . ." she said. "We'll see you tomorrow."

I nodded. "Give Shahzad's father my salaams," I said.

"What 'Shahzad's father'?" she demanded. "We are like your parents now . . . You must call us 'Ma' and 'Papa', like Shahzad does. You are our daughter too now."

I blinked back tears and managed a quick nod as my new ma waved and headed out. Would I cope with a jol so soon after the funeral? I wondered. Would it be decent to celebrate our marriage while still mourning Naani's departure?

<hr>

"I say *have* the jol! It's not some massive wedding. I mean, there'll only be the same people that have been eating here every night anyway," Zeenat stated, lighting a fag and sinking tiredly into the armchair in my bedroom. "The official mourning *is* over. Life must go on!"

"Yah, but Slumurbia doesn't adhere to official three days only." I frowned.

She shook her head. "Hawubo, people will come read and condole for *months* to come! What are you going to do? Wait until they stop?"

"Yah, I know, but it's Kismoos Holidays *and* Ramadan as well . . ."

She shrugged. "What does Shahzad say?"

I lit a fag and puffed thoughtfully. "We haven't spoken about it as yet. I guess he'll go along with whatever I want."

"Which is?"

"Right now I definitely don't feel ready to celebrate." I sighed. "I think . . ." I took a deep breath. "I think we should just have the nikah and leave out the braai." The Herd would no doubt be pleased – spared the shame of an unconventional reception.

Zeenat saluted and grinned. "As you wish, Little Miss Maha," she said.

I managed a weak grin and fluttered my fingers limply as she strode back to her duties down below.

My mind flashed to the bustle downstairs – definitely a positive aspect of Chaar culture – the family rallying around, casting aside all arguments and attitudes and simply *being there*. I sighed into the pillow, grateful I did not have to concern myself with the finer details of post-funeral behwa. We could be leading the way if we just booted out cultural crap and polished the gems.

Once Upon a Time in Slumurbia

I slipped into comfy tracksuit bottoms and a T-shirt and padded downstairs to make myself tea. It was the last day of 1998, the eve of our nikah, but, unfortunately, I had awoken to my period.

Having made myself a cup I wandered back upstairs, locked my door and lit a fag. I switched on the CD player as I sipped thoughtfully at my tea, and flicked some ash into one of the large shells I'd collected on the day of Naani's accident. The pain of losing my parents had been something that I had had to learn to deal with – I had grown used to them not being around – but at that moment the thought that Naani wouldn't see me married to Shahzad was almost unbearable. Suddenly, tears were streaming down my face.

The cigarette had burnt itself out by the time I was calm enough to take a shaky sip of lukewarm tea. I gulped down the liquid and sniffed loudly. At least Naani had been up to speed with my life, and she would be able to inform my parents of my approaching nikah. I smiled at the thought of them being in the know.

I walked slowly over to my wardrobe, yanked it open and stared blankly inside. Moving the jumpers to one side, I pulled out Ouma's old shoebox that I had hidden so long ago. I blew off the dust and sat back, staring at it for a few seconds before lifting the lid and peering inside.

The gaily checked dishcloths had been folded neatly and placed on top. My first clothes! I envisaged my arrival in Ouma's candle-lit kitchen while a storm raged overhead as I unfolded one gently and held it up to my face. It smelt of Sunlight soap.

Setting the dishcloths aside I pulled the box onto my lap and studied the contents – a bundle of identity documents and a leather pouch. I slipped out a little green ID book, opened the first page and giggled at Achmat Jacobs' mug shot. His waanku baal had been suitably teased into the style of the day, framing the solemn expression he offered the camera.

I opened the next one – my mother – and gasped at her youth. Glancing at the date I realised that she had been eighteen when the picture had been taken – rosy cheeked and sparkly eyed.

Putting the ID books away, I fingered the pouch thoughtfully before emptying the contents onto my palm – a small gold ring with three tiny stones and a sturdy silver band. I peered at the rings that lay in my hand and studied the inscription engraved inside Achmat's ring. *Sonnet CXVI*. "Let me not to the marriage of true minds admit impediments," I mumbled and smiled, pretty confident that Maryam Maal's interpretation had also embraced the physical.

I slid them onto my right hand and held them up for inspection –

my father's ring predictably too big. I could give it to Shahzad, I thought suddenly. But what if he didn't like it? What if he lost it? Oh shut up, Maha! You're marrying him tonight. If you trust him enough to marry him then surely you can trust him with your daddy's ring? I exhaled slowly.

I studied my bejewelled hand. My parents had faced oceans of adversity only to have their lives brutally aborted by the apartheid regime. Perhaps I could channel some of their resolve and make it through to the other side – perchance even enjoy some of today. It was impossible to ignore Naani's absence – especially here in the Mahal, I mused – but where else could I go, and quite frankly, did I want to go anywhere?

I refolded the dishcloths, left the box on my desk and headed downstairs for another cup of tea.

Gorinani's voice carried through the open back door and I paused to ponder how she'd made her way outdoors. Grabbing my mug I stepped out into the scorching day to investigate.

I found Gorinani on her veranda in Naani's *old* wheelchair – the newer one still lay in a mangled heap in a corner of the garage. She was picking at a bunch of grapes.

"Nor fasting today?" she asked, gazing at my mug of tea.

I shook my head and sat on the wicker chair beside her. "How are you feeling?"

She shrugged. "Paining still . . . Hard for wudhu bathing toilet . . ."

I nodded. "Your roses are looking nice," I offered as I stared out across the garden.

She nodded. "Hah, grow nice. Bau mashallah this time," she said, shifting about in her seat. "Better you dorn have braai."

I looked at her with a small smile. "It's still a house in mourning. It's not ready for a wedding yet . . ."

"Nor, nor, Maha," she clasped my hand gently, "mustn't say like that. Funeral finish now . . ." She pointed to the flowers. "Cut and put in vase for wedding house. Mus make nice."

My astonished hand lay limply between hers and she gave it another pat. "Allah Paak keep jorru salaamat," she said.

"Aameen," I responded shakily – stunned by her wish for the Good Lord to keep our blessed union safe. I exhaled slowly as I remembered that Naani had made the same dua a few weeks earlier.

Geckos scrambled along the exterior wall, birds twittered in the branches of the nearby tree – sunlight pervaded every inch of the stoep upon which Gorinani and I sat in equable silence. I sipped my tea and she popped another grape.

She smiled at me. "Allah Paak keep happy too," she said.

I blinked – she'd just offered some of her prized roses *and* wished me well. *Twice*. The day had officially turned surreal! I managed a small, watery smile and sniffed.

"Nor, Maha, dorn cry . . . Mus be happy . . ." She leaned forward and stretched her arms toward me and before I knew it I found myself in her generous embrace for the first time ever.

"Shh . . . shh . . ." she said as my tears ran. "Mus make shukar, Maha. Sor lucky, see you got nice *jawaan* mathero too. Never mind is Memror."

That was more like it. I smiled, lifted my head and wiped away my tears. "You're right, Gorinani," I sniffed, "I should be happy even though I miss Naani *so* much . . . I *am* lucky."

"Who's lucky?" Samiha asked, frowning as she stepped onto the stoep with a child in her arms. "Oh, it's *you*! I was wondering who Mummy was talking to."

Samiha placed the child on the ground and busied herself with tidying up. "You not fasting, Maha?" she asked, glancing at my tea.

I shook my head. "Got it this morning."

She clucked. "Shame, wedding night too." She blushed and read-justed the cushions. "Umm, I told Nana *we'll* stay with him, so you can go and stay in Umhlanga for one-two nights."

Samiha making arrangements for *me*? Things were definitely getting weirder.

I shook myself. "Oh, that's very nice of you, Samiha, thanks." I stood up suddenly. "I should tell Zeenat, and maybe pack a few things. There's no food at the flat or anything . . ."

Gorinani shook her head. "Nor-nor worry. Finish tell Zeenat. You gor rest and then wear nice for nikah . . ."

Zeenat was in the know? The Herd had spoken to her directly? Would these wonders never cease?

⁂

"So, has Ma Moosa got everything under control for iftar?" Zeenat asked, bursting into my bedroom as I trimmed the thorns from Gorinani's roses – she had forced Samiha to pick me a dozen before I had left for the Mahal.

"Yes, Ma Moosa has everything under control," I replied as Zeenat, looking flushed and harried, dumped her bags onto the bed and flopped down beside them.

"And why aren't you in your clothes?" she asked.

I smiled. "I was just about to have my tea and fag, then I was going to dress . . ."

Zeenat sat up and brushed the hair off her face. "Well, don't light up just yet, I heard Nana say he was coming to see you."

"Oh? Well, he's already asked me in the presence of the ballies if I want to marry Shahzad Moosa, so I don't know why . . ."

"Maha!" Nana called out from behind my bedroom door, interrupting me.

"Jee, Nana," I replied as I walked across to open it.

"Here . . ." He held out a beautifully crafted gold chain. "Your naani's chain . . . If you want to wear for nikah," he offered.

I reached out and clutched at it. "Jazakallah, Nana, I'd *love* to wear Naani's chain!"

I kissed his wrinkled cheek and he nodded, patently pleased by my decision.

⁂

"Well, you certainly look bright and cheerful in Maryam's sari." Zeenat nodded approvingly as I stood back to admire the way the soft Indian silk lay against my body. I had helped myself to something from my mother's amazing sari collection that Naani had stored in her peti. "Ayyo, sor nice you look and all, sor 'appy too . . ."

"Can you believe that the Goat is actually helping out . . .?" I asked, changing the subject. "She reckons she wants to see me happy!"

Zeenat shook her head as she opened her toolbox. "Tell me about it, I'm still in shock from Samiha calling about sorting out your Umhlanga flat!"

I smiled at her reflection in the mirror. "If someone had chooned me I'd live to see the Goat's good side, I'd *never* have believed it . . ."

"*And*," she grinned, "if someone had told *me* back in ninety-five that in three years' time you'd have been divorced and would be about to marry one Memon you happen to know via your ex-husband . . ." She threw her hands in the air. "I'd have called them an ambulance!"

I grunted. "Come now, Zee . . . *enough* panchaath! Make me look like a happy bride . . ."

She rested her hand on my shoulder and stared thoughtfully at my reflection. "You are happy, aren't you?" she asked.

I nodded and blinked back the tears that threatened. "Of course I am . . . I just can't help being sad as well."

She smiled. "Well, then," she clapped her hands importantly, "monsoon-resistant mascara coming up!"

⁂

The Moosa and Maal women broke their fast in an atmosphere of gentle excitement. I took a steadying breath as I nibbled on a samoosa and sipped slowly at my strawberry milkshake. I would soon be Mrs Moosa, Shahzad's wife, and we would be *living* together at the Mahal! Undiluted contentment coursed through my body and I smiled.

The men returned a short while later – causing chaos in the Mahal as people greeted and embraced, crying and congratulating one another in the same breath. Then, suddenly, Nana was standing before me, smiling through his tears. I fell into his embrace and for a few moments we wept in each other's arms.

Nana broke away. "Allah keep you happy, beti!" he said.

"Aameen, Nana," I choked. "I love you."

Nana faltered, clutched onto my hands and squeezed gently. "Your naani loved you very much, Maha . . . And me too . . ." he managed with a loud sniff.

I smiled at him through blurred vision before flumping onto the closest sofa.

"There you are, gorgeous. Lost sight of you for a moment in the throng!" Shahzad said as he sat beside me. "I need to give you your wedding ring, Mrs Moosa!"

I smiled. "*Oh,* I didn't know you'd gotten me one . . . This is rather splendid by itself," I said, looking down at the rock that already graced my finger.

"Oh, okay then, I'll save it for a special occasion," Shahzad teased.

I punched him lightly. "Do you want to go to my room?" I asked.

"And what have you in store for me there?" he asked with a naughty grin.

"Well, you'll never know if you don't follow!" I stood up and headed towards the door.

"I'll just get a drink," he said as he moved lazily off the couch. "I'll catch up. I promise . . ."

I nodded and floated dreamily up the stairs.

❦

Shahzad appeared ten minutes later with two glasses of milkshake. "One of your connections saw me sneaking up with these glasses," he announced, "and told me in no uncertain terms that it's Sunnah for the husband to give his wife a drink of milk."

I looked up and met his gaze. "Forget about them . . ." I patted the bed. "Come and sit with me."

He grinned as he placed the drinks on the table. "So, you seriously *don't* want the ring?" he asked as he bounced onto the bed beside me.

I shook my head and laughed. "Don't be silly. I'm a woman – I love rings!" I leaned over to my bedside table and grabbed Achmat's sturdy silver band. "And to prove it I have something for you as well. It's my father's wedding ring . . . So it's not exactly modern or trendy . . . I don't even think it's very valuable . . ."

Shahzad placed his palm against my cheek. "Shh . . . It's your father's ring. I'm honoured."

"Are you sure?" I met his gaze – surprised *and* oddly reassured – to find tears in his eyes.

"Go on, then, hold out your hand!" I ordered briskly.

He held out both. "Take your pick."

I stared thoughtfully and smiled. "Well, I *would* choose right, 'cos that's the hand you eat with. But *other* women will look at your left to figure whether you're married or not . . . So, as much as it goes against my feminist principles to mark my man, I'm going with tradition here." I pushed the ring – with some difficulty – down the length of the ring finger on his left hand. "Is it too tight?" I asked.

He moved it about slowly. "It's actually okay." He held up his hand for me to admire.

I pulled it towards me and kissed the ring. "Thank you for wearing this," I said.

"You're welcome, my love," he said, fishing around in his pocket and pulling out a little box. "Now, may I please with this ring thee wed?"

276

Shahzad drove slowly along the busy roads towards the Umhlanga flat – it was late and people were heading off to their different jols. I cast a glance heavenwards and smiled – it was a perfect, star-studded night.

At the flat I unlocked the door and felt about for the light switch.

"Surprise!" everyone shouted.

I blinked and stared at the beaming bunch.

"You didn't think we'd let you get away without *any* kind of jol, did you now?" Zeenat asked.

I shook my head, truly startled as behind Zeenat Farah grinned and Shahzad's younger sister waved gaily.

Zeenat stepped towards me. "There's something else," she stated cryptically.

"Oh?" I looked at her. "Something nice, I hope . . ."

She shrugged. "It's your *wedding* jol, doofus, how can it *not* be nice?" She waved to the throng and they parted like the proverbial Red Sea – exposing the furthest armchair.

"Oumaaaaa!" I squealed excitedly, running through the crowd and flinging myself onto her. "*When* did you get here?"

She squeezed me. "Ah, Maha, kleintjie, dis lekker om jou weer te sien!"

I nodded and kissed her cheeks soundly. "It's *baie, baie* lekker to see *you* too, Ouma. What a *fabulous* surprise!"

I looked up at the cheerful faces. "So whose grand plan was this?"

Zeenat grinned. "Your husband's, actually."

I flew into his arms. "I love you, Shahzad Moosa," I said, hugging him wildly.

Zeenat herded everyone together shortly before midnight – to usher in the final year of the twentieth century. I stood between Ouma and my husband, leaning gently against the latter.

"Ten, nine, eight . . ." Zeenat started the countdown and we all took up the chant, before gasping in unison at the sudden burst of colour in the skies over Durban.

I turned to Ouma and embraced her warmly. "Happy New Year! I hope it's a wonderful one for you!"

She patted my hand gently. "And the same to you, kleintjie."

I straightened up and turned to Shahzad. "Happy New Year, darling husband," I said and kissed his mouth.

Shahzad enfolded me in his arms. "And happy-happy to you too, gorgeous," he whispered.

Corks popped on the beach down below as I turned back towards the glittering night, people cheered and I thanked the Creator for allowing me *this* moment – surrounded by those who loved me.

Farah tapped her mug of tea and everyone fell silent. She grinned at us, cleared her throat and brandished her cellphone. "Firstly, greetings from abroad," she began. "Sabah says congrats!"

"Hear! Hear!" Zeenat called out from the throng.

Farah stuffed the phone into her pocket and raised her mug. "Okay," she continued earnestly, "I'd like to propose a toast to Shahzad and Maha . . . We all know you've been through a helluva hectic time recently, and I'm sure you miss your parents *and* your naani, especially on an occasion that is so very special . . ."

I swallowed at the stubborn lump in my throat as I felt the tears edge slowly out of the corners of my eyes. "It's my party and I'll cry if I want to," I thought fiercely as my heart constricted with equal measures of rapture and meloncholy.

"I don't have to remind either of you that marriage *is* hard work, so I'd just like to say . . . may the Big Baas upstairs bless you guys with a long, happy, safe and peaceful life together."

"Aameen!" Zeenat shouted and lifted her glass to the dazzling skies.

"Aameen!" everyone murmured.

Shahzad drew me closer and kissed my hair.

Farah looked at us. "You *both* deserve it!"

I blinked back tears and grinned.

Farah held her tea aloft and smiled. "So, here's to Maha and Shahzad," her voice quavered, "may you live happily ever after!"

⁂

Glossary

aaj kaal	today
aalu	potato
aari jaath	stubborn ways
ai hu thu handu arrange kare?	what is this that you arrange everything?
ai handu gaandu-gaandu rawadhe aweh	leave all this madness now
akkals	brains/common sense
ardi raathe	in the middle of the night
aweh hudd thayyu	now that's the limit
baal	hair
bandhuk	gun
behwa	sit (refers to visiting in order to condole)
besaram	shameless
bhema	Zulu: smoke
bhenchodh	sister-fucker
bosri	cunt
buggle	armpit
charrbees	fat (refers to being cheeky)
cherr	to wind up
choobie	Durban slang for willing slave
chopras	books
chup reh!	shut up!
chuth/chuthia	cunt

dhaadi	paternal grandmother
daawat	invitation (usually to have people over for a meal)
dala	provoke
dhandhas	nonsense/inappropriate behaviour
dhikri	daughter (loving expression)
dhukh	pain/woe (refers to having worries/troubles)
dohas	old people
dua	prayer
cklcc	alone
Esha	late night prayer
fitnahs	wrongdoings
foi	paternal aunt
fufuyaan	fit/seizure (based on Zulu: fufunyani)
gaandi	mad
gaan	arse
gorni	dim-witted
haaru	good
hachao je	be careful
halgat	completely
hambarr	listen
hambru?	did you hear?
haraam	unlawful/forbidden
hazrat	term of respect for a learned person
heedee	straight
hu che?	what is it?
hunda hu kehe?	what will everyone say?

ifa	Zulu: die
iftar	post-sunset breaking of fast
Istikara	special prayer for big decisions
itar	oil-based perfume
izzat	respect/honour
jaldi kar	hurry up
jalebi	sweet snack made of flour and syrup
jamai	son-in-law
janaaza	corpse/prayer for the dead
jawaab	answer
jawaan mathero	young man
jazakallah	May Allah reward you
jika-jika	Zulu: dance
jor aweh	see now
Juma	Muslim Sabbath (Friday)
jux	eager
kay dhungh waaru perr je	wear something decent
kayyu	said
keewu lage?	how will it look?
khaala	aunty
khabbaddaar!	don't you dare!
khawaanu	food
loko	people
looi	blood
luchee	slag (female)
lucho	slag (male)
maadarchodh	mother-fucker

maangu	proposal
madraajees	non-Muslim Chaarous, word originally used to describe KwaZulu-Natal's South Indian settlers
Maghrib	evening or sunset prayer
marhoom	late (deceased)
masjid	mosque
mathero	man
mazaar	tomb
min gepla	Afrikaans: don't care
mithai	sweetmeats
Molwi	Durban pronunciation of Molvi
moosh	moustache
mota	big
Moulana	priest
musallah	prayer mat
muthlabee	a person willing to use people
naam ni waalu . . . kaam waalu	your name is not appreciated . . . your work is appreciated
naach	dance (to party)
nikah	wedding ceremony
ntombi	Zulu: girl
orhni	long, wide scarf
paiha	money
panchaath	unnecessary chatter
parwaarthi	one with too much time on their hands
peti	chest/trunk
phuza	Zulu: drink

pideli	drunk (female)
pidelo	drunk (male)
poyri	girl
poyro	boy
puchu	ask
raan	mistress/whore
raani	queen
rupaaro	handsome
saali/saalo	stupid
saali khottee	stupid lazy
sabar	patience
sadhu	ascetic
saram	shame
sati	immolation
sawaab nu kaam	reward-earning action
sehri	pre-dawn meal
shukar	thanks (to God)
siyaphila	Zulu: I am fine
sunnah	practice of the Prophet (peace be on him)
ta'leem	regular gathering of Muslim women
talaaq	divorce
Taraweeh	extra prayer in Ramadan
thaakat	strength
thaigi	became
thiku	very hot (too much chilli)
thumme be	you too
thunnee	Indian card game similar to klavejas
toubah-toubah ai hu dhukh?	what hardship has befallen me?

tshebe	beard (based on Zulu: intshebe)
thu bau moti	you're very big
thu daaru piyech'	you're drinking alcohol
thu hu gaandu-gaandu waath karech'?	what nonsense are you speaking?
thu jaach'	you are going
thu ka' jaach'?	where are you going?
waanku	crooked
waath	speak/speech
wudhu	pre-prayer ablutions